ALL OUR YESTERDAYS

CRISTIN TERRILL

HYPERION
NEW YORK

First Edition
1 3 5 7 9 10 8 6 4 2
G475-5664-5-13166

Printed in the United States of America

This book is set in Janson Text
Designed by Marci Senders

Library of Congress Cataloging-in-Publication Data
Terrill, Cristin.
All our yesterdays/Cristin Terrill.—First edition.
pages cm.—(All our yesterdays; 1)
Summary: "Em must travel back in time to prevent a catastrophic time machine from ever being invented, while Marina battles to prevent the murder of the boy she loves"—Provided by publisher.
ISBN 978-1-4231-7637-4 (hardback)—ISBN 1-4231-7637-5
[1. Time travel—Fiction. 2. Love—Fiction. 3. Murder—Fiction. 4. Science fiction.] I. Title.
PZ7.T27532All 2013
[Fic]—dc23   2013008007

Reinforced binding

Visit www.un-requiredreading.com

SUSTAINABLE FORESTRY INITIATIVE   Certified Sourcing
www.sfiprogram.org
SFI-00993

THIS LABEL APPLIES TO TEXT STOCK

FOR MY MOM.
AND FOR MY MARINA.

Tomorrow, and tomorrow, and tomorrow,

Creeps in this petty pace from day to day

To the last syllable of recorded time;

And all our yesterdays have lighted fools

The way to dusty death.

—*william shakespeare,* Macbeth

ONE

em

I stare at the drain in the center of the concrete floor. It was the first thing I saw when they locked me in this cell, and I've barely looked away since.

At first I was just obstinate, dragging my feet in the thin prison slippers they gave me so they were forced to pull me along the hallway by both arms. But when I saw the drain, I started to scream. It grew in my vision until it dominated the little cinder-block cell, and I kicked at the men who held me, trying to wrench my arms out of their iron grasp. I could only conjure the most gruesome scenarios for why they'd need a drain in the floor.

Whatever horrors I imagined haven't come to pass—at least, not yet—but the drain still dominates my attention. It's like a lodestar to me, pulling my focus back to it again and again. Even now, I'm lying on my side on the narrow cot against the wall and staring at the thing as though there's still something to be learned from it. Five and a half inches across, thirty-two little holes, and a dent the size of a nickel just off the center.

"What are you doing?" The familiar voice is faint through the heating vent.

"Baking a cake."

He laughs, and the sound makes me smile. I'm a little surprised my muscles still remember how to make the movement.

"Are you staring at that drain again?"

I don't say anything.

"Em, please," he says. "You're only going to drive yourself crazy."

But I have something else in mind.

Today, finally, I'm going to uncover all of the drain's secrets.

I hear the footsteps of an approaching guard some time later. Time is hard to judge in here, with no clocks or windows or any activity to break up the long flow of seconds. All I have to mark time by are my conversations with the boy in the cell next door and the waxing and waning of my own hunger.

My stomach growls at the sound of the boots against the cement, the sound like a bell to one of Pavlov's dogs. It must be lunchtime.

The heavy metal door slides open enough to reveal Kessler, the guard with the face like the smoldering of a doused fire. Most of the guards are indifferent to me, but he really hates me. Resents being made to wait on me, I guess, bringing me my meals and fresh changes of the plain blue clothes they've given me to wear. It makes me smile. If he only knew what I was accustomed to before the world crumbled around us like a house eaten from the inside by rot.

Kessler holds the lunch tray out for me, and I move quickly to snatch it from his hand. When I'm not fast enough, he drops it with a clatter to the floor, sending bits of food flying in every direction. The indignity of scrambling for anything Kessler offers me burns at my insides, but for once I'm eager for my meal. Though not for the brown, sloppy food on the tray, of course.

For the cutlery that comes with it.

Kessler gives me a sharp, mocking grin and slides the door of my cell shut again. As soon as he's gone, I grab the spoon and fork off the tray and begin examining them. There's no knife; there never is. The soggy meat doesn't require cutting, and they're probably afraid I'd stage a daring escape attempt with the dull plastic utensil, brandishing it at the men with machine guns outside my cell.

I put the tray to one side and sit cross-legged by the drain. I try the fork first, pressing the tongs to one of the screws that holds the grating in place. As I suspected, they're too thick to fit the grooves, so I toss it. It skitters across the concrete and lands by the tray.

My only hope is the spoon. I press the curve of it against the same screw, and this time one edge catches. I hold my breath, as though any change in the air pressure of the room might undo things, and press down onto the spoon, trying to use it to loosen the screw. It slips. I try it again a half a dozen times, but it's no good; the spoon keeps slipping off the screw so that I'm pressing and turning into nothing but air. The curve of the spoon is too severe to fit against the straight groove of the screw head, and I nearly hurl the spoon against the wall in frustration.

I stop with my hand raised in the air. Take a breath. *Think.*

The handle of the spoon is far too thick to fit the groove, and the base too wide, but . . . I touch the rough concrete of the cell floor, which is prickly and cold against my palm. It could work.

When Kessler comes back for my tray, I'm waiting for him. My stomach is hollow and aching, but I haven't touched the food. I need the full tray of slop intact. Kessler slides the door open, and as soon as the space is big enough, I hurl the tray through it.

"This is disgusting!" I shout. "We're not animals!"

Kessler ducks, and the tray flies into the wall behind him with a crack. He flinches and swears when flecks of brown and green food speckle his face and uniform. I suppress a wicked smile for the half second before Kessler raises his hand and strikes me hard across the face. I crumple to the floor, stinging tears rising into my eyes at the blow.

"Crazy bitch," Kessler says as he shuts the door on me.

I can only hope he'll be so angry at having to clean up the mess that he won't notice the missing spoon.

I wait as long as I can just to be safe. One hour, maybe two? Then I pull the spoon out from where I've hidden it under my thin foam mattress. I break off the head, which leaves a sharp edge, and measure it with my fingers, comparing it to the groove in the screw.

I scoot over to the wall and put my face close to the heating vent. "Hey, you there?"

4

I hear the tortured squeak of rusty springs as Finn rolls off his cot. "Just headed out. You're lucky you caught me."

I press my fingers to the cold slats of the vent. Sometimes it's hard to believe that only a foot of concrete separates us. He feels so far away.

Does he ever touch his side of the wall and think of me?

"Could you sing?" I say.

"Sing?"

"Please?"

"Um, okay." Bemused but willing. Finn never says no. "Any requests?"

"Up to you."

He starts singing something that sounds churchy. A hymn, maybe. I didn't know until after everything started—once we were on the road, everything about our old lives left behind us like the exhaust that trailed from the truck smuggling us out of the city—but Finn went to church every week with his mother. He even liked it. I was shocked by that at the time, although I can't remember why now. Maybe because religion was never a part of my life, or because the idea of prayer and church potlucks and sermons seemed so far removed from the Finn I knew then.

The Finn I *thought* I knew then.

His voice is good, a strong tenor with a texture like cool cotton against the skin. You'd never guess it to look at him. Or, I don't know, maybe you would. I haven't laid eyes on Finn in months. Maybe he doesn't look the way I remember.

With Finn's voice reverberating against the cinder-block walls until it fills up every crack and crevice, I press the sharp edge of the broken spoon against the concrete. I drag it back and forth over the rough surface, slowly filing down the plastic. I move faster and faster, the scrape of the spoon against the floor mingling with Finn's voice in my ears.

Despite the chill in the cell, sweat prickles on my forehead from the exertion. I stop and check the width of the spoon against the screw. It's not thin enough yet, but it's closer. I go back to filing, clutching the spoon so tightly that my hand begins to ache. This is going to work; I'm sure of it.

Finn stops singing, but I hardly notice, I'm so focused on my task. "Em, what are you doing?"

"It's going to work," I whisper to myself.

"What is?"

I check the spoon again, and this time the sanded edge fits perfectly into the groove of the screw. I jam it in and feel the temperature of my blood rise. A dull little voice in the back of my mind asks me why I care so much about this stupid drain, but I barely hear it over the pounding in my head, like a drummer leading soldiers to war. I begin to turn the spoon, but the screw doesn't budge, held in place by years of dirt and rust and God knows what else. I turn harder, trying to force it to move, until the plastic creaks and threatens to snap.

"Come on, damn it!"

I pinch the spoon at the very base, as close to the screw as my fingers can manage, and turn. With a squeal, the screw begins to move. I laugh, little huffs of air that feel foreign but wonderful on my lips. When that screw gives way, I attack the next and the next, scrabbling at them with my fingernails until they bleed when the spoon doesn't work fast enough, and finally yanking at the grating when only a few threads of the last screw are holding it in place.

It pops off in my hand, suddenly nothing more than a thin piece of metal, and I drop it with a clang.

"Em, what's going on?"

Finn sounds anxious now, but I don't have time to care. The drain is open and exposed, finally. I reach inside of it, the rational part of my brain telling me that I won't find anything there but a cold pipe, but something deeper and more instinctive inside of me whispering of . . . what? Purpose? Destiny? One of those other big things I stopped believing in years ago?

That something isn't surprised when my fingers close around an object hidden in the drain. My body tenses as something wild and joyful bursts open inside of me, like my muscles know to contain the explosion. I tug the object free, pulling it out into the light, and stare.

It's a plastic freezer bag, ancient and dotted with years of hard-water marks and mold. Such a mundane object—which conjures memories of the peanut butter sandwiches I used to find tucked in my gym bag—seems wildly out of place in my tiny prison cell. Inside is a single sheet of paper, white with blue stripes, like I used in school, with a frilled edge that shows it was ripped out of a notebook.

I open the bag with trembling fingers, suddenly scared. I knew there was something important about that drain from the moment I laid eyes on it. It isn't natural. Nothing about this can be good.

I pull out the sheet of paper and get my first good look at it. The room becomes a vacuum around me. I try to inhale and find I can't, like all the air is gone.

The page is almost entirely covered in writing. Some lines are in ink, some in pencil, the lines at the top so faded with time that they're difficult to read, and those at the bottom looking almost fresh. Every sentence but the one at the very bottom is crossed out with a neat, thin line.

There's a name at the top of the page, written in familiar block capitals, and the line at the bottom is bold and dark, the words carved into the paper like the person who wrote them pressed the pen deep into it.

That person was me.

I've never seen this piece of paper before in my life, but the handwriting is definitely mine: my cursive *e* when every other letter is in print, my sloping *k* and too-skinny *a*. Some primal part of me recognizes it, like a phone ringing in another room.

I start to shake. In this time and place, a letter I don't remember writing means something very specific.

But it's the last line that makes me scramble for the toilet in the corner of the cell.

You have to kill him.

TWO

em

I heave until my stomach comes to terms with the fact that there's
nothing inside to throw up, then lean my forehead against the
cool wall and wipe my mouth with my sleeve.

You have to kill him.

When I close my eyes, I can still see the words. They're seared
into me, but I can't accept them. There has to be another way. I'm
not that hard.

Not yet.

Far down the hallway, I hear the clink of a door. Someone is
approaching. I bolt upright and lunge for the drain. No telling
what the doctor will do if he finds me breaking into it, and if he
sees the sheet of paper . . .

The thought sends ice through my veins. He'll kill me for sure.

Hands clumsy with rushing, I break the spoon into several
pieces and drop them down the drain. I can now make out a pair
of heavy boots against the cement. I jam the grating back onto

the drain and replace the screws as best as I can with fingertips and nails. I swipe up the plastic bag and piece of paper and throw myself at my mattress. I shove them both underneath just as Kessler's face appears at the small window in my cell door.

"Where's the spoon?" he says.

Great. Kessler is not as stupid as I'd hoped.

"Don't know what you're talking about," I say, leaning my head back nonchalantly. I force myself to take normal, even breaths, even though my lungs are burning from the burst of exertion.

Kessler turns to his right, conferring with some person I can't see. Someone who isn't wearing military boots, so I didn't hear them approaching. My toes curl inside my slippers.

Kessler turns back to me. "We know you've got it. Hand it over."

Well, that isn't an option anymore. I'd have to dig the shards out of the drain, and then they'd toss the whole room to find out what I'm hiding. If they find that piece of paper with its laundry list of threats in my handwriting, I'm dead.

Besides, I'll never give these men anything they want, no matter how small.

I fold my hands behind my head. "Bite me."

"It's just a plastic spoon, kid." It's the doctor, his voice muffled by the door. "What are you going to do with it, burrow out of here?"

I jump to my feet at the sound of that voice. "Go to hell!"

"Em?" It's Finn at the heating vent. "What's going on?"

"Last chance."

I spit on the cell window. My skin is electric with fury. Any second the door will slide open, the doctor will walk in, and some fresh new horror will begin. All over a plastic spoon. My legs quake with the need to run, but there's nowhere to go.

Besides, I can take it.

"Open it," the doctor says.

I hear the clank of a key in a lock, the rumble of a door sliding open, but mine doesn't move. Understanding comes a moment later than it should.

"No!" I throw myself at my locked door, my fists making hollow banging sounds against the metal. "Leave him alone! Finn!"

On the other side of the wall, Finn yelps in pain. I hear the faint sizzle of the special military-issue Taser the doctor prefers to use so as not to get his fine hands dirty. It has an array of settings, some of which can knock a person unconscious or instantly stop a heart. I've experienced the first and seen the second, and the idea of that device being used on Finn makes me crazy. I scream his name and throw myself at the door again and again.

The doctor appears at the tiny window in my cell door, and I jerk back like I'm scared he'll reach through the glass and wrap his hands around my throat. Not that he'd need to. Just seeing his face makes me feel as though he's choking the life out of me.

"You can make this stop any time," he says. He looks the same as he always has. I doubt I would recognize myself in a mirror, but time has left him untouched. His voice softens into something like kindness. "Just give me the spoon."

I stare at him with blurry, burning eyes. Finn is moaning in pain now, and there's nothing I can do, because that paper would damn us both. I swallow, and it tastes of bile. "I don't have it. Kessler must have lost it."

The doctor looks sad, and, God, I despise him for that. Then he inclines his head, and Kessler does something that makes Finn scream.

My voice and the sides of my fists are raw from banging on the walls by the time Finn falls silent. Kessler's heavy footsteps and the doctor's lighter ones pass my cell and then die away. Guilt fills me like lead and makes movement slow and exhausting as I pull the pillow and thin cotton blanket off my cot and curl up on the cold floor next to the heating vent.

"Finn?" I whisper. "You there?"

It's silent. Does he hate me as much as I hate myself right now?

"Finn?"

"Just got home. Went out for pizza."

I burst into tears.

"Hey." His voice is soft and hoarse. "Hey, it's okay."

"Shut up!" I cry. "Don't try to comfort me! I just got you *tortured*!"

"Shh, Em, I'm fine."

"You're not!"

"I *am*. I just . . ."

"What?"

He sighs. "I just wish I could see you."

I scoot closer to the wall, until I'm pressed against it, and I spread my fingers against the concrete blocks like it's him I'm touching. It's foolish, and I'm glad he can't see it, but it makes me feel a little better. "Me too."

"Remember when you used to hate me?"

I laugh-sniff-hiccup. "Well, you used to be insufferable."

"I think *incorrigible* is a better word."

I lean my forehead against the wall and let myself imagine for a moment that it's his shoulder, warm and firm, beside me. "You're so full of it."

"Hey, I just got tortured for you. Easy on the ego."

"Finn—"

"Shh," he says softly. "Now, tell me how wrong you were back then and how wonderful I am."

He *is* wonderful. And he doesn't deserve this.

Neither do I.

"I'm going to kill him," I say softly.

"Yeah, I know."

"No, I'm serious. We're going to get out of here," I say, "and I'm going to kill him."

I explain everything—the drain, the paper, and the message at the bottom—in a whisper through the slats of the vent. Finn's silence is as thick and solid as the wall between us. I try to picture him. Shaggy blond hair probably in desperate need of a cut, curling around his ears and the nape of his neck. Blue eyes wide and unfocused with shock. Or are they green? No, definitely blue. Blue like deep, clean water. His mouth hanging open, but no matter how hard I try, I can't remember what that mouth looks like. Lips thin or full, pink or pale?

I'm not even sure what *I* look like anymore.

"Can we do it?" he finally asks.

Can we kill him is what he means, but maybe he can't say the words. "I'm not sure we have any choice."

"But first," he says, "we'd have to break out of here. Go back. You think it's possible?"

"Judging from the note, we've done it fourteen times already."

"How?"

"I don't know. But I'm sure I would have told me if I needed to know."

He laughs. "I can't believe the insanity of that sentence."

"Can't you?" I envy Finn's gift for finding humor in every situation, but nothing about this is funny to me.

"Em . . ."

"Don't tell me we don't have to do this." I must have had a damn good reason for writing that sentence, and the twisted little creature inside of me, the one made up of all my anger and bitterness, isn't sorry. "Don't tell me there's another way."

"Actually, I was going to ask what you're wearing."

I bite my lip to stop the smile. Okay, *that* was kind of funny.

"God, I miss you," I say, and instantly wish the words back again. I turn my face away from the vent, irrationally afraid he'll see me blushing.

"I know," he says, voice soft. I imagine him pressing his hand to the other side of the wall. "But I'm right here."

Days pass. Finn and I spend the time that spans three meals talking over what I've discovered.

"What time should we go to?" he finally asks. We've both

been avoiding the subject. It's painful, and we get enough of that in here already.

"I've been thinking about that," I say. "We need to be there for January fourth. Four years ago."

Silence.

"Really?"

I get his hesitation. It's not a time I want to relive, either.

"We can't do it before he's figured out the formula," I say. "The paradox would be so massive that there's no way to predict what would happen. It has to be after."

"Okay," he says, "but why the fourth?"

"Because he'll never think to look for us there," I say. "Remember when I got the documents?"

"Of course. It was that day."

"But the doctor doesn't know that," I say. "He thinks I stumbled on them sometime later. Know why?"

"Why?"

"Because he *doesn't remember* discovering the formula that day," I say. "He thinks he first wrote it down three days later, on the seventh."

"So if we go to the fourth," Finn says, "we'll have at least three days before he expects us."

"Exactly." I sigh. "Plus, he'll be weak because of what's just happened. Any later in time and he'll be too powerful. Too protected."

Finn agrees. He knows as well as I do that there's no other time that will give us as good a chance. We go over everything again, working out every detail we can in advance. By the end,

I've memorized every struck-out word of the note and think I know the chain of events that led it to my hands. I don't remember the events that compelled me to write these lines, but those past versions of myself, copies of me that no longer exist, left me enough clues to figure it out.

With nothing left to discuss and without the drain to obsess over, there's nothing to do but stare at the ceiling. The bad food, the pain, even the visits from the doctor, I can handle. But this tedium? This waiting for *something* to happen? I'm sure it'll drive me crazy.

"Finn, you awake?" I say, rolling over onto my side.

No response. His ability to sleep under any circumstance amazes me. He must spend sixteen hours a day sleeping just to stave off the boredom.

"You suck," I whisper.

I stare at the door for a while to give the ceiling a break. Somehow, one of these days, I *must* get out of this cell. At least I have before, every earlier version of me who's escaped and added to the note under my mattress. How do I do it? I wish I could remember the events those other Ems experienced, because escape seems impossible. I work through every option in my head for the hundredth time. I could overpower the guard who brings me my meals, or get a hold of the doctor when he comes for one of his midnight visits and use him as a hostage. That would get me out of my cell and maybe get Finn out of his. But even if I were able to do that—and, let's face it, that's a huge *if*—there's still a massive government facility beyond my cell that I only glimpsed once, months ago, on the day they dragged me in here. It's full of armed soldiers standing between me and Cassandra, even if I knew where I was going, which I definitely don't. Every plan I come up with leads to a dead end or a bullet through the head.

Like everything else, contemplating my escape and/or death eventually gets boring. So boring that I'm almost relieved when my door opens to reveal the doctor and the man Finn and I have dubbed "the director," the puppet master who pulls the doctor's strings.

Almost.

I pretend to yawn, because I know it rankles him, but my heart is hammering. "Is it time again already?"

The director inclines his head, and a soldier comes forward to yank me to my feet and sit me down in the metal folding chair they've brought with them. He secures my hands to the supports of the chair with the same kind of zip ties our gardener used to use on the rosebushes.

"Her feet, too," the director says. I'm gratified to see he remembers what happened last time.

Once the defenseless teenage girl surrounded by the men with machine guns is properly restrained, the interrogation begins. I used to count how many times the doctor and the director visited for one of our little chats—thinking each time might be the last, that their patience would run thin and they'd finally kill me—but I lost track somewhere in the twenties. That was weeks ago.

"Where are the documents?" the director says.

"You're not even going to ask me how my day's been first? Didn't your mother teach you any manners?"

The director slaps me across the face. Unlike the doctor, he doesn't mind bloodying his hands. My vision swims. The movies didn't prepare me for this, for how much getting hit actually hurts, and somehow it's always still a shock.

"I've got no time for your games today," the director says. "We need to know where the documents are. Who did you give them to? China? India?"

"Lives depend on this," the doctor says quietly from the corner of the room, as though he gives a damn.

I blow the director a kiss as best I can without the use of my hands. I know very well that the moment I tell them where the documents are, my last bargaining chip is gone. That I have that information and they don't is the only thing that's kept Finn and me alive this long. Even when I'd rather give it up and get my death over with already, knowing I also hold Finn's life in my hands keeps me silent. No matter what they do.

And they do their damnedest.

I'm sure my screams wake Finn from his nap, but at least I don't give us up.

THREE

em

Another day passes. I'm only half awake, staring at the ceiling, trying to make out the cracks I know are there in the faint bluish light from the hallway. I finger my bruises idly. From the way they feel when I press my fingers against them, I think they're probably that purplish-red color that's like the bedspread in our old guest room. My mother always liked that color. I suspect it had something to do with her affinity for a good cabernet.

I hear boots in the hallway and frown. I'm not hungry; is it time for breakfast already? But no, the lights are still off.

My door opens slowly, and the guard behind it is one who's only recently been assigned to us. I like him. There's still the glimmer of basic human decency in his eyes, and, unlike Kessler, he always hands me my meals and even says thank you sometimes when I hand the tray back. I'm unsure of his name. Connor? Cooper?

"When you were little," he says, hovering in the doorway,

"you had an imaginary friend named Miles. He was a purple kangaroo."

I bolt upright. "What?"

"Come on. We have to go."

"What do you mean?"

"I'm getting you out of here."

My mouth goes dry, and my tongue feels suddenly too large for my mouth. This is what I've been waiting for. The way out. I never told anyone about Miles, not in my entire life.

Except, apparently, this guard.

"What about Finn?" I say.

"Him too. Hurry up."

I jump to my feet, and my legs are surprisingly solid beneath me. I reach under my mattress and pull out the sheet of paper in the plastic bag, stuffing it in my pocket. The guard—Connor?—is already gone, on his way to free Finn. I step toward my cell door slowly. It's wide open. I touch the door frame with the tips of my fingers, examining the place where the walls that have been my boundaries for so long end and become nothingness. I take a tentative step through, and for one stupid second I think I might cry.

I hear the rattle of a key in a lock, and turn, watching Connor struggle to open Finn's cell. Oh my God. The realization crashes over me like that rogue wave at Kiawah Island that knocked the air from my lungs: I'm about to see Finn.

Connor finally manages the lock and pulls the door open, and everything slows until the silence between each heartbeat in my ears is expansive and deafening. If I reacted to our sudden freedom like an animal who had forgotten the world outside its bars, Finn flies out of his cell like a bird from a cage. I barely have time to look at him before he collides with me in a tangle of arms and legs, holding me so tightly I can't breathe and don't care.

"Oh my God," he says over and over. "Oh my God."

"Let me look at you." I pull away and put my hands on his cheeks, examining his face. Blue eyes, of course. And how could I forget that mouth? Thin pink lips with one crooked corner always suggesting a mocking smile. My God, how had I never noticed before how handsome he is? "You need a haircut."

He rubs the side of his thumb over my cheekbone. "You're beautiful."

I've been scared for years. On the run, isolated from everyone I love, and then locked in this cell, tortured and interrogated with the threat of death always hovering over my shoulder. But I swear I've never been as scared as I am when Finn leans forward to kiss me for the very first time.

He presses his lips to mine so softly that I think he must be afraid this is a dream that will dissolve at the best part. His hands press tighter to my back, pulling me close, and for a second all my fear is drowned out.

"I'm sorry," Connor says, "but we've got to get moving."

Finn shoots me a shy smile as we disentangle ourselves, and Connor draws his gun as he starts down the hallway. I take Finn's hand and weave our fingers together. Now that he's beside me, I don't want to lose him again, even for a second.

Connor leads the way, and we follow just behind. My head is constantly moving, taking in everything around us. It's my first glimpse of the place since they locked us in here however many months ago, and I wasn't in a state then to take in the scenery. There are three more cells next to mine and Finn's, reinforced like ours with cinder-block walls and metal doors, but they're empty. The rest of the hallway seems to be used for storage, and it's so banal that I'm shocked and not a little offended. It looks like the doctor packed Finn and me away with the rest of the old junk, like a box of winter clothes put away for the summer and eventually forgotten.

"Where is everyone?" I whisper once we're through the locked door that separates our hallway from the rest of the facility. So far we haven't spotted a single soldier.

"It's the middle of the night, skeleton shift," Connor says over his shoulder. "And I drugged the coffeepot in the break room."

"You know," I say, "I'm really starting to like you."

"Don't decide that until we get to Cassandra."

We creep toward the heart of the facility, which I see now is huge. Connor has to be careful to keep his boots from thumping against the concrete floor, while Finn and I pad silently in our thin prisoners' slippers. My breathing grows more labored with each step, the center of my chest burning from the effort. I didn't realize what a toll living in a room only four steps across was taking on my body until this moment. I glance at Finn to see if he's starting to sweat and shake the way I am, but he seems unaffected. He's probably been working out in his cell, the vain little bastard.

I'm wishing now I'd thought of it.

"You okay?" he says. I've been slowing down, and he's now pulling me forward where our hands are still clutched together.

I nod, take a deep breath, and force myself to quicken my pace.

I'm so focused on putting one foot in front of the other that I don't hear the door open at the other end of the hallway or see the dark-haired man step through it. But Connor does. His arm crashes into my chest, shoving Finn and me into the recess of another doorway, and I only catch a glimpse of the man as I'm shuffling backward, out of sight.

It's the doctor. I plaster myself against the door and try to rein in my ragged breathing.

Connor walks toward him, and terror slices through me like a knife. I'm suddenly sure this has been some setup of the doctor's, another trick to break us down. Connor will turn us back in to him now, and we'll never leave our cells again. I'm seized by the wild desire to run.

Maybe sensing what I'm thinking, Finn squeezes my hand, holding me in place.

"Connor, what are you doing in this part of the building?" we hear the doctor ask from our flimsy hiding place. All he has to do is take a few steps in our direction and the recess in the wall will fail to hide us any longer. "Aren't you supposed to be watching the prisoners?"

"Yes, sir. Abrams is covering me. The sergeant sent me to find you."

The doctor sighs in irritation. "I'm not even on duty; I just came in to finish some paperwork. What does he need?"

"Not sure, sir. All he said was that he needed to see you in cent-comm."

Footsteps approach us. Not Connor's heavy-soled boots, but

what I'd bet my life is fine Italian leather. I press myself so hard against the door at my back that I'll have new bruises to add to my collection if we survive the night.

"I need to go to my office first," the doctor says, "and then—"

"He said it was urgent, sir."

The footsteps stop. "Take your hand off me, soldier."

Oh God. I ball my free hand into a fist. If the doctor comes this way, at least I can give him a few bruises of his own before he kills me.

"Excuse me, sir," Connor says in a shaken voice. "I only meant that the sarge really needs you, and there's not time . . ."

The silence stretches, and with my eyes closed I can almost see the evaluating expression on the doctor's face as he looks at Connor. To my ears, Connor sounds wildly guilty, and the doctor would have to be deaf not to realize something is amiss. I can only hope his obliviousness to people and his own sense of invincibility will win out.

"Fine," the doctor finally says. "I'll go to cent-comm, and you get yourself back to those prisoners. And next time, remember your place."

"Yes, sir."

The doctor's lighter step moves away from us, and I release the breath I've been holding.

"We've got to move now," Connor says when he returns to us. "He'll know something's up when he gets to cent-comm and no one's there. It's on the other side of the facility, though, and Cassandra is close."

We run through the corridors, Connor ten or fifteen feet

ahead to scout for other soldiers and Finn practically dragging me alongside him. When we stop, I double over, resting my hands on my knees as I struggle to catch my breath. Finn rubs my back in soothing little circles, but Connor's attention is entirely focused forward. He has his gun pulled up to his chest, poised at a turn in the hallway. He holds a finger to his lips.

"Control room's right around the corner," he whispers. "It'll be guarded—nothing I could do about that—so you two stay back."

Finn tenses beside me. "What are you going to do?"

"Does it matter? Once you go back, none of this will have ever happened, right?"

I swallow another gulp of air. "That's the idea."

"Don't move." Connor tucks his gun back into its holster and turns the corner at a run. We hear him shout, followed by the sound of fists banging on glass. The control room. Finn puts his arm around my shoulders, and I tuck myself close to his body. God, he's warm. It's been so long that I'd forgotten how warm another person could be.

"Fire in A-Wing!" Connor cries. "We need all units. Come on!"

There's a pause, then the barely audible swish of a door opening.

"There's no alarm," a soldier says, "or radio call."

"We can't leave our post," a second adds.

The sudden pop of two gunshots reverberating off the hard walls is deafening. I clap my hands over my mouth.

"Come on!" Connor shouts.

Finn starts to run, so I do too, rounding the corner and approaching the control room, which is surrounded floor to ceiling with bulletproof glass. The two soldiers are slumped in the doorway, a pool of dark blood beneath them, spreading with each second. I never could have imagined so much blood. The movies didn't prepare me for the sight of two men whose heads have been blown off, either.

Connor stands inside the control room, on the other side of the guards' broken bodies. His face and uniform are speckled red, and I shudder when he holds a hand out to me. It's his right hand, the one he used to shoot with, and the blowback has left a shadow of tiny red dots across his skin. I force myself to take it, and he helps me jump over the bodies of the dead men. Finn leaps after me, but his foot lands in the edge of the spreading pool of blood and slips out from under him, sending him sprawling to the floor. I help him up, and he kicks off his sodden slippers.

"I hope to God you know how this thing works," Connor says, staring at the rows and rows of machinery and flashing lights on the console. Above them is a viewing window that looks into a second, smaller chamber that's only accessible from a door in the corner of the control room. The tiny room is an arresting sight, eerily devoid of color and texture, a smooth, empty box in shades of gray.

"I have an idea," I say. "Someone used to talk my ear off about it. Finn, can you—"

"On it," he says, already sliding into the chair in front of the main computer terminal. "If I know anything about our doctor, the system was designed to be simple to use."

Finn taps away at the keyboard, a faint line of concentration crossing his brow. I know he'll get snappish and stressed if he's interrupted, so I turn to Connor. "Thanks for doing this."

He wipes the back of his hands on his trousers. "No problem."

"Why are you helping us?" I ask. "I mean, how did I convince you? I'll need to know."

He shrugs. "I was a glorified security guard, and you gave me the chance to be a hero. Besides, some of the things I've seen . . ."

"How bad is it out there?"

"Bad."

Connor looks scared, and that terrifies me. This is a man who calmly drugged his very well-armed colleagues and just shot two men through the head without blinking, but whatever's going on in the outside world has him tight-lipped and tense. When Finn and I were captured, American drone planes were attacking China, Israel was in a nuclear standoff with Syria, and a good chunk of Houston had just been wiped off the map. It was hard to imagine that things could get worse.

But I guess they did.

"You really think you can change all of this?" Connor asks, and I can see now the desperation hiding deep in the back of his eyes.

I run my finger along the edge of the plastic bag in my pocket. "I think we won't stop until we do."

"Oh, here," he says, reaching into his own pocket. "I almost forgot. You'll need this." He pulls out his wallet and works a small photograph of a woman with honey-colored hair and a bright, toothy smile from the photo flap. He hands it to me.

"What's this?"

He grins. "That's the real way you convince me to help."

I smile. "Oh. She's pretty."

"And she said yes to a loser like me, can you believe it?"

I put the photo in my pocket along with the note in plastic. "Yeah, I can."

"Okay, I've got it," Finn says, entering a few final keystrokes. "Everything's pretty much automated, so I just need to input the date and then Connor can start up the collider once we're inside."

"Wait," Connor says. "If you input a date, won't he follow right behind you? Or show up ten minutes before you do and shoot you the moment you appear?"

"We've already thought about that," I say.

"I know a code that will hide the real date we use and show something else," Finn says. "Are you *sure* about January fourth, Em? Last chance."

"I'm sure."

"Okay," Finn says. "I'm going to make it seem like we went to the seventh. That's when the doctor will expect us, and it should give us plenty of time to take care of things before he comes back for us."

"How do I start the collider?" Connor asks.

"Once we're inside the chamber"—Finn points at the RETURN button—"press this. The automation will do the rest. It takes the accelerator about two minutes to get the particles to the right velocity for collision, and after that we should be gone."

"Seems easy enough," Connor says. I repress a hysterical urge to laugh. "I guess there's nothing left to say but, you know, good luck."

Finn shakes Connor's hand, and he and I walk to the far side of the control room, where the door to the inner chamber is. When Finn pulls it open, an earsplitting siren explodes through the building. My hands fly to my ears, my body curling into itself and away from the deafening sound, and Finn swears.

"Get in!" Connor hollers over the din. "Before they get down here! I'll hold them off!"

Connor slams the door to the inner chamber behind us. I pull Finn after me into the heart of the room so that we're both standing on the large black circle that marks the center of Cassandra, the miles-long subatomic particle collider that's built deep under the ground of this facility. Connor barricades the door to the chamber, tipping what looks like a backup server rack in front of it. The siren is so loud, I don't even hear the bang of the server hitting the floor. Connor runs back to the computer, and the wail of the siren is joined by another sound, a rumbling so low I think I might be imagining it until the vibrations travel up from the collider thousands of feet beneath me and into my feet. Energy hums around Finn and me, lifting the hair off the back of my neck and sending gooseflesh up my arms.

This is only the beginning, I know. I've never made this trip that fourteen past versions of me have, but I've heard it explained often enough to know what comes next. When the particles whirring beneath my feet around the miles of pipe big enough to drive a truck through finally slam into one another at nearly the speed of light, the explosion will be so powerful, it will fracture time itself.

I'm suddenly very scared. Not of the explosion, which defies my comprehension, but of what I'll have to do when it's all over. Of what all this is for.

You have to kill him.

Either Finn senses my fear or he feels it himself, because he puts his hands on my cheeks, lifting my eyes up to his.

"It's going to be okay," he says, the words barely audible above the roar.

But then things get very quiet, for me at least. Somehow I find silence in Finn's dark blue eyes. God, how did I survive so long in that cell without being able to see those eyes?

I'm hit with a crashing realization. Something so obvious, I can't believe I haven't thought of it until now. My heart breaks and spills white-hot misery into my body.

"Finn," I say, and I tell him the terrible thing I've finally understood, too late to do anything about it.

He looks into my eyes and tells me why I don't have to worry. I memorize the words and hold them close.

Over his shoulder, I see a flash of movement, and the world and its noise are back. The soldiers have arrived. While we weren't looking, Connor cleared the bodies of the dead from the doorway and closed off the control room, but the door's a paltry barrier to them. I watch in horror as they send it rocketing open. Connor fires into the press of bodies that crowd the doorway, taking down soldier after soldier, but they have more numbers and more guns. He's quickly overwhelmed. I hide my face against Finn's chest after a volley of bullets knocks Connor back and he sags to the floor.

But I can't look away for long. Soldiers are pouring into the control room. Most go straight for the server rack jammed against the door to the inner chamber. If they get the door open, Cassandra will automatically shut down, stranding us here.

But the sight that truly fills me with dread is the doctor entering the room in the wake of the soldiers. Our eyes meet through the four-inch glass of the chamber's viewing window, and the fury in his face chills me to my marrow. I think he must know what I plan to do. Even if we get away, I know that look will haunt me across time.

He goes to the computer terminal. The rumbling beneath our feet is like an earthquake now, but between the doctor at the keyboard and the soldiers at the doorway, we only have seconds. I squeeze Finn's hand in mine so tightly, I feel his bones rub together. They'll shut Cassandra down and finally kill us in some slow, inventive way.

But they're too late.

As the soldiers heave open the door, the world explodes, and my body dissolves in an agony of fire.

FOUR

marina
FOUR YEARS EARLIER

I pick absently at the pink polish on my thumbnail as I gaze out over the driveway next door, and Tamsin slaps my hand.

"Stop that!" She examines the nail and sighs. "I'm going to have to do that one over."

"It was uneven anyway," I say. "You'll live."

Sophie, who's sprawled out on my bed, doesn't look up from her phone when she says, "At least she doesn't bite them anymore."

"I know, right? So gross."

Of course, I do bite them sometimes, but I'm careful not to do it around my friends. I still can't get used to the feel of polish; it's like my nails are suffocating. But Tam says she's honing in on my perfect color, something to go along with the plum-colored "Sophie So Fine" and bright red "Tam-erica the Beautiful."

"Marina . . ." Tamsin says as she applies a coat to the fingers of my right hand. "Marina . . . Your name doesn't rhyme with anything."

Sophie's head snaps up. "Aqua Marina!"

"Well, duh, but I'm painting her nails *pink*, genius. Goes better with brown hair."

I'm only half listening, my eyes drifting toward the window and the house next door. Tamsin looks up and catches me.

"He hasn't shown up since you checked ten seconds ago," she says, flashing me a grin.

I think about playing dumb, but end up just rolling my eyes. "Shut up."

There's no point pretending I'm not waiting for James to get home. I got a single text from him in the three weeks he was gone, to let me know he'd be back from Connecticut tonight. Normally we would have been exchanging phone calls and texts the whole time he was gone, but it felt too awkward given what happened before he left.

"He's *totally* going to ask you out," Sophie says, crossing to my closet where she starts to rifle through my clothes. "I can't believe you're going to be James Shaw's girlfriend!"

"I don't know. . . ." I say. I've been in love with James pretty much as long as I can remember, but I've never had any hope he'd feel the same way. Given who he is and who I am, it's basically impossible.

"Oh, please." Tamsin blows across my newly pink nails. "He almost kissed you, and for James that's, like, practically a proposal. Has he *ever* kissed a girl before?"

I doubt it, but even the idea of James kissing another girl

makes my stomach hurt. "He hasn't even talked to me since, though! Doesn't that mean he regrets it?"

"No, he was just freaked out by the realization that he's madly in love with you," Tamsin says. "But now that he's had time to wrap his big brain around it—"

"Bet that's not the only big thing he has," Sophie says, wiggling her eyebrows.

Tamsin groans, and I say, "Gross!" But Sophie just laughs and pulls on my new cashmere sweater, checking her reflection in the mirror.

"I'm serious!" she says. "You know you're going to have to make the first move with him, right?"

"Totally," Tamsin says. "But play it cool."

"How do I do that?" I say. I get shaky and sweaty just thinking about it. "Not *all* of us have jumped so many boys that it's that easy."

"With that boy?" Sophie says. "It sure as hell *should* be easy."

Sophie makes lewd moaning noises and kisses the back of her hand, and Tamsin and I laugh. This is the best thing about Sophie; she's never scared of looking dumb. Maybe because she kind of is. Meanwhile, Tamsin, with her posh British accent and Bollywood-star looks, instantly makes anything she does or says seem cool, so it's really only me who's constantly worrying about making a fool of myself. I just can't bear to go back to being the friendless loser I was before.

There's a knock on my bedroom door, and Sophie claps her hand over her mouth. "Are your parents home?" she whispers.

I wave my hand. "It's just Luz. Come in!"

Luz, who's been our housekeeper since I was little, pokes her head in the door.

"I'm going home, *mi querida*," she says. "Are you okay until your mama gets home?"

Tamsin laughs, and I stiffen.

"I'm sixteen, Luz," I say. "I think I'll manage."

I see a troubled look pass over the woman's face and briefly feel bad. Luz is one of the few people in the world who really loves me, but I wish she wouldn't treat me like such a little kid. It's embarrassing.

"There are empanadas in the refrigerator if you girls want a snack," she says.

"Okay," I say, knowing there's no way we'll eat empanadas. She looks like she might say something else—like *sleep tight* or *you don't eat enough* or *I love you*—so I jump in. "Bye, Luz."

"Good night, *mi querida*."

When she's gone, Tamsin starts on her own nails and Sophie tries on a couple of the dresses I bought during our latest shopping trip. Every one of them looks loose on her perfect body. I decide to eat nothing but salad for the next week before school starts.

I look over at the Shaws' place again. A crew came to shovel the driveway and sidewalk this morning in anticipation of the congressman's return. Any second, a sleek black town car will drive up. It will happen by the time I count to five.

I tick off the numbers in my head, drawing them out. Three, four . . . five.

Nothing.

I reach for my phone and dash off a text to our friend Olivia, who's in Switzerland with her parents for break. She invited me to go with them, but I decided not to just so that I'd be home when James got back. I'm so stupid. Wherever he is, James isn't jittering with anxiety over seeing *me* again, running his mind over the moment three weeks ago where his mouth lingered an inch from mine before drawing away. I'm popular and reasonably smart and very independent; I don't need to be obsessing over some boy like this, like such a pathetic little *girl*.

Tamsin and Sophie stay over until my mom comes home from her planning meeting for the symphony benefit and slams the front door behind her. The sound echoes up the stairwell, and suddenly the air is tense and thick, like Mom brought a thunderstorm in with her. It doesn't take my friends long to decide to clear out. I only wish I could go with them.

"Text me later, okay?" Tam says at the front door. "I want to hear what happens."

"You'll be the first to know."

Sophie kisses my cheek. "Go get him, tiger!"

"Oh my God, you're such a dork," I say, even though my stomach tightens. I push her out the door and wave as they climb into Tam's Cabriolet. She shouldn't be driving without an adult since we're not old enough for licenses yet, but she always sneaks it out of the garage when her parents aren't home. I close the door gingerly behind them, trying not to make a sound, and lunge for the stairs.

"Marina?" Mom calls from her studio at the back of the house.

I groan and stop on the fourth stair. So close. "Yeah?"

"Don't yell across the house; come here!"

I roll my eyes savagely and barely avoid calling back that *she's* the one who started the yelling. I tromp back to her studio, where she makes paintings that no one wants to buy and which inevitably end up hanging in one of our guest bedrooms. I think she actually dreamed of being a great artist once, but the closest she gets now is hosting fund-raisers for the National Gallery.

"What is it?" I say.

"Watch the tone," she says, blending a couple of reds on her palette. "Have you talked to your father today?"

You'd think in this age of e-mail and cell phones they wouldn't need to use *me* as a communication medium, but lately they only seem to talk to me as a means of passing messages to each other. "No."

"Can you call him, please, and ask him if he plans to be home for dinner?"

"Why can't you?"

She levels a look at me over the top of the canvas. "I'm working here, Marina." Like her painting is so important to her. She'll spend hours planning parties for some museum or hospital, or at the salon getting her hair highlighted, but the second she gets home she has to lock herself up in her studio.

I think she just can't stand to be near me.

"Fine." I turn to leave.

"Don't text him!" she calls after me. "You know he never replies!"

I dial Dad's office line as I take the stairs back to my room. It always takes him forever to answer, so I put the phone on speaker and rest it on my dresser as I change into pajamas. Mom hates it when I wear pajamas to dinner. These were a gift from Luz, and my skin sighs in relief when I slip out of the suffocating skinny jeans Tamsin insisted I buy and into the cheap, soft fleece. I feel a brief pang as I remember Luz's face when I snapped at her. Questionable taste in pajamas aside, I do love the woman. She's one of the few people who doesn't make it a total secret that she cares about me, even if that means she embarrasses the hell out of me every chance she gets.

After about fourteen rings, Dad finally picks up the phone. "What is it, honey?"

"Mom wants to know if you'll be home for dinner."

"I don't think so." I can hear him typing in the background. "The lira has gone straight to hell today. Italy's going to need someone to bail them out, but Germany's not biting. Thank God the euro never went through; the whole continent would be screwed."

He's not really talking to me anymore, which is fine, because I'm not really listening. "Okay, I'll tell her."

"We're leaving early tomorrow," he says, "so I may not see you. I spoke to Luz, and she's going to stay while we're gone—"

"Dad! We talked about this!" My parents take off for Vail for a few weeks after Christmas every year. I thought they might skip it this year since they've been fighting so much, but they decided it would be a good opportunity for them to "reconnect." Gross. I wander to the window and look out over the Shaws' driveway. "I'm not a little kid anymore. I can stay by myself."

"I'm sorry, honey, but I'm just not comfortable with that. Luz will be . . ."

I stop hearing him as headlights sweep the yard and a dark car pulls into the Shaws' driveway. The rah-rah-girl-power I'd summoned earlier evaporates in a rush of adrenaline. *James is home.*

"Okay, Dad," I say, cutting off some explanation about post-Christmas burglaries and high school parties. "Gotta go, bye."

I run down the stairs and jam my bare feet into my snow boots, which Luz has wiped down and laid beside the door. I grab my coat from the closet and wrestle it on, suddenly clumsy.

"Going next door!" I cry back to Mom before closing the front door behind me.

I creep carefully down the icy front steps and then run across the yard through ankle-deep snow, slipping on the wet grass beneath, to the Shaws' front door. I press the doorbell twice, which I've always done, and stick my hands into my pockets as I wait.

The door opens, and there's James, all tall, dark, and gorgeous. It's still kind of a shock to see him like this. A couple of years ago, he was just the gangly science kid with oversize ears who was more interested in puzzling out math equations than partying and hooking up with the rest of his classmates. Even though he was a Shaw, I was usually the only one who sat with him at lunch.

Then, practically overnight, James shot up six inches, grew into his ears, and became *hot*. Everyone wanted his attention, because apparently people can overlook your extreme dorkiness once you've been profiled by *Vanity Fair*. Luckily for me, he's just as weird and antisocial as ever.

The girl I was a few weeks ago would have thrown herself into his arms as soon as he opened the door, but I suddenly don't know what to do with myself. Staring at the lips that came so close to mine, I feel like I've become one of those corn-husk dolls we made in elementary school, brittle and fragile to the touch. Everything's different now.

James pulls me into a hug and ruffles my hair. "Hey, kid!"

Okay, not so different. Maybe the almost-kiss never happened. Maybe I imagined it.

I'm so *stupid*.

James pulls back and grins at me. "Nice pajamas."

I punch him in the arm and force a smile. "Shut up. They were a Christmas present from Luz."

"What are they, dancing reindeer?" He bends down to examine the garish pattern more closely. "I like them."

"Are you going to invite me in or not? It's freezing out here."

He steps aside and ushers me in with a sweep of his hand.

"That you, Marina?" James's brother, Nate, calls from upstairs. "Welcome home, Congressman!"

I follow James through the foyer to the kitchen at the back of the house. Once there, James pulls a gallon of double-chocolate ice cream from the freezer, and I smile. He has a whole mouth full of sweet teeth. "Isn't it a little cold for that?" I say.

"Never." He hands me a spoon and lays the tub on the counter between us. "So how are things, Marchetti?"

You'd know if you'd spoken to me in the last three weeks.

I walk around the island counter to stand beside him. "Stand still. I want to look at you."

He grins and straightens, throwing his shoulders back. He's a good eight inches taller than me, with long limbs that made him the best swimmer at Sidwell for the fifteen minutes he was there. His dark hair is a little longer than I remember but perfectly neat as always, and his light brown eyes are so bright when he smiles down at me that I swear my knees weaken.

"Yep," I say, turning to dig my spoon into the softening ice cream. "Still ugly."

He laughs. "Thanks."

"You don't look any smarter, either. Are you sure that fancy school is doing anything for you?"

James blushes—actually *blushes*, which hardly anyone really does—because not only is he a genius, but he's a humble one. He doesn't like people pointing out how very special he is, how he graduated high school three years early, and now, not even eighteen, is already working on his PhD at Johns Hopkins.

"Actually," he says, "there's something I need to tell you."

I'm that empty corn-husk doll again, the slightest breath making me rustle and crack. Maybe Tamsin was right after all. He's only trying to pretend everything is the same as it's always been because he's nervous—James isn't exactly a model of social well-adjustedness—but he wants to tell me how he really feels. I just need to help him along, make the first move.

"Yeah?" I say. "Me too."

He looks relieved. "You first."

"Okay," I say.

Then my mind goes blank.

I should have practiced this. I should have gotten Tamsin and

Sophie to tell me exactly what to say. I spend precious seconds replaying what happened in my head. It was the night of the winter formal at school, and James was leaving for Connecticut the next day. The dance had been a disaster. My heel broke ten minutes after we arrived, Sophie drank too much spiked punch and spent half the night throwing up, and Tamsin broke up with Asher in a suitably dramatic fashion before the first slow dance was even over. After that, my date—Will Denby, who I didn't want to go with in the first place, but of course James was too busy with school to take me—became, like, *physically incapable* of not hitting on her, and I ended up sitting alone at a table in the corner of the room, watching the two of them dance. I fled to the parking lot in my bare feet, holding my broken shoes in one hand and my cell phone in the other.

I knew he was in the middle of a big project for Dr. Feinberg, but I called James anyway.

"Sorry," I said when he picked up the phone. "I know you're working—"

"What's wrong?" he whispered. He must have been in the library. "Are you okay?"

"I'm fine," I lied, my choked voice giving me away.

"Come on, Marina."

"Well . . ." I took a deep breath and the story poured out of me. "Sophie's sick and Tam's dancing with my date, and everything's terrible! Plus I broke my shoe."

"Stay there. I'm coming to pick you up."

I didn't feel the gravel against my feet anymore. I was floating. "James, you don't have to—"

"Twenty minutes."

He showed up in a cab fifteen minutes later with a tube of superglue in hand. He fixed my shoe while the cab drove us to the Diner in Adams Morgan, where James wheedled until I split a stack of chocolate chip pancakes with him. After an hour and more calories than I cared to think about, the tight, queasy feeling in my stomach had dissolved, and I felt happy. Just happy.

Then James hugged me as we parted on the sidewalk outside our houses, and he paused with his face just inches from mine, staring at my lips. The air between us was suddenly electric, and I could feel the heat radiating off of his body. But he pulled away and the moment passed. We said good-bye, and that was the last time I saw him.

It *couldn't* have just been me, could it?

"James . . ." I croak.

"Yeah?"

"I . . ." Oh God oh God oh God. "Did you miss me?"

I could just *slap* myself.

He flashes me his most dazzling smile. "Of course."

"Then why didn't you call?" I say, in a voice roughly similar to one a kicked puppy would use if it could talk.

"That's just it." He moves closer to me, catching my sleeve between his fingers and rubbing his thumb over one of the reindeer in a Santa hat. I can't breathe. "The thing I need to tell you about—"

The chime of the doorbell interrupts the moment. I start, and James drops my sleeve.

"That must be Abbott," he says. "I texted him when we landed."

43

I try to smile and feel my lips stretch uncomfortably tight across my teeth. "Great."

James trots to the front door, so eager to see his *other* best friend, the one he *texted*. I stay in the kitchen, nursing a giant spoonful of ice cream because I'm disgusting. I can faintly hear the two boys greeting each other in the foyer, no doubt engaging in one of those strange boy half hugs or some kind of almost-manly fist bump. I knew from the moment I caught the two of them shooting hoops and talking computers when James came to Sidwell to meet me after tennis practice last year that he was going to be a problem, and I wasn't wrong.

I hate him.

"Hey, Marina!" he says when he follows James back into the kitchen. "Sweet pj's."

I roll my eyes and don't say anything. I don't even look at him.

"I'm sorry," he says. "I didn't mean to break up the party."

I accidentally glance over at him, and his eyes are alight with mocking triumph. Oh yeah, real sorry. The new boy who used to eat lunch at the edge of the basketball team's table but had no real friends is the only one who's managed to worm his way in with James; he knows *exactly* what he's doing. James slides him a spoon as Nate appears from upstairs.

"Hi, Marina," he says. "Mr. Abbott."

"Hey, Congressman."

"You guys know I hate it when you call me that," he says, grabbing a bottle of water from the fridge. Nate's almost twice James's age and has raised him since he was twelve, but he's not like a *dad* or anything. He jogs shirtless through the neighborhood in the summer, is the only person who can beat the boys at Call of Duty, and still helps me sneak into R-rated movies sometimes. "I've got to run to the office for a couple of hours. Top secret spy work."

Nate is on the House Intelligence Committee, and he likes to pretend this makes him James Bond. "So, paperwork?" I say.

"Exactly, smart-ass." He drops a kiss on the crown of my head. "Don't burn the house down while I'm gone, okay?"

James's stupid friend salutes. "Yes, sir!"

"Very funny."

"I'd better go, too," I say, seizing Nate's exit as an opportunity to get out myself. The idea of James asking what I was going to tell him with his friend sitting right there makes me want to vomit. "Mom's going to freak."

"Let me grab my briefcase, and I'll walk you out," Nate says.

"Hey," Abbott says, "don't let me run you off."

"You wish."

"Can we talk later?" James asks, catching my hand. "I have some work to do first, but then . . ."

My chest swells, because I'm pathetic. "Sure."

Nate appears at my side, briefcase in tow and coat already on. "Ready?"

"Nighty-night, Marina!" the idiot says. "Sleep tight, don't let the bedbugs bite!"

I punch his shoulder on my way out. Hard. "Shut up, Finn."

"So, how was Connecticut?" I ask Nate as we walk out of the house.

He shrugs and swings his car keys around his index finger.

"Fine. Good to be home, though. James really missed you."

I brighten. "Yeah?"

"You bet." He musses my hair, too, which is either a Shaw thing or a Marina-is-still-twelve thing. "Me too."

"Thanks. Don't work too hard, okay?"

Maybe it's a trick of the light as we pass out of the shadows and into the glow of the streetlamp, but Nate's expression seems to change, become harder. He smiles at me, but it looks different than usual. "We'll see."

"You okay?" I say, noticing for the first time that there are dark smudges under his eyes and his skin looks oddly tight, like the muscles underneath are rigid with tension. "You look kind of awful."

"Ugh." Nate grabs his stomach like I've punched him. "Way to hit me where it hurts."

I grin. "You know what I mean. Is everything okay? We're not about to be invaded by Canada, are we?"

"No, nothing that terrifying," he says, unlocking his car and tossing his briefcase into the passenger's seat. "I've just been busy with this investigation, ate up my whole recess. It's nothing for you to worry about, though."

"Oh. Okay."

"Do you . . ." Nate runs a hand across his forehead. "I'm sorry, Marina, this is a weird thing for me to ask."

"What is it?"

"Could you . . . keep an eye on James for me?"

I frown. "What do you mean?"

"I'm worried he's working too hard."

I laugh. "He's always working too hard!"

"Yeah," Nate says, "but this seems different. Can you just let me know if he says anything odd, or starts acting different? Different for James, I mean."

A chill runs up my spine, and I pull my coat closed. It's colder out here than I realized. "Sure, I guess."

"Thanks, Marina," Nate says. "You're a good friend. Now get inside before you freeze."

I smile and make my way back across the lawn. "Good night, Congressman!"

"Nate!" he shouts after me, and he waits beside his car until I'm safely inside my own house.

A faint trilling drags me up from the depths of sleep. I manage to crack open one bleary eye and reach for my cell phone, which is glowing blue in the dark of my bedroom. JAMES, the display reads.

"Ugh." I press the answer button. "Why are you calling me, you lunatic?"

"I didn't wake you, did I?" he asks.

"Of course not. It's only . . ." I glance at the clock. "Two thirty in the morning."

"Oh. Sorry. I didn't realize it was so late. I started working after Finn left, and I guess I lost track of time."

I climb out of bed and wrap a throw blanket around my shoulders. With the phone still pressed to my ear, I settle into the window seat across the room from my bed. James sits in the window opposite, surrounded by a mountain of open books and papers, the golden glow of his desk lamp making a halo around him.

47

"Remember when we used to have two soup cans strung between our rooms?" he asks. The sound of his voice through the phone lags a fraction of a second behind the movement of his lips, so he looks like one of the filmstrips we used to watch in elementary school: not quite synced right.

I smile. "Quickly replaced by walkie-talkies, if I remember correctly. Mom said having cans hung from the windows made us look like hobos."

"Yeah, but they were more fun."

"Is this what you woke me up for?"

"I forget how cranky you get when you're sleepy." He smiles. "Actually, there was something I meant to ask you before you ran off earlier—"

"I did not *run off*—"

"Nate's speaking at some DNC fund-raiser at the Mandarin Oriental tomorrow," James continues, ignoring me, "and they need a couple of bodies to fill empty chairs. It'll probably be boring, but he already put your name on the list and had you vetted, so do you feel like having a free dinner while the vice president speaks tomorrow night?"

Is James asking me out? A month ago the thought wouldn't have crossed my mind, but now . . .

"Do I get to dress up?" I ask.

"Black tie. And you thought you'd never have an excuse to wear your winter-formal dress again."

A fancy dinner in a D.C. ballroom with James in a tux. Yeah, I think I can handle that. My mind instantly spins an elaborate fantasy: James's face when he sees me in my dress, the way our hands will brush and linger as we both reach for the butter dish, the impromptu dance he'll sweep me into under a streetlamp. He'll lean forward and say the thing he's been meaning to tell me, that he's been waiting weeks to say: that he's in love with me and can't live without me.

"Finn's coming, too."

The dream shatters at my feet, and I scrunch up my face. Finn Abbott ruins *everything*.

James sees my expression and laughs. "You should give him a chance. I think you'd really like him. He likes *you*."

"Aww, you are so terrible at spotting a liar. It's almost sweet."

"Anyway—"

"I don't get why you're friends with him. He's an idiot."

"No, he's not. He's amazing with computers, you know, even builds his own."

"Okay, so he's a big nerd like you. He's still an idiot."

"He's funny," James says, "and he treats me like a normal person. Could you at least try to be nice to him for one night?"

I sigh. "If the fund-raiser's going to be boring, you have to let me have fun somehow."

He smiles, and I swear the room gets a little brighter. "Fair enough. So, you in?"

It may not be quite the fairy tale I'd hoped for, but it's still James in a tux. Even with Finn there. "Definitely."

"Great! You'd better get some sleep, then. It's late."

"Oh, is it really?"

"Ha, ha." He starts to get up, but then stops. "Oh, wait. What was it you wanted to tell me earlier?"

I don't feel real without you beside me.

I swallow. I can't do it, not now. "Nothing. Tell you later."

"Yeah," he says. "Me too. Probably better when you're not half asleep."

"Yeah," I whisper.

"'Night, Marina."

He hangs up and walks away, and a moment later the light in his room goes out. I press my face close to my window and exhale, fogging up the pane of glass, and draw a heart with one fingertip.

"*What* did you do?" Tamsin says when I open the door.

"Nothing!" I say. "I couldn't say or do *anything*! He said he needed to tell me something, and I said I did, too, but then I couldn't. So I just pretended like things were normal, and then Finn Abbott came over—"

Tamsin makes a face.

"—and I left! I need your help."

She loops my arm in hers. "You're pretty much a hopeless case, Marina, but if anyone can salvage your pathetic love life, it's me."

She leads me upstairs and sits me down on my bed while she goes through my closet, jewelry, and makeup—most of which she helped me pick out—and assembles her tools. Sophie arrives twenty minutes later with a bag of shoes and a rolling suitcase full of cosmetics and hair products. They start to argue about the merits of sparkle versus no sparkle and send me off to take a shower.

When I emerge in my robe, they're both ready for me. Sophie sits me down in my desk chair, where an array of products is lined up, waiting for me. "We've got this," she says. "You're going to look *hot*."

Tamsin starts on my makeup and Sophie on my hair, and I just close my eyes and let it happen. They're good at this kind of stuff, and I'm obviously not. Not *looking* stupid tonight is step number one in not *being* stupid.

Now I just need to figure out how to act.

"We were talking while you were in the shower," Tamsin says, "and we've decided he's definitely just being shy, and you have to take charge."

"Uh-huh," Sophie says, working through a snarl in my hair.

"But how do I *do* that?" I say.

"You've got to embrace your inner hotness." Tam tilts my chin up, and I open my eyes. "You're best friends with *James Shaw*. You live in the best part of town, your dad practically runs the World Bank, and ever since you became friends with us, you're one of the most popular girls at Sidwell. You're D.C. royalty, Marina, and you've got to own that already. The boy would be lucky to have you."

I guess she's right. I have come a long way. James used to be my only real friend at Sidwell, until the stupid genius graduated when I was still thirteen and left me stranded. But then Tamsin and Sophie took me under their wing, and now everyone turns their heads when I walk into a room.

"Okay," I say. "Yeah. *Yeah*. I can do this."

"Of course you can," Tam says. "Just be confident."

"Just rip his clothes off!" Sophie says. "He's a *boy*. He won't be able to resist."

"Oh my God, Soph," Tamsin says. "You are such a slut."

Sophie beams. "I know." Tamsin and I laugh, and Sophie adds, "But I'm not wrong, am I?"

"No, you're not." Tamsin motions for me to open my mouth and starts applying lipstick. "You should totally sleep with him. Hello, you're going to some fancy party that probably has an open bar, and your parents are *out of town*. It's perfect. Plus, you're sixteen already. Go much longer and it starts to get embarrassing."

"And having James Shaw as your first, oh my God!"

Tamsin's words send ice through my veins. *It starts to get embarrassing.* I flash back to me at thirteen, hovering at the entrance to the dining hall, with absolutely nowhere to go, seeing each table as a potential land mine. I ate in a locked bathroom stall for the first two weeks of school just to avoid it, just like James once told me he did for an entire semester, hiding in the bathroom by sitting cross-legged on the toilet whenever the things outside the door got to be too much for him. I can't ever be that girl again.

Besides, I love James. He's sweet and famous and handsome. Why *shouldn't* I sleep with him?

"Totally," I say, and although it sounds weak in my ears, they don't seem to notice.

For the next half hour, I suffer through Tam and Sophie pulling and poking and prodding at me, all while they dispense sex advice that makes my stomach churn with nerves. I'm not a *total* innocent, but Tam still complains that my skin is too flushed for her to do my makeup right.

The doorbell rings while they're putting on the finishing

touches. James is so afraid of being late for things that he usually sets himself a couple of alarms and ends up arriving fifteen minutes early. Even from up here, I hear Luz cry out in pleasure as she answers the door and the muted stream of rapid-fire Spanish that passes between them.

"Okay, all done!" Tamsin says. "Ready to see?"

Sophie covers my eyes as they position me in front of the full-length mirror in the corner, then lifts them away with a "Ta-da!"

I take a long look at myself. My dress is awesome, that much I know. I risked Dad's wrath by buying it, charging it to his credit card and hoping he wouldn't notice that it was twice the budget he gave me. He did, but it was worth it. The dress is deep blue and sparkly, like the sky twenty minutes after the sunset, filled with ten thousand stars.

The rest of me is more problematic, even after the application of Tamsin's and Sophie's considerable skills. I smile at myself in the mirror the way I imagine I'll smile when I see James, so I can see what he will. And what he'll see is: an awesome dress on a girl with a bump in her nose, a giant pimple on her chin that no amount of concealer was able to conceal, fat cheeks, and a total lack of boobs to do her killer dress justice. (Plus softly curling hair and a perfect smoky eye, courtesy of her friends.)

I suppress a sigh for their sakes. The right clothes and makeup fool most people, but just once it would be nice to actually be pretty.

"It's great, you guys!" I say and hope they don't hear the false note in my voice. "You did such an amazing job."

Sophie hands me the crystal-encrusted clutch she stole from my mom's closet, and the three of us head downstairs.

James is sitting at the kitchen counter, looking like a lost movie star in his custom black tux, eating an empanada from the towering plate Luz has put in front of him. He turns when we come in, and powdered sugar clings to one corner of his lips as he stares at me. Or, more likely, at the giant pimple on my face. I lick my lips nervously and taste the waxy, faintly vanilla flavor of Sophie's lip gloss.

"Oh, *mija*!" Luz says. "You look beautiful."

James stands, and I can practically feel Sophie and Tamsin holding their breaths as they hover over my shoulders.

"Ready to go?" he says. My heart sinks, like I was expecting my beauty to so stun him that he would drop to his knees and declare his everlasting love for me right here in the kitchen. Because I'm a moron.

"You bet she's ready," Sophie says, nudging me in the back as she steps forward. Her talent for making even the most mundane statements sound dirty is unrivaled. "Hi, James."

"Uh, hi . . . there," James says, blushing and looking pretty much anywhere but at Sophie. Her perfect blond curls and pillowy lips intimidate a lot of guys, but they scare the hell out of James. Even if he can't ever remember her name.

"How was Connecticut?" Tamsin asks, stepping around me to join Sophie next to James. "We sure missed you around here."

James frowns. "F-fine. Worked a lot. You know."

"Yeah? What are you working on?"

"I, uh . . . It's kind of hard to explain. . . ."

Tam and Sophie look at James like his stuttering is the most fascinating thing they've ever heard. Meanwhile, I think they've completely forgotten me back here.

James looks at his watch and then at me. "Sorry, but we should get going, Marina."

"Right," I say, even though I know it's still early. It's my job as James's best friend to save him from his own awkwardness, but if I'm honest, it's also because I hate watching him talk to Sophie and Tamsin. Maybe I'm just jealous because in my bones I feel like James is *mine*, but there's something almost predatory about the way they act around him. Sometimes I even wonder if it's really me they like or if it's just my proximity to him.

Tamsin and Sophie follow me to the front hall to say their good-byes. They're full of giggles and innuendo, but my smile feels plastered on.

"Call me later!" Tamsin whispers when she kisses my cheek, and then they're out the door.

"You want something to eat before you go?" Luz calls from the kitchen.

"They're serving dinner at the fund-raiser." I pull my long coat and the spotless white cashmere scarf I only wear on special occasions out of the hall closet. Somewhere behind me I can feel James approach, his presence altering the weight of the air.

"But you might get hungry before then!" Luz says. "Take a snack, at least. An apple. You don't eat enough."

"I eat plenty," I say. If she had her way, I'd be plain *and* fat. But

I take the apple Luz rushes into the hallway to give me anyway, just to make her happy.

James likewise takes the orange she hands him and sticks it in his pocket, which looks ridiculous, and then holds my coat open for me. His hand brushes my hair as he helps settle the fabric on my shoulders, sending a tingle of gooseflesh down my arms. I hear Sophie's voice in my head, explaining exactly how best to separate a boy from his clothes.

I wrap my scarf around my neck and briefly contemplate strangling myself with it, just to put me out of my misery already.

FIVE

em

Consciousness returns to me before my body does. I would panic if I had a heart to pound or blood to rush or a brain to process, but I feel nothing. There's no sensation and no thought, just a vast, endless expanse of nothing.

Did it work? Or is this death?

I slowly start to feel things again. First it's the incredible heaviness of my head, which is like a dull block of wood pulling me down, but I don't care because it's such a relief to have a head again. Then there's the scratch of a rough surface against my cheek and an aching tingle in my limbs, which reminds me I *have* limbs.

Finn is my first coherent thought. I try to move, to reach for him, but I'm frozen.

The tingle intensifies until it becomes pain, bright and sharp and stabbing through my solidifying flesh. I try to scream but only hear a low moan that I vaguely realize must be coming from me.

I manage to flutter my eyelids open, revealing glimpses of a blurry, too-bright world. I suck gasping, raspy breaths through lungs that feel brand new.

Somewhere, Finn says my name.

A hot roil rushes over my body, convulsing my muscles in waves of spasms. I struggle up onto one elbow as I heave up the meager contents of my stomach, and it feels like my body is trying to turn itself inside out. Finn's hands are suddenly on me, brushing the hair back from my sticky cheek, and I lean gratefully into his cool skin.

The spell passes, and I'm able to open my eyes. Finn's sitting beside me, practically doubled over, as obviously exhausted and aching as I am.

"You okay?" he asks.

I nod and drag my sleeve across my sweaty forehead. "Think so. That was awful."

"Yeah, give me a flying car over this any day."

He looks around us, eyes sweeping over every inch of the bare warehouse like it's some strange, alien planet. Seconds ago we were in a tiny room surrounded by soldiers, but now we're in some kind of storage space, the labyrinthine halls that stood on top of the particle collider replaced with row after row of unidentifiable junk.

"We really did it," he says. "I don't believe it."

I don't feel the same awe. Time travel isn't a wonder; it's an abomination.

Finn tucks a strand of hair behind my ears, like it's a natural thing, something he's done every day for years. "Do you think you can stand up?"

My body still feels hollow and unsubstantial, as though I accidentally left some of it four years in the future. "I don't know. Will you be able to catch me if I fall?"

"Doubt it," he says, "but I'll let you land on top of me. I'll make a nice squooshy landing."

I smile. "My hero."

The two of us start the journey to our feet, doing each other as much harm as good along the way. When he totters, he nearly brings me down with him, and vice versa, but it doesn't occur to me that I should let go of him until we've moved from our knees to a shaky crouch.

We stand and struggle to stay upright, but once we're steady, Finn grins and hugs me. He's so pleased to have accomplished such a minor feat that I can't help but laugh. He laughs, too, and soon we're both hysterical, clinging to each other and gasping. I don't know if it's the lingering disorientation from the trip or just joy at finally being free, but it's the happiest I've been in months. Years.

But somehow through our laughter, I still hear the click.

"Freeze!"

Finn goes rigid in my arms, and I lift my hands into the air like the good little prisoner I am. The soldier who snuck up on us as we laughed takes a step closer, his gun aimed at my head.

"What are you doing here?" he asks. A fine tremor travels from his hands through the weapon, making it waver before him.

I squint at him, my eyes still watering and blurry, and then I recognize the face.

"Connor?"

He takes some convincing, but once I hand him the photograph of him and his future wife—Laura, I learn, a waitress at the diner he frequents who's already turned him down twice for a date— Mike Connor begins to come around.

Not that I would blame him for shooting us on the spot.

At my request, Connor takes us toward a far corner of the building. In four years, this will be a classified government facility housing the world's largest particle collider, but right now, as Connor explains to us as we walk, it's just a military warehouse storing hundreds of old vehicles, small munitions awaiting disposal, and other odds and ends. Connor is a minor officer in charge of the graveyard shift.

I can't stop sneaking glances at him as we move. Only moments ago I was watching an older version of him die, one with gray hair at his temples and fine lines etched into the corners of his eyes. Only four years separate the two Connors, but this one looks a decade younger and softer. The future aged Connor before his time as much as it did Finn and me. This young Connor looks to me like some kind of apparition, a living ghost.

He's already dead, unless Finn and I save him.

"I don't understand this," Connor says as we walk. "I mean, I believe you, 'cause I saw you appear out of nowhere and you've got that picture, but I feel like my head's about to explode here."

"It's actually pretty simple," I say. "Do you know Einstein's theory of relativity?"

Connor just stares at me. "Let's assume I don't."

"Yeah, I didn't either, until . . . well." I shake my head to clear that line of thought. "Basically, space and time are really one thing, a kind of giant film stretched across the universe called space-time. Dense objects warp the fabric of space-time, like the way a trampoline dips when someone stands on it. If you've got something heavy enough, like insanely heavy, it can punch a hole right through."

"Okay, I get that."

"Well, in the future the government develops this massive particle collider called Cassandra. When they slam the right sub-atomic particles into one another under the right conditions, the particles hypercondense on impact and become heavy enough to punch a tiny hole in space-time. We came through that hole."

"Why?"

"Because the future needs to be changed. We need to destroy Cassandra before it's ever built, or it's going to end the world. People weren't meant to travel in time."

"But . . ." Connor presses his fingers into his temples. "If you destroy the machine before it gets built—"

"Then it will never have existed for us to travel back in time to destroy it?" Finn says.

"Right."

I nod. "It's a paradox. But the thing about time is that it's not actually linear, the way we think of it. This person I once knew, he had this theory about time, that it had a kind of consciousness. It cleans things up and keeps itself from being torn apart by paradoxes by freezing certain events and keeping them from being changed. Action—like us doing something to stop Cassandra being built—sticks, while passivity—us never coming back to stop the machine because we couldn't make the trip—doesn't. When we . . . do what we have to do to destroy Cassandra, it should become a frozen event, safe from paradoxes."

"How do you get back to your time?" Connor asks.

Finn glances at me before answering. "We don't."

"Oh." Connor's face darkens. "Right. Well, here we are."

We've reached the back corner of the warehouse. In front of us is a small drain in the concrete floor. Five and a half inches across, thirty-two holes, but no nickel-size dent yet, and no cinder-block walls caging it in.

"What is it for?" I ask. "I wondered every day I was in that cell."

Connor shrugs. "They're all over. In case the sprinklers go off or there's flooding."

Such a benign answer. I remember all the horrible things I'd imagined it was for, how I'd spent hours staring at it, picturing my blood swirling away down it.

"You need to learn everything you can about this building," I say, "all of its ins and outs. That's why they'll keep you around instead of reassigning you somewhere else when they take over this place. You're loyal and you work hard, and that'll get you promoted. Someday you'll hear about me stealing a spoon, and that's when you'll know we're ready for you to break us out."

"Jesus, I can't believe you're really saying these things," he says. "It sounds so impossible."

"I wish it were."

"How did I know to break you out the very first time?" he says. "You weren't here to tell me before it ever happened."

"I don't know," I say. "I guess that version of you and me must have learned to trust each other somehow."

Connor tilts his head back, like he's trying to see past this building and into the horizon. "Is the future really so bad?"

Finn steps forward and touches the outer wall of the warehouse, which will one day make up a part of his cell. "Worse."

I look Connor in the eyes. They're numb with shock right now, but someday they'll be the only kind eyes that look on me for months. "We can't change things without you, Mike. You're the key to it all."

He takes a moment to process this and sighs. "Well, I guess you already know I'm going to say yes, don't you?"

"We do now."

Connor pulls a multi-tool from his pocket and begins to unscrew the grating across the drain. I take the piece of paper that I carried across the years out of my pocket to look at it one last time. There's nothing for me to cross out. Earlier versions of me, Ems that I've never known and that have been spawned by each attempt to change time, have left evidence of every plan they ever tried to prevent the future. There's only one option left, and it falls to me. If killing him doesn't work, nothing will.

I kiss the piece of paper and put it back inside the plastic bag. If I fail, maybe the next Em—who's out there somewhere, walking around happy and carefree, with no idea of what's coming for her—will succeed. I tuck the plastic bag deep inside the drain, and as Connor screws the grating back into place, I hope to God she will never be in that cell to find it.

Connor hides us in a particularly desolate corner of the warehouse for the remainder of his shift. He brings us peanut butter crackers and chips from the vending machine and leaves us hidden inside a broken-down Humvee. Finn divvies up the snacks—I notice he gives me more than my fair share, and I don't stop him—and we eat silently, curled up on the cracked leather in the back of the massive vehicle.

"Oh my God," Finn groans, licking orange dust from his fingertips. "Do you remember Doritos being this good?"

"I don't remember anything being this good." I peel a strip of peanut butter off a cracker and suck on it, trying to make it last as long as possible. "How soft is this seat?"

Finn bounces on the leather cushion. "It's heaven."

The upside to being imprisoned for a few months? It doesn't take a lot to please you.

We spend the rest of the night in the Humvee. He sits close enough to touch me but doesn't, and I'm grateful. My insides are mixed up enough right now without that. Instead we just talk, and in the dark of the vehicle's interior, it's so hard for me to make out his face that it's almost like being in our cells again. I find it surprisingly comforting. He and I spent so many hours talking through the wall that separated us, saying things to each other in the safety of our own little prisons that we could never have said face-to-face. It's nice to be able to remember how to be in the same room as him slowly, by degrees.

"Remind me, what did we try before this?" Finn says. "I mean, the last version of us."

"We—*they*—got rid of Noah Hickson," I say. It was item number fourteen on the list. I stared at it so long that I can still see each word when I close my eyes.

"Oh, right. The engineer?"

"Yeah. I guess they thought the doctor wouldn't be able to design Cassandra without his help."

"Still can't say his name, huh?"

I shake my head. The thought of that name on my tongue makes me queasy.

"Me neither," Finn whispers. "So . . . got rid of him how? Did they kill him, do you think?"

"I don't know," I say. I hope not, which is silly. Why should I care what a different version of me once did to a complete stranger?

"But Cassandra still got built."

"Yeah."

"So we really have no choice, do we?"

"I don't think so."

"Em?"

"Yeah?"

"I know things are still kind of weird between us, and this is going to make me sound like a total girl, but . . ." He scoots closer to me in the dark. "Can I hold your hand?"

With a knot in my throat, I offer him my hand. He laces our fingers together, and we hold on to each other until we fall asleep.

Connor wakes us up sometime later, and in the light it's hard for me to look Finn in the face.

"Brought you some shoes," Connor says, dropping a pair of faded sneakers on the concrete in front of Finn. "Can't save the world barefoot."

Finn slips his feet, whose soles are still stained with the blood of the soldiers who died in the future, into the shoes. My prisoner slippers are thin, but they'll get me wherever we're going. Finn does up the laces while Connor explains his plan for sneaking us out of the warehouse, which involves the loading dock and half a dozen old wooden pallets Connor told his boss he wants to turn into tool storage. Twenty minutes later, we're in the bed of Connor's pickup, lying underneath a tarp along with the dusty pallets, as he drives past the guard station on the road leading away from the warehouse.

"Well," Finn whispers. "This feels familiar, at least."

Once we're a few miles down the road, Connor pulls over, and we squeeze into the cab of the truck. He takes us to his house, where he lets us shower and gives us fresh clothes of his own to wear. I emerge from the bathroom with my wet hair dripping down the back of Connor's giant black hoodie, and go looking for Finn. I find him—wearing dark jeans worn thin at the knees and a long-sleeved T-shirt—eating pancakes at the kitchen table. Connor slides a plate toward me.

"It's all I know how to make," he says.

I sit and just stare at the stack of pancakes, which are dripping with syrup and dotted with little puddles of butter, for a full minute. I want to curl up with them.

I don't know how long Finn and I eat, but I do know Connor has to make up another batch of batter because we polish off the first in minutes. By the time I finally put down my fork, I'm so stuffed with pancakes that I think I'll be sick, and it's the best feeling ever. I *treasure* my nausea, and judging by Finn's low groan, he does too.

While Finn does the dishes, Connor disappears from the kitchen and comes back with a duffel bag in one hand and a plastic case in the other.

"Extra clothes," he says. "Some first-aid stuff, a couple of protein bars. It's not much, but—"

"It's great, Connor," I say. "Thank you."

"I've also got . . ." He opens the case, and inside is a semi-automatic pistol and a box of ammunition. Finn and I glance at each other; we didn't tell him we were planning to shoot anyone. "You're going to need this, right?"

Finn forces a laugh. "No! We don't need a *gun*—"

"Not yours," I cut in. Connor deserves the truth, at least, for all he's done for us. And he's obviously not stupid. "We can't have it traced back to you. You *have* to be working at Cassandra in four years, and that'll never happen if your gun is used in the commission of a crime."

"I got it at a gun show when I was living in Arizona. No

registration required. It'll never get traced back to me." He offers me the case again. "It's okay. I know the world doesn't get changed without people getting hurt."

I stare at the gun. Truth is, we'll probably need it. With a gun, you can kill from a distance; you don't have to look the person in the eye as you end their life. Finn and I are going to need that. I reach for the case.

"Em—" Finn says.

"You know how to use it?" Connor asks me.

I check the safety on the 9mm, latch the case, and stow it inside the duffel bag.

"Yeah," I say, remembering the hours of target practice Jonas put us through in the mountains, shooting at crude, hand-drawn targets tacked to trees. "We know."

With that, the pleasant warmth of the little kitchen and the lingering taste of syrup on my tongue evaporates. This isn't a vacation back to our comfortable past; it's a mission. I can't let myself forget that again, even for a moment, because the remembering hurts so badly.

Connor drives us to the bus station in the next town over, which I learn is Oakton, Pennsylvania. All these months, Finn and I have had no idea where we were. I lean my head against the cool glass of Connor's truck window and stare at the world that passes by outside. First it's nothing but cropland, dusted with sparkling white frost and broken up by the occasional house or candy-red barn or grazing horse. The sky is like a perfect blue bowl placed upside down over the world—the color vibrant above us and fading to white on the horizon—and it's bigger than I ever could have remembered. We drive into the little town where the bus stops, and my breath catches in my throat.

There are colored awnings over the doors of the shops along the main street, and the wrought-iron streetlamps are still decked with fat Christmas lights. People walking down the street don't hurry with their heads down or glance behind them for fear of approaching soldiers. The last time I was out in the world, there were Marines with machine guns on every busy street corner who could demand your ID for no reason at all. We were at war with China and fearing impending air raids against California, while a group of terrorists was setting off bombs in smaller cities up and down the East Coast. Even your home wasn't safe. With the government monitoring cell phones and Internet usage, one questionable word was enough to have the DHS breaking down your door and dragging you off to a FEMA camp as a suspected terrorist.

But here, in the past, there are Christmas lights. I turn to Finn and see that his eyes are as wide as mine.

"Was it always this beautiful and we just never noticed?" I say.

He takes my hand but doesn't reply, and we continue staring at this old world of ours in awe until Connor pulls into the Burger King parking lot where the bus is waiting.

Connor pays the driver for our tickets and gives me the rest of the bills in his wallet. I wish I could protest, but I know we'll need them. He shakes Finn's hand and gives me an awkward hug while the driver loads the last of the luggage.

"When I was little," I say into his ear, "I had an imaginary friend named Miles. He was a purple kangaroo."

"Um." Connor lets me go. "Okay."

"No one else knows that," I say. *"No one."*

"Oh, so that's how—"

"That's how I'll know to trust you," I say.

"Got it."

Finn touches my elbow. "Bus is ready to go."

"See you later, I guess," Connor jokes. I blink and see him riddled with holes, his kind face spattered with blood as he falls to the floor. I blink again, and he's standing in front of us, smiling and young and whole.

"You're the best, Mike," I say, and when he walks away, I add him to the list of people I hope I never lay eyes on again.

SIX

marina

James eats his orange in the back of the hired car as it drives us toward the Mandarin Oriental. Somehow he misses the powdered sugar still clinging to one corner of his lips from Luz's empanadas. If I were Sophie or Tamsin, I would lean forward and wipe it off for him, my fingers lingering seductively at the edge of his mouth. It would drive him wild with lust, and he would take me in his arms and kiss me. I try to make myself move. I reach for him but lose my nerve with my hand hovering in the air and reach for my hair instead, brushing a nonexistent strand back into place. I can't do it. Instead I sit frozen in my seat and don't say a word about the sugar. At least I can appreciate how cute it looks.

Finn, in an ill-fitting tux, is waiting for us outside the hotel. He performs an elaborate bow as we climb out of the car. "My Lord Shaw! And Lady Marina of the House of Snobs!"

He reaches for my hand and actually *kisses* it, and I snatch it back before anyone can see. Why does he always have to try to make me feel stupid?

"Did you bathe in that cologne?" I ask. The cloud around him is thick enough to choke a cat. "You know, there's this thing called *soap*—"

"It's *Eau de Homme*," he says, straightening his bow tie. "You know you can't resist it."

I gag.

"Oh, by the way, man," Finn says, inclining his head at James, "you've got food on your face."

James wipes the sugar from his lips and shoots a mock glare at me, and I hide a smile.

We walk inside, following the stream of well-dressed people to the hotel ballroom. The vice president is speaking tonight, so security is tight. Secret Service agents are posted at regular intervals throughout the hotel, and our invitations and IDs are checked thoroughly before we're directed through metal detectors. Once we're cleared, an attendant leads us to our seats, three chairs at a large round table near the back of the ballroom. Two other couples are already seated, and I see the distinct darkening of their faces as three teenagers join their table.

The expression on one woman's face changes when she recognizes James. She raises her wineglass with a hand weighted down with jewels—*new money*, my mom would say—and whispers to her husband behind it. The man's head swivels to stare at James, who's too preoccupied with turning off his cell phone to notice. I'm about to ask them if their parents taught them it was rude to gawk, which will make dinner a little uncomfortable but be worth it, when Finn clears his throat loudly beside me. Everyone automatically looks at him, and he's staring at the woman and her husband with a steeliness I've never seen in his goofy expression. The couple immediately turns away.

James looks up from his phone. "You okay? I think they're bringing water around."

"Nah, I'm cool," Finn says, winking at me, and I turn away.

Dinner is served by waitstaff in tails and white gloves, and the speeches begin. I can tell James is taking in every word, but after twenty minutes, Senator Gaines begins to sound like one of the grown-ups from a Charlie Brown cartoon episode to me: *mwamp mwamp mwamp.* In between stealing glances at James—James in *a tux*—I toy with my salmon and push the vegetables on my plate into neat little piles. After a while, I make a landscape out of them: a green broccoli valley at the base of Salmon Mountain, which rises toward puffy clouds of basmati rice.

I catch Finn watching me, his expression lit up with mocking. *How old are you,* he'll say, *four?* I wreck my landscape with my fork and lean my head against James's shoulder.

"Bored?" he asks.

"A little," I whisper.

"Well, at least you look beautiful."

I forget about Finn entirely. I forget to *breathe.* Suddenly the idea of parting James from his clothes doesn't seem quite so ridiculous.

"Hey," I say softly, hearing the words come out of my mouth as though I'm separate from my body. "Want to come over to my house when this is over? My parents left for Vail this morning."

James is watching the speaker at the podium. "Yeah, sure."

He often stays at my house when my parents are away, which is constantly, so he's not getting it. But I can't just *say* it, especially not here, with Finn Abbott two feet away. So instead, I put a tentative hand on his leg.

Any closer to his knee and it would be merely friendly. If I gave it a quick pat, it would be friendly. But my hand is just a little too high on his thigh, and I try to channel Sophie as I give it a light squeeze. It may seem like a cool move from the outside, but my chest is so tight, I legitimately wonder if I'm having a heart attack.

James looks up at me, and I see the cogs beginning to turn in his head.

"Hey," Finn says. "Nate's up."

I jerk my hand back, and James turns toward the stage. I die in about forty-six different ways as I add this to the list of reasons I hate Finn Abbott, and I clench my trembling hands into fists underneath the tablecloth.

Nate is the second-to-last to speak, right before the vice president. Mayor McCreedy, who's an old friend of my mom's and comes to every party at our house, introduces him. A "rising star" in the Democratic Party, recently elected Minority Whip and climbing the ranks in the House Intelligence Committee.

Plus, he's a *Shaw*.

"Do you think Nate will run for president someday?" I ask while the crowd applauds, trying to sound normal. Tamsin or Sophie wouldn't be all mute and trembling, so I won't be, either. I'm casual.

James shrugs. "He's never said anything to me about it."

"He will," Finn says. "Not the next time around, but after that, maybe. After he's been a senator or governor."

"What makes you so sure?" I ask.

"He's got it all. The lineage, the resources, the perfect presidential hair. He'd be crazy not to run."

James laughs, not hearing the undertone of mocking in Finn's words that I do.

"Well, I think he'd make a great president. He's smart and compassionate and tough. Plus, you know"—I shoot Finn a withering look—"he has such great *hair*."

"You shouldn't discount the importance of a good haircut, M. It really—"

I cut in. "I'm being serious here, Finn, can't you—"

"—says a lot about the man!"

"—quit being an idiot for ten seconds?"

"Guys, shh!" James says. "Nate's coming on."

em

I sit on the frozen asphalt, leaning against the side of a salt-dusted Civic with Finn beside me. He rubs his hands together to keep off the chill, while I stare at the gun that lays in my own open palm.

It's heavier than I remember a gun being. It's been a while, but I didn't think I would forget that kind of thing, and now, for some reason, it's all I can think about.

"You sure you're okay to do this?" Finn says. "Because I can."

I shake my head. "I'm a better shot than you, and we might only get one chance."

"You're *barely* a better shot than me."

"Oh please, Abbott. You suck, and you know it."

"Maybe, but I didn't grow up with—"

I stop him finishing the sentence. I can't bear to hear it.

"I'm doing it," I say. The words come out icier than I intended, like the air froze them as soon as they left my mouth, and Finn doesn't argue with me anymore.

marina

Nate takes the podium to thunderous applause from the ballroom, ducking his head and smiling in a way that both he and James inherited from their dad. Next to me, Finn puts two fingers in his mouth and lets out an ear-piercing whistle that makes me jump and slosh mineral water over my hand. The rest of our table turns and glares, and I shove him, while he and James just laugh. James hands me his napkin to dry off with.

Nate adjusts the microphone. "Thank you. First I want to thank the National Committee for having me and all of you for coming. It's your support that helped our party take back the White House, and hopefully with your continued support, we'll soon be taking back Congress. So I sincerely hope you're enjoying your eight-hundred-dollar piece of salmon."

Gentle laughter ripples through the crowd. Finn looks down at his empty plate and my barely touched one in horror.

"Our political system is broken," Nate says. "Money and special interests speak louder in D.C. than the voices of our citizens. But the beauty of our democracy is that it's always evolving, and nothing that has been broken is ever beyond repair as long as we proceed with courage, integrity, and an eye toward our common interests as a people."

I may not understand politics, but I understand Nate. Most of the men in this room only care about power, but when Nate talks about working for the good of all people, I know he means it. He really cares, when most of us just say we do. I glance over at James and smile at the earnest, worshipful look in his eyes as he looks up at his brother.

"It is up to us to rebuild our government and the promise of our democracy. If we don't—"

Something explodes. A concussion rips through the air, the sound so loud that it feels more like being hit than hearing something. I discover myself hunched in my chair, hands jammed over my ears, with no memory of having moved. Around me people are screaming and scattering, some running, others falling out of their chairs and flattening themselves to the red and gold hotel carpet.

On the stage, Nate has crumpled and fallen behind the podium. I stare at him, frozen, the shouts around me going silent in my ears. He's staring out at the crowd, his cheek pressed to the floor of the stage, and for a second I swear he's looking right at me.

What's going on? Why is no one helping him up?

Then I see the blood. It's blooming from his chest the way the garish red rhododendrons in Mrs. Murphy's yard unfurl when the sun comes out.

The world regains its speed and noise with a crack. My throat feels raw, and I realize I'm screaming.

Nate's been shot.

James lunges toward the stage, tearing through people to get to his fallen brother. Finn, along with a half a dozen other people, turns and runs in the opposite direction, out of the ballroom. I go after James.

Secret Service agents have bundled the vice president out of the ballroom, and a line of them forms a barricade across the front of the stage, pushing back against the people who are being thrust toward them by the surge of the fleeing crowd. Behind the agents, the men who were already on the stage are clustered around Nate, including Mayor McCreedy and Senator Gaines, who's kneeling over Nate, pressing a hand to the wound on his chest. James runs full force into the line of agents as though he doesn't even see them. They catch him around the arm and the collar, holding him back.

"That's my brother!" he screams, voice barely human. "That's my *brother!*"

I find my voice. "He's James Shaw, let him through!"

Thank God the mayor looks up and says, "It's okay, gentlemen!" Otherwise I think James might have torn them apart. He's incandescent with terror, on fire with it, and no force of nature could have held him back. He leaps onto the stage, crashing into the second layer of men between him and his brother and battering his way through. I can only watch helplessly from behind the agents' line as he kneels at Nate's side and clutches his hand.

Nate's eyes roll around the scene horribly, as though he can't focus them, and I turn and vomit all over the ballroom's ornate carpet.

SEVEN

marina

Time passes. I don't know how much. The Secret Service herds us out of the ballroom—the crime scene—and I end up sitting on the floor in the lobby, a few feet from where the front doors open and close, sending gusts of frigid air over me, not caring about the years of embedded dirt I'm getting on my beautiful dress. Somewhere I lost one of Sophie's shoes, and a bruise is rapidly darkening on my arm, which I don't remember hitting. All around me people are huddled in small groups, crying or answering questions from the agents who spread out to take statements, but I don't really see them. I know I should be finding Finn or calling Luz or hailing a cab, but all I can do is sit and stare and remember the day James put his parents in the ground.

James seemed to be carved from marble the day of the funeral. Twelve years old, dressed in a new black suit and shoes that were too big for him, with an expression like hard white stone. I stood at the back of the church with my parents on either side of me, two tall columns of black as solid as the walls of my house, and tried to see James's face, all the way in the front pew with Nate at his side.

He was silent and still, and I kept waiting for him to cry. I would have cried.

My parents told me to give him some space, but as soon as we reached the Shaws' reception, I ran off and left them at a buffet table collecting plates of crab puffs. I slipped through the crowds like a little fish through a school, bobbing and weaving at waist level, looking for James's dark head and pale face. I did two laps of the first floor, but he was nowhere. Nate—who was clerking for Justice MacMillan by then and had his own place in Capitol Hill but still came home most weekends—was shaking hands and taking condolences. When he saw me, he inclined his head toward the staircase and mimed opening a book.

In the library upstairs, I found James's suit jacket laid over the back of the sofa and his shiny leather shoes flung into a corner, but there was no sign of James. I called his name, but only silence greeted me. I stepped farther into the room and finally found him curled up in a large wing chair that faced away from the door, so folded in on himself that he was invisible until you got close. I sat down cross-legged on the floor beside him, even though I knew Mom would be mad about the wrinkles in my best navy dress.

"You okay?" I said. I knew he wasn't, of course, but I didn't know what else to say.

"Why did your parents name you Marina?" he asked, his voice steady and normal, like it was any other day.

His unnatural calmness unnerved me. "It was my grand-mother's idea. It's after a character in a play."

"Shakespeare, right? *Pericles, Prince of Tyre*," he said. "Marina was born on a boat during a storm."

"Yeah."

"Mom and Dad named Nate after my grandfather, who was the governor of Connecticut. They never expected to have me. Mom said they argued for months over what to name me. She wanted James, and Dad wanted Michael."

"How did your mom win?"

He finally met my gaze, and the look in his eyes was like falling and falling and never hitting the ground. "I never asked."

My tiny heart broke, because I think, even at ten years old, I was already a little in love with him. "James—"

He jumped to his feet before I could finish my sentence, and then the lamp on the table beside him was flying into the wall and shattering into a thousand pieces.

"This wasn't supposed to happen!" he cried, his hand bleeding from where he'd hit the lamp with the side of his fist. "How could it just *happen* and there's no way to change it? One stupid second and a wet road and everything's ruined forever?"

The table followed the lamp as he heaved it over. It fell onto its side with a crash. I clambered to my feet and away from him.

"I'm so sorry," I said tearfully.

But James couldn't hear me anymore. He was beyond words. He howled like a wounded animal as he tore the library to pieces. I knew I should stop him, comfort him somehow, but I couldn't. My best friend in the world was suddenly something alien and absent, and it frightened me. I ran from the library and back to my parents' side, and when the sounds of James's cries began to filter down the stairs, Nate excused himself and the staff showed us out.

I didn't see James again for three weeks, and we never spoke about that day. I tried to forget it ever happened.

But now it's all I can think about.

"Marina?"

I feel a hand on my shoulder and dimly realize there's someone crouched beside me. I turn and focus my bleary eyes on him. "Finn?"

"Get up, okay?" He helps me to my feet, and I don't resist. "God, you're freezing. Where's James?"

"The, uh . . . The paramedics came, and . . ." Finn's jacket is suddenly warm on my shoulders.

"James went in the ambulance with Nate?"

The sound of Nate's name throws the real world into sharp relief. I really *see* Finn for the first time, and I hit him hard in the chest with both hands.

"Where did you go?" I cry as he reels backward and crashes into a decorative end table supporting a lush flower arrangement.

"Marina—"

I hit him again, but he's ready for it this time and catches my hands in his. "You left us! James *needed* us!"

"I ran after the gunman!" he shouts over my hysterics. He squeezes my hands hard, and the pressure brings me back to earth. "The shot came from behind us, and I thought—it was stupid, but I thought maybe I could catch him. I don't know what I was thinking."

I dissolve into sobs, and Finn's arm comes tentatively around me. He's practically holding me up, but I still push at him, shoving my hands between us, hitting his chest, unable to stop, and he just lets me.

"I hate you," I say.

"I know," he says, and he holds me until I can breathe again.

I pull away and wipe my eyes. "Sorry," I mumble.

"It's okay. I'm sure I'll deserve it someday."

"We've got to get to the hospital. James'll be—" I choke and can't finish the sentence. "He can't be alone right now."

"Are you sure that's a good idea?" Finn says. "What if we're just in the way or . . ."

"Things gotten too serious for you?" I snap. "James needs us, and we're going. You're the one who's so desperate to be his friend. You're not getting out of it now."

"Yeah, okay." Finn raises his hands in surrender. "Let's find your shoe, and we'll get a cab."

There's already a small crowd forming outside of the hospital. Someone is passing out candles. How do they do that so quickly? Did someone run to the CVS and clear them out? The sight almost starts me crying again, but I clench my teeth together so hard it hurts and concentrate on that instead.

I march toward the desk inside the sliding glass doors with Finn trailing me. One nurse is busy with a line of ER patients who are coughing or clutching bleeding wounds or screaming babies, and another is busy entering information into a computer. I push my way past the sick people to the front of the desk.

"I need some help," I say.

"You'll need to go to the back of the line, miss," the triage nurse says, barely glancing at me.

"Hey, excuse me!" I wave my hand at the second nurse in front of the computer. "This is important. I'm looking for James Shaw, the congressman's brother? I need to know where they've taken them."

"We're not giving out any information about the congressman," the nurse says, "and you need to get to the back of the line."

"Look, you don't understand. I *know* Nate Shaw, okay, and his brother will want me—"

Finn pushes me aside roughly. My vision goes red, but before I can tear his head off, he's speaking to the nurse in a smooth, calm voice. "Nurse Shapiro? I apologize for my friend. She doesn't mean to be rude; she's just worried. See, we're friends of James Shaw and we were with him tonight at the Mandarin. He's just a kid, like us, and you must know what happened to his parents. I know you're only trying to do your job and we've barreled in here making demands, but isn't there anything you could do?"

Unbelievably, the nurse's face softens. She picks up the phone on her desk. "Just a moment."

Finn turns to look at me and sees my openmouthed shock. "What? Some people find me charming."

"Apparently."

"Plus, you might find people more helpful if you don't order them around like they work for you."

"Well, considering how much money my family contributes to the hospitals of this city, they might as well."

Finn rolls his eyes and turns away from me, and I watch Nurse Shapiro speak quietly with the person on the other end of the line, trying to figure out what they're saying. After a moment, she covers the receiver with one hand. "The duty nurse upstairs has gone to speak to Mr. Shaw and the special agents on the floor. You'll need their permission to go up."

"Do you think—" I turn to Finn and stop when I see his expression. He's staring into the ER waiting room, which is separated from us by a glass dividing wall. Sometime in the last thirty seconds, his face went from normal to a sick shade of gray. His focus seems to be on a white-haired woman in a wheelchair who's playing cards with a little girl sitting beside her. "You okay?" He doesn't hear me, so I tap his arm. "Hello?"

He turns and blinks at me, as though remembering I'm here. "Yeah."

"What's wrong with you?"

He looks away. "I just really hate hospitals."

"Well, sorry I dragged you here," I say. "Nate was only *shot*, after all."

"That's not—"

"Miss?"

I spin around to look at the nurse. "Yes?"

"An agent is coming to escort you upstairs."

I release a breath. "Thank God."

The nurse directs us to an elevator at the end of the hall and tells us to wait there. When the doors ding and slide open, a plainclothes agent from the Capitol Police stands inside with

Mayor McCreedy. Finn does a double take that would be funny if everything weren't so horrible.

"Oh, Marina, thank goodness you're here. James is frantic." The mayor turns to the agent beside him. "She's fine, I know her. This is your friend?"

"Finn Abbott," I say. The agent takes the ID Finn offers. "He was with us at the fund-raiser."

"Come in, come in." The mayor waves his hands, and we step inside the elevator. "They're fine, right?"

The officer nods once he's checked Finn's ID against the list of names in his hand and presses the button for the third floor. My stomach drops as we start to rise.

"How's Nate?" I ask.

"No word yet," the mayor says. "But not good, I think."

"Has someone called Vivianne?" I ask. She's Nate's fiancée, and she's been in New York on business.

"She chartered a plane from JFK. She should be here soon."

So James is alone. Enclosed in this tiny space, sandwiched between the mayor of D.C., a Capitol Police agent, and Finn Abbott, I have a sudden, wild desire to bolt. James will be a wreck; what good will I possibly be to him? God, what if Nate *dies*? Finn was right; we don't belong here. I should be at home under my covers, with Luz bringing me mugs of warm milk and murmuring to me in Spanish. I can't breathe in here.

There's a ding, and the elevator doors open. My choking claustrophobia should get better, but it doesn't. It gets worse. We're here, and there's no going back.

The floor is nearly deserted. Two nurses—a woman in peach scrubs and a man in green—sit at the nurses' station, and there are Capitol Police in black uniforms, plainclothes special agents, and a few members of the Secret Service gathered in small groups up and down the hall, but there are no rushing doctors, no patients ambling along trailing IVs, no loved ones with flowers. The floor has been cleared. Everyone's here for Nate alone.

The waiting room is across the hallway from the nurses' station and is also walled in glass. There are several men inside—I recognize Senator Gaines—all talking together in low voices, and an officer stands beside the door. He nods at us as we approach.

James is sitting by himself in a corner of the room, hunched over in a chair with his hands clasped in front of him. For a second, he's that little boy hiding in a library armchair again.

He looks up, and his eyes meet mine. I rush to kneel at his feet. "Oh my God, James—"

"H-he's in surgery. They don't know if . . . if . . ."

He crumbles forward, burying his face in the place where my shoulder meets my neck, and I feel hot tears against my skin. I glance up at Finn, who's edged closer to us, and we exchange a helpless look. He sits beside James and puts a tentative hand on his shoulder.

"Why would someone do this?" James says between sobs. "Why Nate?"

"I don't know," I say helplessly.

"There's no reason, man," Finn says. "You can't make sense out of this."

"I wish my mom and dad were here," James says.

I rub my hands across his back. "I know."

James eventually pulls away from me, wiping his face clean with his sleeve. He leans back in his chair to rest his head against the wall, and I see for the first time that his white tuxedo shirt is stained with blood. A large red patch on his chest, where he cradled his brother, has dried and turned brown and stiff. Nate's blood. Dry and dead on James's shirt.

I can't look at it.

I'm suddenly filled to the brim with can'ts. Can't comfort James, can't fix Nate, can't change what's happened.

But damn it, I can get James a clean shirt.

"I'm going to find you something else to wear, okay?" I say shakily.

James looks down at his chest and frowns, like he's noticing his bloody shirt for the first time. He touches the stain softly, almost reverently.

"There was so much blood," he whispers.

I swallow. "I know. We'll get you cleaned up."

"Yeah." Finn jumps to his feet. "Come on, Jimbo. Let's go to the bathroom."

James doesn't resist. He barely even seems to notice Finn pulling him to his feet and maneuvering him toward the men's restroom at the end of the hall. I head for the nurses' station.

"I need some scrubs or something," I say, "for my friend to wear."

The nurses look taken aback. Nice, Marina.

"Sorry," I say. "But do you have anything he could change into? His clothes are . . ."

I can't finish the sentence.

"I've got some extra scrubs in my locker," the male nurse says, rising. "I'll get them for you."

He comes back with a neatly folded pair of blue scrubs. As I take them in my hands, I don't feel completely useless for a whole half a second.

I got James a clean shirt. What an achievement.

I rap on the bathroom door. "Guys? I've got some clean clothes."

"Come in," Finn calls.

I've never been in a men's restroom before, and with everything happening right now, it shouldn't feel as weird to me as it does, but I still push the door open slowly, like I'm afraid of getting caught. Inside, James is leaning against a sink, and Finn is wiping tiny droplets of blood off of his neck with a damp paper towel. James's blood-drenched shirt and jacket are draped over a stall door, and his stomach and chest are wet from the recent washing. I try not to look at James's bare torso. I get an impression of skin pale from months of winter and a stomach taut from hours of laps in the pool, and then I close my eyes. I don't trust myself not to think terrible things.

"Marina?" Finn says. "Can you hand me those?"

I open my eyes again and find Finn looking at me, annoyed. He has one hand paused with the paper towel against James's neck and the other outstretched.

"Sorry," I murmur and step forward to hand him the scrubs. James looks at me with dazed eyes, and with his body naked to the waist, he suddenly seems incredibly vulnerable. Like I could break him with one hand.

"Arms up," Finn says. He gathers the clean shirt in his hands, and when James raises his arms, Finn expertly slips it over his head like a parent dressing a toddler. It's an odd sight. James emerges from the shirt with his hair rumpled, which makes him look as young as Finn is treating him.

"Pants," Finn says, all business, and James obediently reaches for the fly of his tuxedo trousers.

"Oh. God." I turn away. "I'm going to go."

"I told you, man," I hear Finn say as I leave. "Taking off your pants is *not* the way to get a girl. Just scares 'em."

Before I close the door to the restroom, I actually hear James laugh.

A few minutes later, a freshly cleaned and changed James follows Finn back into the waiting room. He sits down for about ten seconds before rising to pace across the length of the small room, mumbling under his breath.

"How did they do it?" he says softly. "How did they get in?"

Mayor McCreedy thinks James is talking to him and replies, "Someone will be coming to brief us—"

"It's like Bobby Kennedy, right?" James continues, as if the mayor never spoke. "It's just like that, only . . ."

Mayor McCreedy, Senator Gaines, and the other officials from the fund-raiser try to hide their puzzled looks. They mostly fail, but James doesn't notice. He doesn't notice anything when he's like this. Sometimes when James has a problem—like how to work out an equation for Dr. Feinberg or even something as trivial as what kind of takeout to order for dinner—he retreats into his mind to work it out. Unlike the men in the room, Finn and I have seen these episodes enough times that it doesn't faze us.

The mayor takes a step toward him. "Son, are you—"

I catch his sleeve. "Please, don't disturb him. It's just something he does. It's better if you don't interrupt."

Whatever's going on in James's head, it's something he needs to work through. If he's prevented or distracted, he can fly off the handle. James doesn't lose his temper often, but when he does, it's spectacular.

The mayor pats my hand. "I'm glad you're here for him, Marina," he says, and leaves James alone.

"Nate was on Intelligence, so maybe he . . ." James mutters. "But the *vice president* was there! It shouldn't have happened. It *shouldn't* have. . . ."

James is still pacing and talking to himself when Nate's fiancée, Vivianne, rushes into the room, her coat mis-buttoned and a chalky undertone to her brown skin. I'm the closest one to her, and she grabs me, clutching me like a drowning woman.

"Oh, Marina," she says tremulously. She sees James over my shoulder and pulls away. "Oh, no. How long has he been like that?"

"Not long. Twenty minutes."

"Great." Her fingernails dig into my shoulders. "Marina, what am I going to do?"

I don't know what to tell her. There's nothing to tell her.

"Can I get you anything, Viv?" Finn asks. "Water or coffee?"

"An herbal tea would be great, thank you."

Finn goes to get her a drink from the vending machine, and Vivianne, without letting go of me, sinks into a chair, pulling me down beside her. She and Nate are supposed to get married this summer. They've been together on and off since law school, soul mates who couldn't quite get the timing right. She was working in New York at a high-powered litigation firm, trying to pay off her student loans, and he was here, raising his kid brother. It took him years to convince her to quit her job and come to D.C. to work for one of the nonprofits she loves, because they pay next to no money and she didn't want him supporting her. But he finally wore her down and convinced her to marry him.

Which she may never get to do now.

"Have they told you anything yet?" she asks.

I shake my head. "Just that he's in surgery."

"Viv?"

She and I look up. James has stopped pacing and seen Vivianne for the first time. She stands and enfolds him in a hug.

The next hours are a blur. Nate's in emergency surgery deep into the night, and there's nothing for us to do but wait. Mayor McCreedy is called away, and once he leaves, Senator Gaines and the others begin to drift away with murmured apologies. After a while, it's just the four of us and the Capitol Police agent at the door.

Vivianne keeps up a near constant monologue. "I called your cousin Alice, and she's flying down from Westchester. She said

Nancy is looking for someone to watch the kids—you know Benjamin only just turned two and apparently their nanny is on vacation—but then she and John will be on their way. William is in Shanghai, but I'm sure he'll be here just as soon as he can. . . ."

Meanwhile, James doesn't speak, just stares at the floor with a fine line creasing his brow. Like the thin maroon carpeting has insulted him.

I excuse myself from the waiting room and pull my cell phone from the clutch Sophie stole from Mom's closet. I texted Luz when we first arrived to let her know where we were—I couldn't bear to hear her voice, because I knew I would break down like a baby—but then turned it off because of the constant stream of text messages from friends and people I barely know. I turn it back on and wait to see if I have any voice mails. Just two, both from Tamsin. I fiddle with the phone. I've been thinking about making the call for hours, but even now, with my finger poised over the number, I'm not sure. Why haven't they called me? They must have heard by now. If I don't call, then they can't fail to answer. If I don't *want*, I can't be disappointed.

I press the number, labeled DAD'S CELL, and the phone starts to ring. I close my eyes and try to figure out what I'll say when he picks up. *Daddy, the world's ending, please make it stop.*

"Hello. You've reached Daniel Marchetti. I'm not available—"

I jab my finger at the phone to end the call. I try Mom. Her phone goes straight to voice mail, and I'm willing to bet a million dollars she's in the spa. Dad goes to Vail for the skiing, but she spends almost every moment being massaged or plucked or exfoliated.

Or so I hear, since they've never taken me with them.

I jam the phone back into the bag, my fingers curling into the material as I make fists. The delicate Swarovski crystals that adorn the outside strain against their threads, and I claw at them with one hand, my fingers catching and popping a half a dozen glittering pieces off. Mom will kill me, and I don't care.

I go to the restroom and splash some cold water on my face. I try not to look too closely at my reflection. My hair and makeup are a wreck, and I suddenly don't recognize the person looking back at me. She's like a photograph of some distant cousin. Vaguely familiar, but strange. Not me.

"You okay?" Finn asks quietly when I throw myself back into a waiting room chair. He's looking down at my mangled bag.

"Yeah," I say. "Did you call your parents?"

"I texted. Didn't want to wake my mom." He cocks his head at me. "What did your parents say?"

I look away from him. "Nothing."

My eyes go back to James, who's sitting in the corner of the room, just like he was when I left, except now he has his head bent over a yellow legal pad and is scribbling furiously. The ghostly expression has left his face, and his distant eyes are now focused as he stares fiercely at the pad.

"What's he doing?" I whisper.

"Not sure," Finn says. "He went and asked the nurse for a pen and paper after you left, and he's been like that since. Think he's okay?"

"I don't know." James's eyes are lit up with such a fire, I'm afraid he might ignite the paper. It's a little frightening, but less frightening than the lost, blank look he's been wearing for hours. "At least he's doing *something*."

"Yeah, I guess I just worry what."

I look at Finn and am trying to decipher his furrowed expression when I hear the pad of paper hit the ground behind me. James has jumped to his feet, and I follow his line of vision to the doctor in a surgical gown standing in the doorway.

Oh God, this is it.

Vivianne stands beside James on one side and me on the other, and I search the man's face as he pulls off his mask. I'm looking for some hint about the news he's bringing, but his features are perfectly inscrutable, like a second mask. At first I'm relieved. If Nate died, he would look upset, wouldn't he? But if everything is fine, it's almost cruel for him not to smile.

The four of us face the doctor like he's the firing squad and we're the prisoners.

"Is he okay?" James asks.

"Congressman Shaw was very seriously injured," the man says, and I barely resist the urge to shake him. We know he was seriously injured; we were there. "We're still working on fixing the damage done by the bullet, but he's made it through the most difficult part."

James sags, and I put an arm around his waist to steady him. Thank God. I turn my face into his shoulder.

"He's still in critical condition, though. The next forty-eight to seventy-two hours are crucial."

James straightens, his muscles going rigid under my hand. "What does that mean?"

"Let's sit down, and I'll explain everything." The doctor turns to Finn and me. "I'm sorry, but details of the congressman's condition are confidential, so I'm going to need you two to wait outside."

Finn squeezes James's shoulder before he leaves the room. I stand on my toes to press a kiss to his forehead, and he catches my hand as I go so that our fingers catch for a moment and then slide apart. It's such a little thing, but the touch leaves me shaking. I hate myself for feeling this way when Nate's fighting for his life down the hall, but for a second it was almost like James needed me beside him.

Finn and I sit in two chairs against the wall to wait. We don't speak. He's surprised me the last few hours, being so patient and kind and not the least bit idiotic. I hardly recognize him.

The doctor soon leaves, nodding at us as he walks back toward the operating room, and I rush back to James's side.

"It's bad," Vivianne says. "He's alive, but he's not breathing on his own. The doctor says there's only a fifty-fifty chance he'll make it past—past the next few days."

"Jesus," Finn whispers.

"Oh my God." I want to touch James, but I'm scared to, and my hands flutter uselessly at my side.

James's paper-white face is blank. "He said we should be able to see him in a few hours, but . . ." He suddenly loses the will to speak, and his head falls into his hands. I think of James the day of his parents' funeral, bleeding from the cut on his hand he couldn't seem to feel, hurling furniture across the library. I can almost see the string holding him together right now beginning to fray. If nothing changes, I'm afraid it'll snap.

I put a tentative hand on his back. "How about we go back to my house and you get some sleep? We'll come back first thing in the morning, when Nate's ready to see you."

"I think that may be a good idea," Vivianne says.

James shakes his head, voice muffled by his hands. "No. You guys can go, but I've got to stay. I could never forgive myself if . . ."

. . . *if I left and Nate died.* I hear the words even in the silence.

"Okay." I look at Finn and shrug. "We'll stay, too."

I pull out my phone and dial Luz. If we're staying, I'm going to need something less ridiculous to wear.

Of course, the real reason I call Luz is because I can't take another second of pretending to be strong. If that's what I've been so far. I need someone to put their arms around me and tell me it's going to be okay.

It takes Luz over an hour to be searched and cleared to enter, in no small part because she's brought two enormous bags along with her. Once she gets the okay, she bustles past the agent posted outside the waiting room door and comes right for James and me, scooping us up in her fleshy arms and pressing kisses to our heads.

"*Ay, Dios mío,*" she murmurs. "My darlings. God bless you."

I hide a smile as I suffer the indignity of having my face squashed to Luz's breast, but James looks gone, like part of him has fled and left his body behind.

Luz unpacks her bags. One contains a change of clothes for each of us, and the other holds more food than the entire hospital could consume in a week, from sandwiches and fruit to a casserole dish of enchiladas and a batch of freshly baked cookies. Luz cooks when she's worried, and judging by the contents of the bag, she's been *freaking out*.

We've had nothing but vending machine food since the eight-hundred-dollar salmon, so Finn dives into the food, Vivianne takes a peach, and even James manages to nibble at a peanut butter sandwich. Finn offers me the plate of chocolate chip cookies, but I shake my head and grab the clothes Luz brought instead. I excuse myself to the restroom to change. It's hard to imagine why I was once so in love with this dress. When I get home, I'm going to burn it.

I come out of the bathroom stall clad in jeans and a sweater to find Luz leaning against the sink, arms crossed over her chest.

"*Mija*, are you okay?"

I burst into tears.

Luz folds me up in her arms, rubbing circles against my back with her palm like she used to do when I was little. I'm making these incredibly embarrassing, ragged noises, and I'm pretty sure my nose is running on Luz's sweatshirt, but she doesn't let me pull away, and I'm glad.

"I'm sorry for last night," I say. "I know I'm a real bitch to you sometimes."

"Shh, shh." She pushes my hair away from my face and mops my cheeks with the end of her sleeve. "Have you called your *mama?*"

I shake my head. Somehow it's easier to pretend I never even tried. Luz squeezes me tighter, until my ribs ache. I don't know what I was thinking, waiting so long to call her.

We return to the waiting room, where Finn is shuffling a pack of cards he found, Vivianne is staring at her phone, and James is back to scribbling away on the legal pad. No one looks up when we enter. Luz takes a seat by the door and pulls some knitting from one of her bottomless bags. I sit between the boys and look for something to do with my own hands. I finally give in and start to chew on a fingernail while I watch James.

This frantic writing is starting to worry me. It's too intense, even for him. I want him to look at me and say something, anything to stop the manic scratching of his pen against the paper, so I ask, "Did you eat, James?"

"He ate," Finn says. James crosses something out on his pad with feverish strokes.

"You mean that sandwich with the three bites out of it?" I say, nodding at the forgotten peanut butter and jelly on the table. "'Cause I'm not really sure that counts as eating."

"And you're one to talk?" Finn says mildly.

I feel the blood drain from my face. Luz glances up at me but quickly turns back to her knitting. "What does that mean?" I say.

"Nothing."

"No, tell me!"

"It means lay off, okay, Marina? He'll eat when he's hungry."

"I'm just trying to look out for him, not—"

"Jesus, I'm still *here*, you know!"

I whip my head around to look at James. He's on his feet, and he flings the legal pad into the far corner of the room, where it smacks against the wall and flutters down behind a chair.

"Nate's the one dying," he says. "Not me."

The air leaves my lungs. "James—"

"Oh, sweetheart," Vivianne says. "They're just trying to help."

James pulls on his coat. "I'm going to get some fresh air."

I jump up. "I'll go with you."

"No, Marina! I need . . ." He takes a deep breath and lowers his voice. "I just need a minute, okay?"

I sink back into my seat and blink back tears. "Yeah. Okay."

When he's gone, I rest my forehead on my knees and cover my head with my hands.

"Let him breathe, M."

"Shut up, Finn!" I say.

EIGHT

em

My legs are starting to cramp from sitting in the cold so long. I extend them in front of me, flexing and pointing my feet to stretch the muscles and get the blood moving again. I try to focus on the ache in my calves and the tingle of numbness in my toes rather than the deep black pit in my stomach.

Finn looks up at the sky. I'm not sure why; there are no stars in the city, nothing to see but blackness and the hazy blue glow of the streetlamps.

"It must be close to time," he says.

"I know."

"How do you feel?"

"How do you think?"

He puts his hand over my clenched fist. My first instinct is to pull away, but I make myself stay still. The feel of his skin against mine is still new and strange, his touch strangely hot after so many months of touching no one. He rubs his fingers over mine until I start to relax, my fingers loosening.

"We can think of another way," he says. "This is too messed up."

I shake my head. "There is no other way. We've already tried everything else."

"I'm so sorry, Em."

"Don't be," I say. "I hate what he's done. I hate *him*. The world will be a better place when he's gone."

Finn wraps an arm around my shoulder. "Okay," he says in a placating voice. He obviously doesn't believe me, but does he think I'm lying to him or to myself? Maybe my hatred isn't simple, maybe it's complicated by lots of other things, but it's true. It burns inside of me like the bluest, hottest flame.

I can do this. I stamp down the weakness I feel building inside of me. *I can do this.*

I lean into Finn and inhale the smell of him. Well, the smell of Connor, I guess. Detergent with stale cigarette smoke hidden underneath. When I close my eyes, I can remember the way Finn used to smell, like soap and that terrible cologne he wore too much of on special occasions, and later the dirt and sweat of life on the run. I burrow closer to his skin. I think of the scars he's hiding under his shirt, the bruises that are probably still visible from his last beating, anything to fan the flame of my anger until it burns away everything else.

I hate him. I hate him. I hate him.

"Don't think about him," Finn says, like he can read my thoughts. He rubs his hand up and down my arm, warming me. "Think about her."

Her. Marina. She's in that building somewhere, hurting and

confused, probably biting her nails to the quick. Finn's right. Marina's the reason I'm doing all of this. More than anything, what I want is for her to be happy and have the life she deserves. My love for her is a stronger motivator than my hatred of him could ever be.

Finn presses a kiss to the crown of my head, and I shiver. His lips travel down to my temple and my cheek, skimming kisses there, too.

"Em," he hums.

I tilt my face to look at him, and we're so close, I can feel his breath against me. "Yeah?"

"I know you know already," he says, "but I always wanted to be looking at you when I finally said it for real. I know my timing is terrible here. . . ."

Oh God, Finn. Don't.

"But soon we'll be gone, so this is my last chance." He gives me a shy little smile. "I love you."

He's right, I *did* know, but I suddenly can't hold his gaze. It's too much. My face is hot in the cold air, and I look away from him, turning automatically toward the doors of the building we've been watching.

They're opening, sliding silently apart, and a figure is walking out.

"It's him," I whisper.

I would know him anywhere, even in the dark, even with his shoulders bent and his lean frame clad in borrowed scrubs. I try not to look at him too closely. I don't want to see his face.

I scramble to a crouched position behind the Civic, Finn at

my shoulder. His rapid breathing puffs out around us. For once, he doesn't say anything, just touches my back to remind me he's there.

My fingers shake so violently that I can't flip off the safety of the gun. I close my eyes and try to find a single piece of stillness inside of me to focus on.

Marina.

The shaking stops, and I flip the safety. I won't remember who he was. That person is dead and gone. I'll only think about who he'll be.

I'll only think about Marina.

With one last deep breath, I stand, aim the gun straight at James Shaw's head, and pull the trigger.

The gun kicks violently in my hand, and it throws me back.

And *back and back and back . . .*

A fist tightens around my belly and jerks me away, wind rushing through my hair, the world blurring around me. I'm flying and falling at the same time. Finn and the gun and the hospital smear into gray streaks, and a different world materializes in their place.

I'm going to do it this time, I'm sure.

Other kids get their parents to give them a push to start out, but I don't have that, so I poise my bike at the top of our inclined driveway and let gravity do the job. I fly down the driveway and into the quiet street, and I'm finally riding. My heart soars. The houses on the block whoosh by impossibly fast. I'm free.

No. I'm not riding. I'm falling. The big wheel beneath me

wobbles out of control, jerking the handlebars to the left and the right, nearly pulling them out of my little hands. So little. The ground rushes up at me, and before I can cry out, I'm sprawled across the pavement, my palms and knees stinging. I roll over and pull one knee up to my chest, see the abraded skin and blood through my ripped tights. These are my favorite pair, the bright pink ones with the white polka dots. When I pictured this moment in my mind—flying down the street on my bicycle, riding away from this place with my hair streaming loose behind me—I was always wearing my favorite tights, so I insisted on putting them on this morning. And now they're ruined.

Hot tears roll down my cheeks, and I don't try to stop them.

"You okay, kid?"

I look up and see the boy next door through my watery eyes. When we moved in a few weeks ago, Mom told me I should ask him to play, but I was too scared. He's a *boy*, and at least eight. He would laugh at me.

My jaw tightens. "I'm fine."

"You forgot to pedal." He grins and offers me a hand.

"No, I didn't!"

"Yeah, you did." He sits down on the curb beside me. "It's okay. I did the same thing when I was learning to ride. Fell into a big bush."

"Really?"

He nods. "It was full of stickers, too. You hurt?"

I shrug, but he takes my hands in his and turns the palms to face him. They're scratched and covered with grit from the road.

He leans forward and blows across them, clearing away the dirt and cooling the burn in my skin.

"Want some help?" he asks.

I nod. He stands, and this time he looks like a giant to me. I gaze up at him in wonder—in *worship*—before he loops his arm under mine and helps me to my feet.

"I'm James," he says.

"I'm Marina," I say.

Far away, someone is calling my name. I turn. It must be Luz or Mom. . . .

But no. They're not calling for Marina. They're calling for someone else.

There are hands on my shoulders, shaking me. I look up into James's face, and it blurs, becomes another. I blink, and James becomes Finn.

"Em!" he says.

"Finn?" I slam back into my body from whatever strange place I was in. I'm on the ground, the barrel of the gun resting in my lap, the metal hot even through my jeans. Finn is crouched over me, his eyes wide with panic. "What happened?"

"I don't know," he says, hauling me to my feet, "but we've got to run."

Finn is dragging me away, but I stop and look back at the hospital, where there's a sudden swarm of people. "Did I kill him? Is it over?"

He pulls on my arm. "Run, Em!"

And we do.

NINE

marina

After James storms out, Vivianne excuses herself to the restroom, and I wander to the waiting room window, watching the back entrance of the hospital. It only takes a minute for James to emerge. He looks like any other hospital employee in his blue scrubs and black coat, but I could recognize him with my eyes closed. He paces back and forth beside the ambulance bay and then sits on the low stone wall that lines the driveway. His head sinks down into his hands.

Behind me, Finn is shuffling and reshuffling the deck of cards. Even the sound is an angry one, the impatient *fuht-fuht-fuht* of the cards seeming to judge me for not being able to let James have even this tiny moment to himself.

My eyes unfocus, and in my mind I see James standing in the doorway, barking at me to leave him alone. The stupid puppy always following at his heels.

This is *not* how I imagined this night would go.

Luz leaves off her knitting to squeeze my hand, but I don't

want to be touched right now. I cross my arms over my chest and pinch the inside of my elbow to keep from crying. I won't cry in front of Finn Abbott again. Down below, James stands and starts to swing his arms to keep warm.

Then there's a bang.

It's not like the sound from the hotel ballroom. Three floors up, filtered through the city noise and the thick panes of glass, it's more like a pop than an explosion, but I still shriek. I'm back in that ballroom, watching blood spread across Nate's chest, only this time it's James, and I can't breathe.

"It was only a car backfire," Finn says.

"No, it wasn't!" I press my face to the window. James is still standing, still whole, but he feels a hundred miles away. I put my hands against the window, like I could reach him somehow. I follow his gaze out into the parking lot, and that's when I see her. A girl, her face obscured by shadows. Holding a gun.

The air leaves my lungs, and time slows to a crawl. The girl falls behind a car, and a boy I hadn't noticed before bends over to haul her back to her feet. They start to run, but the girl stops under a streetlamp and turns back toward the hospital. Her face and that of the boy with her as he tries to pull her away are suddenly illuminated, their features clear.

The world sways in front of me, and I clutch my head with my hands. I'm hallucinating.

Officers in black uniforms run out of the hospital, and things move quickly again. They surround James and bundle him back inside even as he's pointing at the parking lot and struggling against them.

I *didn't* imagine it.

Someone just shot at James.

I run from the room.

I skip the elevator and take the stairs down to the first floor two at a time. Somewhere behind me, I hear Finn saying my name. I run through what I saw again in my head: a girl with a gun, a boy helping her up, stopping under a streetlamp to look back at the hospital—

That's where my mind judders to a halt. Because the faces I saw, even with the distance and the darkness, were so familiar, looked so much like . . .

I hit the first floor landing and run into the ER, where James is seated in the waiting room, surrounded by a cloud of black suits and uniforms. The hospital is swarming. The agent in charge is barking orders at a nurse, who relays everything he says through the PA system. They're putting the whole building into lockdown, no one allowed in or out, and I'm swimming against the stream of panicked people to try to get to James.

"James!" I call. "James!"

"Marina!" He spots me in the crowd and waves me over, and the officers surrounding him part to let me through.

"Are you okay?" I ask. "What happened?"

He looks a little dazed, but unharmed. "Someone shot at the hospital."

Finn's caught up to me and hears him. "Oh my God."

I shove him. "See! I told you. I *saw* them shoot at him."

An officer standing at James's side abruptly stops speaking

into his radio. "Excuse me, miss, you said you saw the shooter?"

"Yes, I was watching out the window." I turn back to James. "Are you okay? You're not hurt?"

"I'm fine," he says. "You're white as a sheet, though. Are *you* okay?"

I nearly laugh, but it comes out as a kind of strangled sob, and I throw my arms around his neck. Even with my eyes closed, the world is still spinning. I bring a hand up to his head to hold him tight and feel something warm and slick between my fingers.

"Miss, what did the shooter look like?"

I pull away and look down at my hand. It's smeared with blood, vivid red against my skin.

"He's bleeding." My voice comes out small and weak, and I have to work to raise it. "Someone help, he's bleeding!"

James touches his dark head and pulls back bloody fingers with a bemused expression. The swarm descends on him once more and sweeps him off into a nearby exam room. I go to follow, but the agent who was giving orders earlier blocks my path.

"Miss, I'm Special Agent Armison," the wall of a man dressed in black says. "I need to know now: what did the shooter look like?"

em

"Damn it!" I slam my hand against the side of a brick building six blocks from the hospital. It stings, but I deserve it.

"It's okay, Em."

I pace back and forth. "It's not, and you know it! That was our chance, and I blew it. I can't *believe* I missed."

"Did you miss," Finn asks, "or did you jerk away?"

"I-I don't know." I clench my fists until my nails bite into my palms. "I really don't."

"It's okay. We've still got two days before the doctor comes back for us. All we have to do is follow him and wait for another moment when he's alone."

I shrug off the hand Finn's put on my shoulder and lean my forehead against the rough wall. "I just . . . I saw his face. And he was *James* again, you know?"

"I know."

"And whatever that was that happened to me . . ." I turn to look at him. "What the hell was that?"

"As soon as you pulled the trigger, your eyes went blank, and you started blinking like crazy." He shakes his head, like he's trying to stop himself from picturing it. "You couldn't hear or see me. It was like you were *gone*."

"I saw the first time I met James," I say. "It was like I was living it again."

"Oh man," he whispers. He reaches for me again, but stops himself. "I'm sorry."

"He just . . ." I bite the inside of my lip. "He hasn't done anything wrong."

"Not yet." Finn takes my face in his hands, so gently that he must think anything more will break me. "But we both know it won't last. The James we knew is already gone."

For the first time in months, I cry. Not the girlish tears I used to shed, sniffling and pouting, letting the tears roll down my cheeks like someone in a movie, but deep, guttural sobs that shake my whole body.

Finn holds me tight, like he's afraid I'll shake myself to pieces and his arms are the only thing that can hold me together.

I think maybe he's right.

marina

"The shooter," Agent Armison says again. "What did the shooter look like?"

"I . . ." I can't think with James on the other side of that wall, bleeding, maybe dying. I try to follow him, like I'm caught in the pull of his gravity, but the agent steps in front of me. "I-I don't know. . . ."

"Yes, you do." Agent Armison bends his face close to mine, so that his eyes are the only thing I see. "Focus, now. What did the shooter look like?"

I have to do this. It's the only way they'll catch the people who shot at James. But how do I say it? How do I tell him what I saw? "There were two of them. . . ."

He gets on his radio. "This is Armison. Stand by for description." He looks back at me. "Okay. What did they look like?"

"One was a g-girl, and one was a boy," I say. "They looked like . . ."

"Like what?"

"They looked just like"—I turn to Finn—"the two of us."

Agent Armison stares at me for a second. "You mean they were about your age? Had your same hair color, what?"

"No, I mean they looked *exactly* like the two of us. Maybe a little older, but otherwise . . ." I stop at his expression. "I *know* it sounds crazy, but—"

He gets back on his radio. "This is Armison. Disregard my last."

"No, don't!" I say. "You have to catch them!"

"Marina . . ." Finn touches my elbow.

"Miss, you've had a shock—"

"No!" I pull my arm away from Finn. "I'm not imagining things; that's what I saw!"

"I know. It's okay," Agent Armison says. "Let's go into one of the rooms here, and I'll ask you some more questions, all right?"

"What's the point?" I say. "You won't believe me. Is it even legal to question me without my parents here?"

"You're not under arrest, Miss . . . ?"

"Marchetti," Finn oh-so-helpfully supplies.

"Come with me, Miss Marchetti," Agent Armison says, "and you can explain to me exactly what you saw. Your friend can come with us, too."

"He's not my friend," I say, but I go because I can see there's no getting out of this.

We're at the door of the employee break room where Agent Armison is leading us when Luz and Vivianne find us. Vivianne, who's a lawyer but also the closest thing James has to family right now, is clearly torn about where she's needed most. She turns to Luz.

"Can you go be with James?" she says. "And come get me if he's badly hurt or asks for me?"

Luz nods, and I point her toward where they took James. At least someone will be with him. Armison leads us into the employee break room, but my mind follows Luz to the exam room down the hall. If James isn't okay, I don't know what I'll do. I once saw a woman on *Good Morning America* who was stabbed in the back with a kitchen knife by an ex-boyfriend and walked around the mall, totally oblivious, for an hour before someone in the food court suggested she go to the hospital. If that could happen, maybe James was shot and didn't even know it.

Finn is less rattled. "It was just a cut or something, M. Don't worry so much. It'll give you wrinkles."

"Maybe you should worry a little more," I snap. "I know this is hard for you to grasp, Finn, but some of us actually *care* about things and can't just mock everything—"

"Hey." Finn's eyes flare. "I care about things. You have no idea what you're talking about."

He brushes past me to sit at the lunch table and leaves me standing in his wake. Agent Armison gestures for Vivianne and me to sit, draws a fancy fountain pen from his breast pocket that looks out of place in his big square hands, and flips open a small notebook.

He takes down our names and basic information, and then

says, "Okay, Miss Marchetti. Now, tell me again what you saw."

The gentleness in his voice sets my teeth on edge. It's the way you talk to children or mental patients.

"I was watching James out of the window." I bite off each word. "I heard a shot and looked into the parking lot. There was a boy and a girl running away, and when they turned back, I saw their faces. They looked just like Finn and me. Same build, same hair, same *faces*."

Armison turns to Finn and Vivianne. "Did either of you see anything?"

They both shake their heads. They were right there, but I was the only one at the window. I'd give anything for one of them to have been standing with me so they could back me up.

"Have you seen anything else strange today, Miss Marchetti?" Agent Armison asks gently, like a wrong word might break me.

"No!" I bang my fist against the table. "I know it sounds crazy, but it's true! You have to believe me!"

Vivianne puts a hand on my knee. "It's okay, Marina."

"I believe you're sincere, Miss Marchetti," the agent says, "but you're under a tremendous amount of stress. The mind reacts to that in funny ways sometimes."

"Fine." I press my lips together to stop the sob of frustration I feel rising in my throat. "But they're out there, and they're getting away because you won't listen to me."

Agent Armison looks down at his notepad, unable to meet my eyes, and I feel Finn shift in the chair beside me. Good. I *hope* I'm making them uncomfortable.

"Now, what about earlier, when the congressman was shot?"

Agent Armison says. "You were both there, correct? What did you see?"

I cross my arms over my chest and don't say anything. I don't have any useful information, anyway, since all I saw was what everyone else did: Nate falling to the floor, people scattering. Of course, I could have gotten the shooter's fingerprints and Social Security number and it wouldn't make a difference to this guy.

Finn's more inclined to be helpful than I am. "I already spoke to one of the agents at the hotel about this," he says, "but I'm positive the gunman shot from inside the fire exit in the back right corner of the room."

Vivianne bends her head and closes her eyes. I wonder if what she's imagining is even worse than what we saw.

"A few other people and I tried to run after him," Finn continues. "The door led to a service hallway, but it was already empty by the time I got in there, and there were probably a dozen doors going off to different parts of the hotel. We checked a few that weren't locked, but the shooter was long gone."

Surprise clouds my anger for a moment. Finn told me he ran after the gunman, but I guess the reality of that didn't hit me until this moment. While I was cowering in my chair, unable to do any good for anyone, Finn was chasing after a would-be killer.

"Did you see the gunman?" Armison asks.

Finn shakes his head. "Another guy said he got a glimpse of him. Dark clothes, baseball cap over his face. That was it. How was the shooter able to get through the Secret Service?"

"We're investigating that," Armison says as he makes a note

on his pad. "Do you know of anyone who'd have a reason to want to hurt the Shaws?"

"Of course not," I say.

Vivianne shakes her head. "No one."

"Well . . ." Finn says.

I gape at him. "You have *got* to be kidding me."

"Maybe Nate," Finn says. "Just because he's a congressman."

"Fine. Some right-wing loony maybe, but—"

"But not James. No one could have a grudge against James."

I forgive him, just a little.

"It *is* possible the second shooting was only a coincidence," Armison says.

"That's a hell of a coincidence, isn't it?" Finn says.

"I know it seems that way, but it would have been extremely difficult for someone from that distance to recognize Mr. Shaw in the dark, wearing hospital scrubs. I'm inclined to think it was a mentally unbalanced person looking for attention, or possibly some gang activity. We'll check out the security cameras from the parking lot, and until we have whoever it was in custody, the Capitol Police will assign a protection detail to stay with Mr. Shaw and make sure he's safe."

"Are those all your questions?" Vivianne asks.

"Can we see James?" I add.

"We're done for now. You'll have to check with the doctors."

Finn and Vivianne shake the agent's hand across the table, but I'm already at the door. The same agent who'd been guarding the waiting room upstairs is now standing in front of Exam Room A, and he nods at me and waves me in when I approach.

Inside, James is sitting on one of the beds, his feet dangling off the edge like a little boy. He's pale but beautifully whole, and my stomach unclenches. Luz is patting his hand, and a doctor is bandaging his scalp above the left ear.

James gives me a wan smile. "Looks like I got hit by a shard of brick. Not very dramatic."

"That's okay," Finn says, coming up behind me. "Boring suits you."

"We gave him a couple of sutures just to be safe," the doctor tells Vivianne, stripping her gloves. "You're all set, James."

"Can I see my brother now?" he asks.

"Let me call upstairs to check."

The doctor gets on a phone attached to the wall, and I take a step closer to James. I touch his head lightly. "Does it hurt?"

"They numbed it up before the stitches. How does it look?"

They cut the hair away from the wound, leaving him a bald patch above his ear. "Ridiculous," I say, all of the residual fear pumping through my veins turning into a totally inappropriate urge to laugh. He's still here, still safe. And only slightly less gorgeous with a divot of hair cut out of his head.

The doctor hangs up the phone. "You can see the congress-man now."

TEN

marina

My momentary relief disappears. Luz says she has to go home and check on her grandkids before heading to work, so she hugs me tight, and then Finn and I follow James and Vivianne to Nate's room in the ICU. All I can think about is the way that lamp shattered when James slammed his fist into it when we were kids. I knew from that day on that there was a hairline crack running through him. I've only ever seen glimpses of it in the years since, but I'm afraid the sight of Nate might put enough pressure on him that he finally shatters.

One of Nate's doctors pulls Vivianne aside to talk with her, so it's just the three of us who enter his hospital room. James stops inside the doorway so abruptly that I bump into him. His shoulders are rigid, and I crane my head to look around him.

Nate is barely recognizable in the bed, he's so obscured by wires and IVs and bandages. He's hooked up to a ventilator, the thick tube taped into place, disappearing into his open mouth and down his throat. The machine hisses softly as it pumps air into his lungs and lets it out again, its robotic rhythm creating a syncopated beat with the heart monitor beside it. Nate is bare to the waist, his chest covered in bandages. What little skin shows through is stained with either disinfectant or blood. His face is a chalky gray color, except for his eyelids, which are such a dark purple that they look bruised. He's like a battered and discarded shell, no spark of animation to show that anything of Nate is still inside there.

He looks dead.

He looks, somehow, *worse* than dead.

The nurse who led us here goes right to his side and checks one of his IV bags and then looks back at us, clustered in the doorway. "It's okay. You can touch him if you want."

I take James's hand and squeeze it. Neither of us moves. I don't want this image of Nate in my mind; if he dies, I don't want to remember him this way. I wish I'd never followed James here.

Finn is the one who steps forward. He leaves us cowering in the door like children, sits in one of the chairs at Nate's bedside, and takes his hand gently.

"Hi, Congressman," he says. "It's Finn. James and Marina are with me."

"Can he hear him?" James asks the nurse.

"No harm in trying, right?" Finn interjects. "The doctors fixed you up nice, Congressman. You'll be kicking my ass at basketball again in no time, sir."

James takes a small step forward, and then another. Eventually he makes his way to the second chair by Nate's bed. I watch from the doorway, hating myself for the way my feet are cemented to the floor. Finn didn't even want to come here. He would have left James to deal with this on his own, because he hates hospitals, but now he seems . . . he seems . . .

I realize with a shock that Finn has done this before.

"James is looking pretty rough," he continues. "I think he could use his brother right now, so you've got to hang on, okay, Congressman?"

I pray for Nate's eyes to open. I can imagine exactly how it will go. His eyelids will flutter. We'll gasp, and the nurse will whisper that it's a miracle. Nate will turn to Finn, and in a quiet, raspy voice he'll say, "I told you to call me Nate." And we'll all know everything will be okay.

But he doesn't. Aside from his chest rising and falling in time with the hiss of the ventilator, he's still.

"Don't worry, though," Finn continues. "We're taking care of him. Marina hasn't let him out of her sight. She's like a very protective, terrifying little dog."

James reaches forward and slowly takes his brother's hand.

Finn gets up and takes my arm. "Let's go."

For once I don't argue, and I leave James alone with his brother.

Finn and I sit in the hallway to wait while Vivianne joins James inside. I pull out my phone and check the text messages I've been ignoring. I'm up to forty-three now.

Tamsin: OMG are you okay?

Tamsin: What's happening? Are u w/ James?

Sophie: I just heard! Text me back and let me know how you are, k, bb?

202-555-9054: Hi Marina, it's Alex Trevino from your bio class. I heard you were there tonight, what happened?

TAMSIN: MARINA! TEXT ME BACK, I'M GOING CRAZY HERE!!1!

SOPHIE: Watching the news. This is the biggest thing ever, and you're actually there! What's going on??

I turn my phone back off.

Now that I'm off my feet, exhaustion crashes over me. I didn't realize how tired I was until this moment. I lean my head back against the wall, and soon I can't keep my eyes open anymore. I let them fall shut, telling myself I'll just rest for a minute.

"Marina." A hand touches my knee. "Marina, hey."

I drag my gritty eyes open and lift my head from Finn's shoulder. God, I fell asleep on him.

"Sorry," I murmur.

"Don't worry about it." He nods toward Nate's room, where James and Vivianne are standing in the doorway speaking with one of the doctors. "While you were out, Viv asked me if we could try to get James to leave for a little while. She's worried he's going to make himself sick."

I look at James, who's wearing my father's rumpled clothes from Luz's bag and stitches in his head. "He'll never go."

"He might if we both ask him to," Finn says. "He's got to get some sleep, or . . ."

The hairline crack. Maybe Vivianne and Finn see it, too.

"Okay," I say. "Worth a shot."

We stand and meet James and Vivianne in the middle of the hallway. His eyes are red, but I can't tell if it's from crying or being awake for almost twenty-four hours. He looks ready to drop.

"The doctor says we should leave him alone for a while," he says. "His immune system is depressed because of the trauma, and they don't want him catching anything while he's still in critical condition."

"In that case, I think you should go home and get some sleep," I say.

"Yeah, man," Finn says. "You can't stay here."

James shakes his head, but Vivianne doesn't let him start. "I think they're right, sweetheart. I'll stay right here, and I'll call you if anything changes."

James's eyes darken as he realizes we're ganging up on him. "I can't leave you alone here, Viv."

"I won't be alone long," she says. "Alice should be here any minute."

James grimaces. His cousin Alice is probably the most overbearing woman I've ever met—and I live with my mother—and she has a particular fondness for interrogating James.

"Better run while you still can," Vivianne says.

"We'll come back in a few hours," Finn says, "once you've gotten some sleep and a shower."

"Please, James," I add.

James leans against the wall, letting it take his weight. "You two *agree* on this?"

"I know, it's weird," Finn says. "I feel dirty."

James sighs. "Fine. But just for a couple of hours."

Finn goes to the waiting room to collect our things, and James and Vivianne go back into Nate's room so he can say good-bye. I hover in the hallway, waiting.

"Excuse me, miss?" one of the nurses at the station says.

I turn. "Yes?"

"We found this in the waiting room," she says, extending a yellow legal pad toward me. "I think it's your friend's?"

I take the pad; it's the one James was scribbling on with such intensity for hours. There are half a dozen pages littered with mathematical formulas and notes. There's only one bit that makes any sense to me at all. At the top, he's scribbled, *Is this what's been missing?* Whatever these symbols mean, they're important. I rip the sheets from the pad and put them in my pocket, thanking the nurse, and imagine the hug James will give me when he remembers they're gone and finds out I saved them for him.

ELEVEN

em

Finn and I split up when we head back to the hospital. He joins the candlelight vigil and swarm of press at the front entrance, and I make my way around to the back. I stand across the street from the parking lot and keep an eye on the ambulance bay. The area is being kept clear of press and mourners so that emergency vehicles can still move through, so my view is relatively clear, but I'm far enough away that I shouldn't attract any unwanted attention.

A couple of reporters are back here, doing stand-ups about the second shooting, but most are in the prime real estate in front, where Finn is. I pretend to watch them as I keep an eye on the back of the hospital. It's important that we keep track of where our younger selves are, because things are different now. Once I took that shot at James, I changed the future, so I now no longer know what Marina is going to do or where she's going to go. My old memories are useless.

In the pocket of the hoodie I borrowed from Connor is a

protein bar and one of the prepaid cell phones Finn and I bought as soon as we arrived in D.C. Finn has the rest of our supplies in his backpack: the gun and extra ammunition, some food and a couple of spare T-shirts. I hope we won't need the clothes or the food; I hope we won't be here that long.

I watch the glass doors at the back of the hospital slide open and shut from across the street and rip into the protein bar. I'm not hungry, but I've got to do something with my hands. I thought watching James slowly become hard and merciless was the worst thing I'd ever experience, but I was wrong. This is worse. Maybe I was naive to think I could do this. Somehow I'm *still* finding ways in which I'm just a child.

Looking at his face, remembering the boy he'd been and how much I'd loved him, had instantly turned me back into that sixteen-year-old who thought the sun rose and set with James Shaw. I miss that girl, and that boy. I've missed them for years, even if I haven't been able to admit it. And now I have to end one's life and devastate the other.

It's unbearable.

The phone in my pocket buzzes, and I jump. I fish it out and press the button with unsteady fingers. "They leaving?"

"No," Finn says on the other end. "Just wanted to say hi."

I smile. "You checking up on me?"

"Please, like I care. I'm just bored."

"I'm fine, okay?"

"Well, that makes one of us."

The ambulance bay doors slide open, and a guy in a suit with "dignitary protection" written all over him steps out. I edge behind one of the news vans as I watch him walk to the car—a black, unmarked Crown Victoria—and pull it up to the side of the hospital, right in front of an emergency exit.

"I think they're coming out," I whisper.

The emergency exit opens, and someone whose face is covered with a coat dashes out, flanked by a uniformed officer and another agent, and slips into the back of the car. Even without seeing his face, I know it's James. The two television crews still back here must think so, too, because they start rolling.

"I'm on my way," Finn says in my ear as I watch the other Finn—God, he looks so young—climb into the car after James. "What are they doing?"

"Getting into a car with a couple of agents."

He swears.

"Finn, if they're taking him into protective custody, we'll never—"

"I know." I can hear the exertion in his breath as he runs toward me. "I'm coming."

Marina comes out next. That is, *I* come out next. It's my first glimpse of my old self, and my heart constricts in pure longing for the girl I was. She's catty and shallow, but only because she hasn't learned how to like herself. How can she not see how beautiful she is, how special? All she sees is James, bending toward him like a flower to the sun.

"Come on, Finn!" I say.

He comes racing around the corner of the hospital as the Crown Vic begins to roll out of the opposite end of the parking lot.

"Hurry! They're going to get away!"

Finn runs past me. "Keep an eye on where they go," he says into the phone. "I'm going over a couple of blocks."

I watch the car take a right out of the parking lot and stop at the light on the corner. It takes a left when the light changes, and I follow its every movement until it turns out of my field of vision. I turn and go after Finn, finding him two blocks away from the hospital.

"They're headed north," I say when I catch up to him.

He's weaving among the parked cars by the curb, rubbing the frosted glass to look inside the windows. He finds what he's looking for with a dusty blue Honda and grabs the gun out of the backpack. He uses the butt to smash in the back window. The tinkle of broken glass sounds impossibly loud to me, but no shouts or sirens follow. "Headed toward Georgetown, then," he says.

"Maybe. Hope so."

He reaches through the jagged teeth of the broken window and pops open the lock on the driver's door. He slides behind the wheel and opens the passenger's door for me, and I watch him dig into the wire beneath the steering wheel and go to work on hot-wiring the car the same way he did a dozen times in our years of running.

After several tries and lots of swearing, the car roars to life beneath us, and we take off in the direction the Crown Vic went. Back toward Georgetown.

Back toward home.

marina

The front exit is choked with mourners and press, and the ambulance bay has to be kept clear, so the officers and men in dark suits lead us to a small fire exit door on the side of the building that's only used for emergencies. One of the agents—I think his name is Morris—goes to get the car, while his partner, Spitzer, waits with us inside the door. Spitzer assures us they've combed the parking lot and tightened security around the perimeter of the hospital, but I'm still tense with waiting for the sound of a gunshot because now I feel like they can come from anywhere at any time.

When Morris pulls up, Spitzer and an officer guard James from both sides as he climbs into the car. Finn goes next, slipping in the opposite door, and then me, practically diving in the door nearest us so that James is sandwiched between us. Spitzer climbs into the passenger seat, and we set off toward Georgetown. The sky outside the window is a steely gray, the night almost over. I'm not sure whether I'm surprised that so much time has passed or shocked that it's been so little.

"Want us to take you home first?" Morris says, glancing at Finn in the rearview mirror.

"It's fine," Finn says. "I'll take the Metro."

Morris frowns. "You sure?" he says. "I don't even think the Metro is open this early, and—"

"I'm sure," Finn interrupts, and I realize I don't know where he lives.

James is silent, watching the streets roll past outside the window.

"You okay?" I say. It's an idiotic question, but I have to say *something*.

He doesn't hear me.

We turn onto our street, and I've never been so glad to see it before. The Shaws' house is dark, but the kitchen light is still on in mine. Luz has probably been cooking up a storm since she left the hospital. I'm not letting James stay in his home; the investigators have been in there, and there will be reminders of Nate everywhere. We'll stay at mine. The agents can protect him just as easily at my house, where there will also be a thousand pancakes and beds with freshly washed sheets waiting for us.

"You can take us to the house with the light on. James is going to stay with me." I pause. "You can stay, too, Finn. If you want."

Before either boy responds, a flash of light explodes in my eyes. I scream and cover my face, expecting an explosion of noise and blood and pain. Morris swears and the car accelerates sharply beneath us. I force my eyes open and blink away the floating halos of light that swim in my vision.

"Are you okay?" I grab at James blindly. "Are you hurt?"

"I'm fine," James says shakily. "What was that?"

"Photographers," Spitzer says. "Camped out across the street. News crews'll be here any minute."

"Son of a bitch!" Finn says.

I sag back into my seat. I can't even summon rage for the creeps who would invade James's privacy like this. I'm too relieved he hasn't been shot.

"Is there somewhere else you'd rather go?" Morris asks. "We can secure your house, but there's nothing we can do about the press."

James is still pale. "No, I don't want to go back there. You can drop Marina off, though. The photographers will go away once they see I'm not with her. I'll go to a hotel, I guess."

I start shaking my head before he's even done with the sentence. "No way."

"I'll be—"

"You say you'll be *fine*, and I swear I'm shoving you out of this car!" I snap. I hate it when James gets like this, so perversely determined not to be a bother to anyone, like last year when he broke his wrist and insisted on scrawling his equations in an unreadable script with his bad hand rather than letting me write for him. He doesn't see how much I *want* to be bothered by him, how that means I'm actually important to him. "I'm not letting you stay alone in some hotel."

"Then I'll go back to the hospital."

"There's even more press there! You'll be mobbed!"

"I don't need you to take care of me, Marina."

"You need *someone* to—"

"Guys," Finn says. "*Guys!*"

We both turn to look at him.

He's slunk down in his seat and is staring up at the roof of the car. "You can both stay with me, if you want."

James blinks. "Really?"

"Sure." Finn sighs. "Why not?"

James's voice is soft. "Finn, you don't have to."

I look back and forth between the two boys in confusion.

"You can't go home or to Marina's, and you can't go to the hospital," Finn says. "You go to a hotel, and someone who works there will recognize you. Jesus, man, you were just *shot* at. No one would ever think to look for you at my place. It's the best option you've got."

"So where are we going?" Morris asks.

"Columbia Heights," Finn says. "Gresham Place."

I go still. Finn stares resolutely out of the window, not looking at us. I'm not stupid; I've noticed Finn's cheap shoes and the fact that he takes the Metro everywhere when he's old enough to drive, so I knew he must be on financial aid. But I always figured he was some middle-class teacher's kid or something, because poor people just don't go to Sidwell. But Columbia Heights? It's, like, *beyond* poor. Mom would have a two-Xanax-level fit if she knew I was spending time with a boy from that part of town.

We make our way across the city as the sun begins to rise, and both boys are silent. I try to look out of the window at the streets around us as inconspicuously as possible. Misty gray light is creeping into Columbia Heights, illuminating the shuttered storefronts and cracked pavement. It sends the people who linger on the streets scurrying toward home like rats looking for a hole to hide in until dark. Some streets aren't bad. The main drag is lined with chain restaurants and boutiques, but stray a couple of blocks from Starbucks and Urban Outfitters, and you're in gangland.

Yeah, we should be a lot safer here.

Finn directs Morris to his house, and at least it could be worse.

Gresham Place isn't Georgetown, but it's not *quite* the Murder Central we passed a few blocks ago. Finn's small row house is in bad need of a new coat of paint, and the lawn is wildly overgrown, but there aren't any bars on the windows, and there's a bench and two pots of pansies on the tiny porch.

"Home sweet home," Finn says in a flat voice as Morris parks the car by the curb.

James and I follow him up the porch steps and into the house. The lights are off, but even with nothing but the watery sun through the blinds, I can see that the place is worn and cramped and cluttered. None of the furniture matches, and practically every surface has something on it that shouldn't be there: a stack of old newspapers, a half-full coffee cup, a discarded sweater. There's a pile of dishes in the sink and a stack of folded laundry on the sofa, like someone hit the pause button on life. This would never happen in my house. Even without Luz, I think it would drive my mother crazy enough that she'd clean up herself. Or at least make me do it.

"Sorry for the mess," Finn mutters, shoving a stack of unopened mail into a drawer and sweeping a handful of crumbs off the countertop and into the sink.

"It's fine," James says. I can't say anything. I'm trying not to be the terrible snob that Finn thinks I am, but I've never known anyone who lives like this. The whole house could practically fit inside my living room. I imagine what Tamsin and Sophie would say if they knew.

"Finn, honey, is that you?" a voice calls from another room.

"It's me, Mom!"

"Can you come help me in here? Your father got called in early."

Finn barely glances at us. "I'll be right back."

When he's gone, I turn to James, who's moving the stack of laundry so he can sit on the sofa. "Did you know Finn lived here?"

He shakes his head. "He would never tell me; we always stayed at my house. I knew his family didn't have the kind of money ours do, but I didn't think it was this bad."

I perch on the arm beside him. "How can they afford to send him to Sidwell? Even with financial aid?"

"He's on a full scholarship. He didn't want anyone to know."

"You mean Finn's *smart*?" I ask, only half joking.

"I hide it pretty well, huh?" Finn asks as he turns the corner back into the living room. There's a sharpness to his grin, like a knife's edge. "James, you can take my room."

"No, that's okay," James says. "I don't want to kick you out—"

"I insist, so shut up, okay? It's the first door on the left."

James sighs. "Okay. Just a couple of hours. Then I'm going back to the hospital."

"Of course."

James stands, and I'm about to get up and hug him when I see Finn watching me. I stop myself, suddenly self-conscious.

"Good night," I say.

"Good night." For a second James looks like he's going to say something else, but then he turns and leaves.

Finn lifts the lid of the wooden trunk that serves as a coffee table and pulls out a pile of extra pillows and blankets.

"You can take the couch," he says. "I'll take the floor."

"Okay."

He cuts his eyes up at me. "You could do me the courtesy of arguing for at least a *second*."

"Oh. I, uh . . ." It never even occurred to me to offer to take the floor myself. But it *is* his house. "I guess I can take the floor. . . ."

That makes him laugh. "I was joking, M."

Thank God.

We make a decent pallet for him on the floor, laying the back cushions from the couch down in the small space between the coffee table and the doorway to the kitchen. My bed is more easily made, just a pillow and an old quilt that smells like lavender and mothballs dumped onto the sofa. It's not Egyptian cotton and hypoallergenic down, but I swear it feels even better than that when my body sinks into the cushions. I'm half asleep before my head hits the pillow.

"Marina?"

"Hmm?"

He pauses so long, I nearly fall asleep in the silence.

"You in love with James?" he finally asks.

My eyes fly open. Those five little words in Finn's hushed voice chase away any thought of sleep. "What?"

"You heard me."

"That's none of your business."

"I know."

I roll over and find him looking up at me, his hands folded behind his head. I can barely meet his eyes. "Then why do you care?"

He shrugs. "I just do."

"Well, I'm not, okay?" I say, hoping my voice sounds steadier than I feel. "He's my best friend, that's it."

Finn's expression doesn't change. "Okay."

"Can I go to sleep now?"

"Sure."

I roll over again, turning my back to him.

"Good night, Marina."

His voice is so oddly kind when he says it that I burrow deeper into the quilt to get away from the sound of it and don't say anything back.

TWELVE

em

Finn and I catch up with the Crown Vic at one particularly long light and follow it from a discreet distance to James's house. I tuck my hands under my legs to keep them from fidgeting as we approach. I'm going to see my house again. I haven't seen it since the night I snuck out to meet Finn and escape from D.C. I even left my key in the flowerpot beside the front door after locking it behind me, because I knew I was never coming back.

We watch from around the corner as the Crown Vic turns onto my street. A group of photographers jumps at it, and the driver hits the gas. Finn goes after them, and my house flies past the window so quickly that it's little more than a blur. I'm not sure if I'm disappointed or relieved.

"Where are they going?" I ask as the Crown Vic turns east.

He frowns. "Not sure."

We follow them for a few more minutes, and then Finn abruptly steers our car into a gas station. The Crown Vic flies through a green light ahead of us.

"What are you doing?" I say.

"Getting gas."

"But they're getting away!"

Finn gets out of the car and goes to pay the attendant. I open my door and clamber out.

"Finn!" I call after him. *"Finn!"*

But he waves me off and disappears inside the station. What the hell is he doing? I slam the door shut and cross my arms over my chest, like I could contain the panicked beating of my heart. Every second takes Marina and James farther away from me and deeper into the unknown.

I'm still leaning against the car waiting for Finn when he comes back. "What the hell was that about?" I say. "We've lost them now!"

"No, we haven't." He starts to pump the gas. "I know where they're going."

"What? Where?"

"My house."

"Oh." My anger instantly cools. I don't know what to say. Even when things were really bad and we were trying to think of a way to get past the checkpoints and out of D.C., Finn always wanted to meet in coffee shops and fast-food restaurants. He said he didn't want his family getting involved, which I believe, but I think he also didn't want me to see where he lived. "You okay?"

"Yeah. I just . . ." He replaces the pump. "That poor kid. He's not ready for this."

We drive at a more leisurely pace now that Finn knows

exactly where we're headed. I watch the houses outside the window get smaller and smaller, grubbier and grubbier. Finn hadn't told me how badly off his family was until we'd been on the run together for a couple of months, and even then it was only little hints at first. I don't think he was ashamed, exactly. More like he was scared how James and I, and the other privileged kids at our school, would react if we'd known, how differently we might have treated him. He was right to worry. The shallow, sheltered girl I was then *would* have treated him differently, but once he and I were traveling across state lines in the back of trucks and going days without seeing a bar of soap, his fear of judgment and my snobbery quickly became things of the past.

But his seventeen-year-old self, who is so sensitive under his bravado, is now showing my spoiled sixteen-year-old self his secret, exposing his weakness to her. I can only hope she won't hurt him. I cover Finn's hand where it rests on the console between us.

He parks a block away from the Crown Vic that's stationed outside of the small row house I now know is his. With Marina and the younger Finn in there with James, there's nothing to do but wait. We can't risk coming face-to-face with our younger selves; we have to wait until James is alone.

"I wish I could see my mom," Finn says. "It's weird that she's right there."

I nod as though I understand, but I don't. Not really. Even when we'd been right outside my house, my parents had barely crossed my mind. I never really missed them after I ran away. When I was scared or tired and would close my eyes and wish for someone to hold me and take my burdens away, the face attached to those arms was more often Luz or even James than it was Mom or Dad. There was a bitterness in that, a special pain that came from *not* missing them.

But Finn was always different, especially when it came to his mother. He wrote his parents postcards while we were gone, and he'd give them to people we met on the road to mail when they got wherever they were going so we couldn't be traced by the postmarks. Once I found him sitting in the dark outside the motel we were crashing in, crying like his heart was breaking. We'd already been to hell and back running from James, but that was the first time I ever saw him cry. It was a night of firsts. It was his mother's birthday, he said, and he wasn't even sure if she was alive or dead. He told me about her for the first time, and it was the first time I ever really understood him.

It was also the first time I ever hugged him. He held on to me so tightly that I could feel his heart beating against me.

"Just think," I say. "When we're done here, you'll never have to leave her."

He goes suddenly, unnaturally still. He's looking at me, but his eyes have gone vacant, like he's no longer seeing me.

"Finn?"

His eyes roll back in his head and his eyelids start to flutter spasmodically, the only part of his body not frozen into place. I put a hand on his arm, which is rigid under my touch. When he doesn't respond, I shake him.

"Finn?" I say again. I can feel the hysteria rising within me. I'm sure he's having a seizure or something when it hits me that this must be what happened to me earlier in the parking lot. Finn has been swept away to some other place inside his mind, like I was when I saw the day I met James. He neglected to mention how terrifying it is. Finn is gone, and nothing but his body is left. I shake him again, even though I know it will do no good.

I'm not sure how long the fit lasts—thirty seconds? forty?—but it feels like longer. Finally he blinks, slowly, and the light comes back into his eyes. I let out the breath I've been holding.

"Em?" he says.

"You okay?" I try to sound calm. "You sort of went away there for a minute."

"Yeah, I think so."

"Did you see something?" I ask. "Was it a memory?"

He rubs a hand over his face and nods. "It was that house we stayed in for a few weeks in Delaware. Remember? It was right after the attack in Providence, and everyone was jumpy as hell. Pete and I were watching the news in the basement. It was the night the president announced that Congress had pushed through Patriot Act IV. I went to wake you up so you could watch with us."

"I remember," I say. I had shoved him for waking me, but he caught my hand and quietly told me about the new laws Congress had passed in the middle of the night. No unauthorized interstate travel, harsher punishments for citizens refusing to present government-approved ID cards, a repeal of the ban on military personnel policing American streets. We both knew James was behind it.

"What is this? Why does this keep happening?" I say. Seeing Finn yanked away from me like that, feeling so suddenly alone in this world that's not really mine, has left me shaken.

"I don't know," he says.

We sit in silence and stare at the little green row house down the street, and I cross my arms to ward off the chill from the cold air that blows in through the smashed window. I don't want to remember these things. But James always said time is complicated, that it has a mind of its own. Maybe this is its way of punishing us for messing with it.

Finn eventually falls asleep, his forehead pressed against the glass. I swear he can sleep anywhere. My eyes are heavy and itching but remain fixed on the house. My resolve has returned. I don't want Marina to ever have to hide out in Nowhere, Delaware, and watch the world end on an ancient little television in a basement that smells like mold and stale air freshener.

I try to imagine what Marina is doing at this moment. It's so strange that she's experiencing things now that I never have. It makes me feel distant from her—from myself—like we're really two different people. In a way, I guess, we are now.

Which is sort of the point of all of this.

Marina has finally seen Finn's secret, which he hid so carefully from me for so long. Maybe she's even met his mother, who he would only ever speak to me about when it was dark and quiet and he could talk in a whisper, as though keeping her a secret between us and the night would keep her protected somehow. Marina comforted James after his brother's shooting, which I did once, but also after someone shot at him, too. She could be doing anything right now: sleeping or showering or booking a plane ticket to Buenos Aires for all I know.

The thought sends a shiver up my spine. Is she okay, there

inside that house, divorced from me? I suddenly have to know. I can't stand this feeling of separateness from myself.

Quietly, careful not to wake Finn, who would only tell me what a monumentally terrible idea this is, I unfold my frozen limbs and slip out of the Honda. I don't close the door behind me, just let it rest shut. The agents assigned to James are still camped in front of Finn's house, but the street is deserted and silent this early in the morning. I hop the fence into the backyard of the house on the corner. That's one advantage of row houses: there are no spaces in between where the agents might glimpse me approaching the Abbotts'. As long as I'm quiet, they should never know I'm here. The yards are separated by chain-link fences that are easy to climb over, and I'm soon in Finn's tiny backyard, which is even more overgrown than the front. I creep up the back steps, freezing when one squeaks under my weight. I take the next two steps more carefully, keeping my feet as close to the edges as possible.

I inch toward one of the two windows, which is dark with dust and the netting of a black screen.

Inside is a woman in bed, an oversize sweater pulled around her body, her hair swept up into a messy ponytail. She shares Finn's coloring, and she was obviously pretty once, before illness dulled her skin and hollowed her cheeks. She's watching television, flipping the channels in a listless way, like she's already been through them a dozen times.

I don't linger at the window. Spying on Finn's mother like this makes me feel like some kind of thief.

Instead, I tiptoe to the second window and peer inside.

What I see stops my heart.

THIRTEEN

marina

I sleep fitfully. I'm exhausted but I can't seem to get comfortable or switch off my brain. Maybe I'm *too* exhausted. I fade in and out of consciousness, dreaming that I'm still at the hospital and waking up grasping for things that aren't there before slipping under again.

At some point, I open my eyes and the drowsiness drops away long enough for me to realize how thirsty I am. I get up and creep over Finn, who's sound asleep on the floor, his face buried so deeply into his pillow that I have no idea how he's breathing. I slip into the kitchen and drink straight from the tap, cupping my hands under the flow of water, too sleep-addled to bother looking for a glass. I take gulp after gulp of the water, which is too warm to be refreshing but tastes almost sweet against my parched tongue.

"Finn, is that you?"

I straighten and twist off the tap. "No, Mrs. Abbott. It's Marina."

"Oh, come here!" she says. "I want to have a look at you."

I pad on bare feet toward the door of the master bedroom and push it open. Mrs. Abbott is lying down, flopped back against a sea of pillows. There's a bar along her side of the bed, which gives me a terrible flashback to Nate in the hospital, looking pale and absent. In fact, there are bars all over the room and a walker by the bedside table, which is littered with prescription pill bottles. Suddenly Finn's demeanor in the hospital makes sense.

"Oh, Marina," she says. She looks just like Finn—blond-haired, blue-eyed, with the same mischievous curl to the lips—except she seems faded, like a bad photocopy of herself. "It's so good to finally put a face to the name. Finn's told me so much about you."

"Really?" I hover in the doorway, feeling uncertain and foolish. I've never been around a sick person before. And . . . Finn's told her about me?

"Oh yes," she says. "You and James are practically all he talks about."

I don't know what to say. Mrs. Abbott struggles to sit up straighter against the pillows, and I think maybe I should offer to help, but I can't move from this spot.

"That's nice. . . ." I say.

"Well." Mrs. Abbott smiles at me. "I'll let you get back to sleep. It was nice meeting you."

I swallow. "You too."

I close the door and turn back to the living room, but my gaze snags on the door to Finn's bedroom. Has James managed to fall asleep? I don't like the idea of him lying there awake and alone. Finn may think I'm smothering James, but I know him better than Finn does, and he shouldn't be alone right now. Besides, the last time I left him alone, he was *shot* at. I knock on the door with one knuckle, lightly enough that it won't wake him if he's asleep.

"Come in, Marina."

I push open the door and find him sitting up in Finn's bed, the blanket twisted around his feet.

"You haven't slept?" I say.

"A little, I think," he says, "but my mind keeps going around in circles. I just . . . I can't believe things changed so much, so quickly."

I sit beside him on the narrow twin bed, which dips under my weight, tilting him toward me. "I know."

"If he dies . . ." James stares forward at something I can't see. "I can't live in a world with no Nate in it."

"He's going to be okay," I say, even though the words taste empty on my tongue. "Everything'll be fine."

James's face collapses, like the facade of a building crumbling into a pile of bricks, and he starts to cry into his hands. I'm relieved. Racking sobs shake his whole body, but it's so much easier to take than the blank face and dead eyes he's been wearing for hours. I wrap my arms around him, and he leans into me.

"Can you stay?" he asks.

I nod, and we lie back on the bed. His arms curl around my waist, and he buries his face into the crook of my shoulder. I've never been this close to him, and I'm a terrible person for enjoying it a little. How many nights have I lain in bed by myself, imagining James beside me? Just last night I was plotting to have sex with him. My mind knows this is only a sick mockery of my fantasies, but my body doesn't quite realize it. He's so warm. I run my hand up and down his back, and I'm sure no one else would feel this good.

When his sobs start to subside, James presses a kiss to my jaw and rests his forehead against my temple.

"I don't know what I'd do without you, kid," he whispers.

My chest constricts into a hot, tingling ball. "You too."

James kisses me again, this time on the cheek, only a breath from the corner of my mouth. He lingers there, his mouth hovering an inch from mine. My mind goes white and fuzzy, the world narrowed to the space between our lips.

James moves away, resting his head on my shoulder, and I inhale sharply. God, I don't think I was breathing that entire time. I should get up, go back to the sofa, but James is heavy against me, his body pressed to mine from shoulder to knee. His breathing has slowed, and I think he might finally be asleep.

He might not have kissed me for real. But maybe I'm just what he needed.

I close my eyes.

em

I stare at the two of them, tangled up in each other, until the bitter wind makes my eyes water and blur.

I could do it right now. The gun is tucked into the back of my belt. I could take it out and shoot James through the window and be done with this forever.

But there's Marina curled up next to him, her fingers clutching at him even in sleep, and I remember so vividly what it was like to be that girl, to clutch with those fingers, to be close to that boy. The feel and smell of him. How much she—*I*—loved him.

I pull the gun from my belt and hold it in front of me. It's warm from being pressed against my skin, and my hands are suddenly clammy as I flex my fingers around it. I flip off the safety, and the soft click is like an explosion in my ears.

I should do it now. Spare myself and Finn any more of this misery. In five seconds it could all be over. I won't exist anymore to regret this horrible step I've been forced to take.

James shifts in his sleep, pulling Marina closer.

I close my eyes. The sight of them weakens me. I try to remember that the boy in the bed is already gone. The man who wears his face in the future has been twisted and warped beyond recognition, made cruel by ambition and his own perverse determination to do what he thinks is right.

I squeeze the gun in my hands as I picture Luz, my dear Luz, thrown away like a piece of trash. Vivianne dying in a one-car crash in the middle of the night on the Baltimore–Washington Parkway. Mrs. Abbott, who will have nothing left of her son but a few scribbled postcards. Finn screaming as they torture him for information he doesn't have. All the people who will suffer and die because of James.

I open my eyes and look at the two of them, lying together in that bed, so beautifully unaware of what's about to crash down on their heads, and I raise the gun. Two feet, maybe less, separates the barrel from James's head. It will be quick.

My eyes drift to Marina. God, was I ever really that young? I'm not sure what will happen after I fire the gun. Finn and I will cease to exist, our time line snuffed out along with James's life, but where—or when—will Marina wake up? Will she see what I've done? The thought makes me shudder. It would destroy her.

Maybe I can give them one more moment together.

I start to lower the gun, and as the barrel tilts toward the ground, a familiar sensation grabs hold of my belly like a cold hand. I don't have time to panic or resist before it yanks me backward.

Back and back and back.

I fall through nothingness at dizzying speed. When I finally open my eyes, I'm in the little white cell that was my home for so many months.

James is sitting across from me. He has a Taser held lightly in his hand.

"Please, Marina," he says. "Tell me where the documents are. Then I can help you."

"Oh really?" I say. "The way you helped Vivianne? Or Luz?"

He stiffens. "That wasn't my fault. I never would have—"

"Vivianne's dead, James!" I shout, my voice leaping out of my control. "I guess she knew too much, but Luz didn't know anything, and when she couldn't tell you where we were, you had her put in a detainment camp. For *terrorist activities!*" Tears sting behind my eyes as I vacillate between grief and rage thinking of

Luz, her careworn face and her strong, gentle hands. "A sweet old lady who never got so much as a traffic ticket, imprisoned as a terrorist. That woman loved you, and you ruined her life just because you could!"

He stands so abruptly that the legs of his chair scrape against the concrete. I can see the tension coiled in his body, ready to snap, as he clenches his hands into fists over and over. For a second he could be the James I loved, pacing the room as he tried to work out some mental puzzle, but the line of his jaw is too harsh, the look in his eyes too cold.

"I did it because I needed you to understand how important it is that you hand over the documents," he says. "If anyone else gets a hold of them, the consequences are beyond your imagination!"

"Yeah, I never was smart enough to understand any of this," I say with a grim smile. "I guess I don't get how planting bombs all over the country is supposed to make us safer. Or how your quest to save the world is doing anything other than serving your ego. Stupid me."

He looks down at me, and he actually looks sad. "Please. They'll hurt you."

I stare back at him. "And you'll let them."

He turns away. "Sometimes you have to hurt someone you love for the greater good."

"Why do you get to decide what the greater good is?" I say. "These are *people* you're talking about, not just numbers in one of your equations. Don't you get that? Did you *ever?*"

His face doesn't change. "Just tell me what you did with the documents."

I spit at his feet.

He sighs and knocks on the door to my cell, summoning the guard. I see him swallow before he says, "Make her talk."

The guard nods and slaps me with the back of his hand as calmly as if he'd been told to make his bed. He hits me again and again.

"James!" I sob when he heads for the door.

He pauses, but then slides the cell door shut without looking at me, leaving me alone with the guard. I swear to myself in that moment that I'll never say the name again. James is gone. There's only the doctor now.

I come back to myself with a gasp. I'm lying on the Abbotts' porch, writhing with the pain of the remembered beating, the gun beside me. How long was I gone? I scramble to my knees and peek into the bedroom.

Marina and James are gone.

FORTEEN

marina

The sliding sound of wood on wood wakes me. I blink, not recognizing the faded blue paint or the piles of what look like computer pieces heaped onto the desk in the corner.

Or the arm slung around my waist.

My head starts to feel heavy as it all comes back to me. Nate. The blood. The hospital. Each thought weighs me down until I can barely turn my head toward the sound that woke me.

Finn is standing at a dresser near the foot of the bed, staring down at James and me, curled up together in his bed.

"I just came for some clean clothes," he says.

"Finn—"

"I'll be in the kitchen."

He leaves and closes the door behind him. My chest aches when I inhale, like the look in his eyes rubbed me raw, though I'm not sure why. I slip out from under James's arm and follow him to the kitchen, where he's cracking eggs over an open skillet.

"So, you finally reeled him in, huh?" he says, wiggling his eyebrows at me.

"What?" I say, thrown by the sudden change in his demeanor.

"You've got to give James credit." He stirs the eggs with a spoon so forcefully that some slosh over the edge of the skillet and onto the burner, where they sizzle and turn black. "He put up a good fight, but I guess your feminine wiles—or is it graces? I'm never sure—anyway, your feminine *qualities* finally hooked him. Your friends will be so proud; did you text them yet?"

"You're an asshole," I whisper. "His brother was *shot* last night."

He ignores me. "What'll you name your kids, you think? I'm sure you've already got some options picked out."

I push him. "Shut up."

He holds up his eggy spoon in surrender and laughs. "Easy, M. Chill."

James enters the kitchen, all rumpled and creased, his hair sticking up in ten different directions. Normally I would find this unbearably charming and add it to my mental photo album of James, but Finn's teasing has shaken me for reasons I can't quite pin down. The way it made me and my friends sound so . . . mercenary? The creeping insecurity that James just needed *someone* and I was the one *there*?

If only he would look at me, but his eyes are firmly fixed on a spot on the linoleum.

"I need to go back to the hospital," he says. "It's been almost five hours. Vivianne must be going crazy with Cousin Alice."

"You should eat something first," Finn says.

"I'm not hungry."

"Too bad."

I want to shake him. *Look at me!* But he doesn't, and the sick feeling in my stomach builds. Was Finn right? Am I really so stupid that I was about to start picking out baby names when what happened meant nothing to James?

From the back of the house, a door opens and a *bang-shuffle-bang* sound moves toward us. Finn shoves the skillet of eggs and spoon into my hand. I stare at it for a moment and then push the eggs around uncertainly.

"Mom," Finn calls. "What do you need?"

Mrs. Abbott, leaning heavily on a walker, her sweatpants and sweater hanging off her thin frame, enters the kitchen. "Just getting some juice."

"I'll bring you a glass. Get back to bed."

I glance at James and see he's as surprised about Mrs. Abbott's condition as I was.

"I want to say hello to your friends," she says, resisting Finn's attempts to steer her back toward her bedroom. "It's good to finally meet you, James. I'm so very sorry about your brother."

James fidgets. "Thank you, ma'am."

I think the eggs are beginning to burn, so I take the skillet off the stove.

"Mom," Finn says softly. "You're going to wear yourself out."

"I'm fine, honey. Quit fussing." She takes a few labored steps toward the refrigerator and leans hard against her walker with one hand while she uses the other to pull it open. Finn fetches her a glass, and she reaches inside the fridge for a carton of orange juice. "How is he doing, if you don't mind my asking?"

"The doctors, um, they say he's critical, and he's still uncon-scious." James's voice is barely audible, and he doesn't look at Mrs. Abbott. He's never been good with strangers, even under the best conditions. "I'm heading back to the hospital now."

"Yes, of course," Mrs. Abbott says. Finn scoops the juice car-ton out of her trembling hand and pours her a glass, and she pulls his face down to kiss his cheek. "There are some travel-size board games in the closet that are good for waiting rooms. You should take them. Finn, go get the games to take with you."

"I will." Finn takes his mother's elbow and helps her from the room. But it's a small house, so James and I still hear every word they say as they make their way down the hallway back to the master bedroom.

"I'm staying home," Finn says softly. "I'm not leaving you alone again."

"Oh, honey, I'll be fine. And your father will be home soon. You should be there for your friend."

"But what if you need something—"

"Finn." It's a tone of voice I recognize from Luz. "I'm the par-ent here, okay? You don't need to worry about me."

When they're gone, the master bedroom door closed behind them, I turn to James. "You didn't know, either?" I ask, trying to sound normal.

He shakes his head and doesn't meet my eyes. "Looks like MS."

"Why didn't he ever tell us?"

"Probably didn't want things to get too serious."

I shrivel. I hurled those words at Finn like a weapon only hours ago, with no idea of how serious his life actually is. I can't imagine what he thinks of me, how selfish and spoiled I must look to him. Selfish, spoiled, and in love with a boy who will never love me back. Selfish, spoiled, and completely delusional.

I am starting to hate myself.

Morris and Spitzer drive us back to the hospital, and James calls Vivianne on the way.

"Anything?" I ask when he hangs up.

"The same. They said once he's stable enough, they're going to move him to Walter Reed, where the security is better."

"Did they say anything about the person who shot at you?" Finn asks. I look over at him sharply. "I mean, uh, the *people*."

"People?" James says.

"Yeah. Marina saw them."

"You did?" James looks at me for the first time since I climbed into his bed. "I didn't know that."

I shrug. The whole episode is just another reminder of how useless I am. "No one believed me anyway."

"Why?"

"Because she says the shooters looked just like her and me," Finn says.

James frowns. "What do you mean, just like you?"

"I mean there was a boy and a girl with a gun, and they looked exactly like Finn and me, okay?" I say. "Whatever, it doesn't matter. Obviously I was just being stupid."

"The agent in charge thought she was nuts," Finn says.

"Thanks a lot!"

He laughs. "Well, he did. But *I* believe you."

"I'm so very comforted by that," I say. "Because what you think about *anything* really matters to anyone."

Finn smiles, but there's no mirth in it. He looks out of the window, and I push down my brief rush of guilt. My foul mood isn't his fault, even if he started it by needling me about James, but it's so easy to take it out on him.

Between us, James has bowed his head and is running his fingers over his brow. Wheels are starting to turn in his head over something, but if we lose him to his thoughts now, who knows when we might get him back? I have to stop him before he gets in too deep.

"So, *did* Viv say anything about the shooters?" I ask. "Have they caught them?"

James looks up at me, and it takes him a second to latch on to my question. "Not sure. They won't tell her anything. Of course."

"I'm sure they'll find them."

"Yeah." He sits up straight again. "Yeah."

When we arrive at the hospital, we find it no longer in lockdown. They must not be too worried about the shooting in the parking lot. Even the third floor has people on it again, although there's a healthy buffer of Capitol Police between Nate's room and the rest of the floor. Maybe the whole thing really *was* a coincidence, just like Agent Armison said.

As soon as we step into the waiting room, Cousin Alice

descends on James, fussing with his hair and screwing up her face at his wrinkled clothes, like it's beneath a Shaw to look like a normal human being who's had a rough night. A couple of other Shaw relatives I vaguely recognize from the annual Christmas party also stand when we come in. Aaron Shaw, who's shouting something lawyer-y into his cell phone, and Julia Shaw-Latham, who I thought was still in rehab, greet James but ignore Finn and me. Only Uncle Perry—who isn't really their uncle, just a family friend who used to give me hard candies from his pocket and taught James and me the sign language alphabet so we could send each other secret messages from across the room—comes over to give me a hug. Behind their backs, Vivianne sags in relief at not being alone with them all anymore.

"I'm fine, really, Alice," James says, ducking away from her as she tries to examine the stitches on his head. "It's nothing."

"Nothing! It's a *bullet wound.*"

"It's just a scratch from some debris—"

"I never liked the idea of you in this city, practically on your own," Alice says, sitting him down beside her. "Nathaniel—God have mercy on him—is too young and too busy to have a teenager under his guardianship. You're coming to live with me."

James's eyes widen in alarm. "I can't leave Nate. Besides, I have school—"

"School you're too young for. And your brother is in no position to take care of you right now!"

Vivianne rubs her temples wearily, like she has a headache she can't shake. "Alice, we discussed this—"

"Yes, but no offense, Vivianne, this is a *family matter*—"

"Please don't fight—"

Finn and I sit on the opposite side of the room, and I try to blend in with the wall. Alice doesn't approve of me any more than she does James, who's a saint. Finn picks up a magazine and starts doodling on the back, and I turn on my cell phone to wade through the dozens of texts waiting for me. The phone dings with a new one the second it comes alive.

TAMSIN: **Are you still w/ J??**

I text back: **Yes, at hospital.**

TAMSIN: **MARINA! THERE YOU ARE! What's going on??**

ME: **Just waiting. Nate's still unconscious. Can you tell everyone I'm okay and to stop texting me?**

TAMSIN: **Ok, but I'm DYING to know what's going on!**

My stomach lurches. Tam's not exactly the world's most sensitive person, but I can't believe she just said that. A little voice in the back of my head, which I've tried to muffle and strangle for years, has always wondered if Tamsin and Sophie decided to be my friend back in seventh grade just to get closer to James. This text—and the dozens of others I've received, many from people I don't even know—makes me feel like this is just entertainment for her, like I'm her personal *People* magazine. I silence my phone and jam it back in my pocket.

"Tamsin?" Finn says.

"Yeah."

"That girl's a bitch," he says mildly. "I don't know why you're friends with her."

Normally a statement like that would piss me off, but since

I agree with him right now, it's hard to get too worked up. "Me neither."

Finn smiles, and for once I don't feel like he's mocking me. I even smile back a little.

A nurse soon comes and tells us it's okay for Nate to receive visitors again. The whole family clambers to their feet, and she quickly adds that there isn't room for all of us.

"You go, James." Vivianne gives him a weak smile. "We saw him a little while ago."

"Okay." James looks a little pale and turns to Finn and me. "Will you guys come with me?"

We stand and follow him to Nate's room. Just outside the door, James says, "Sorry. I just feel kind of weird being alone in there with him."

"It's okay, man," Finn says. "We understand."

Finn and I stand against the back wall to give James a semblance of privacy. He holds Nate's hand and talks to him in a low voice, while Finn goes back to his doodle and I chew the last of the pink nail polish off my thumb.

"Hey, you know you don't have to be here," I whisper. "If you'd rather, you know, be at home."

"You don't have to be here, either," Finn says.

The thought had honestly never occurred to me. I'm here as long as James is here.

"James is *my* best friend, too," he says, looking down at his crude drawing of a dog dressed in a suit, "and his family is scary as hell. If our places were reversed, he wouldn't leave me."

"You're right, he wouldn't," I say. "He'd never make you go

through something like this alone. If you told him what was going on."

Finn only glances up at me before looking back down at his drawing and adding a bow tie to the dog's neck.

". . . is absolutely *unacceptable*!" Alice's voice comes ringing down the hall.

"Don't raise your voice to me today, Alice!" That's Vivianne, sounding frayed.

James groans and stands from his seat at Nate's bedside. "I'll be right back. Can you . . . ?"

"Sure," Finn says, and goes right to Nate's bedside. I follow a few steps behind as James rushes away to deal with his family. Nate looks better today, at least. Someone has cleaned him up, and his skin looks less gray.

"Hey, Congressman," Finn says. "James'll be right back. So, Cousin Alice is a handful, huh?"

I think about taking Nate's hand but can't quite make myself do it. For some reason, I'm afraid it will be cold.

"You're really good at this," I say softly.

"Well, I've had some practice."

"Did you mean what you said earlier," I say, "when you said you believe me about the shooters?"

Finn shrugs. "You may be a drama queen sometimes, M, but you're not crazy. And if you were going to hallucinate something, I don't know why it would be the two of us shooting at James, so yeah, I guess I do. There must be at least one extremely handsome delinquent with a handgun out there."

I roll my eyes but can't quite stifle my smile.

"But they'll never catch him," I say, "since everyone thinks I imagined it."

"Are you kidding?" he says. "There are about ten thousand CCTV cameras in that parking lot. The shooter's face is going to be everywhere."

"Really?" Now that he's said it, I vaguely recall Agent Armison mentioning the security cameras last night, but obviously it didn't sink in. I go to the window and look out over the parking lot, and Finn's right. On each light post is a cluster of cameras pointing in all directions. A tightness I didn't realize I was carrying in my chest eases. "I forgot. That actually makes me feel—"

"Marina!"

I turn around. Finn is perched on the edge of his chair, leaning over Nate.

Whose eyes are fluttering.

"Congressman?" Finn says. "Can you hear me?"

I rush back to Nate's bedside. His eyelids continue to move and then open halfway, like that's all he has the energy for. His fingers jerk in Finn's hand. I cover my mouth to stop the sob in my throat from escaping.

"I'm going to get a doctor," Finn says. "Stay with him."

Finn runs from the room, and I take Nate's hand. His fingers scrabble at my skin, and his lips move, like he's trying to say something.

"You've got a tube helping you breathe, okay, Nate?" I say. "You can't talk just yet. Finn's gone to get a doctor."

But Nate doesn't relax. He seems to be struggling with his body, his eyes that won't open all the way, his fingers that won't grasp, his voice that won't work. He looks up at me with urgent intensity, like he's desperately trying to communicate something to me.

"It's okay, Nate," I say, maybe more for my own comfort than his. He's scaring me. "Shh, it's okay."

Nate moves his head in an almost imperceptible shake against the pillow, and his hand clenches to a fist inside of mine. I snatch my hand back, afraid I've hurt him. Slowly, he raises a shaking pinky finger.

It's not a natural movement. At first I wonder if he's having some kind of spasm, but then I look down into his face and see that look in his eye, that one that begs me to understand. I remember James and me signing painstaking words to each other across a crowded cocktail party. Nate signing with Uncle Perry's wife, Gretchen, who is deaf, whenever they came to visit.

A fist. *A.*

A fist with the pinky straightened. *I.*

"*A-I.* Right, Nate?"

He closes his eyes briefly, and I understand the gesture as relief. With great effort, he straightens his fingers and crosses the first two. What is that? I don't remember. God, why didn't I pay more attention? Why am I not smarter?

"*T?*" I say. "*U?*"

He keeps making the sign.

"Oh!" Suddenly I remember. "*R?*"

He closes his eyes again.

"*A-I-R?*" I say. "Oh God, can you not breathe?"

I look at all of his machines, as if I'd be able to tell if something was wrong or know how to fix it, but the hiss of the ventilator is as even as it's always been. Nate shakes his head again and makes another sign.

"*J*," I say. I remember that one. "James is coming. I'm sure Finn went to get him."

Nate shakes his head. Nate makes his hand into a curve against the stiff bedsheets and then tucks his thumb between his first and second fingers.

"*C-T*? Connecticut?"

Nate closes his eyes.

"What's in Connecticut, Nate?" My blood goes cold, like I'm standing out in the snow in my pajamas again. I remember the odd conversation I had with Nate beside his car the night they got back from his home district. I told Nate he looked tired, and he said . . .

I've just been busy with this investigation, ate up my whole recess.

And then, right on the heels of that, Nate asked me to keep an eye on James. Said he was worried about him and would I let him know if he started acting differently. I thought it was a strange request, and odd that Nate would jump from the topic of an investigation to his brother's behavior, but maybe—

I look down at Nate's hand again, and he's tracing a shaky *J* against the sheet with his pinky. Maybe the two things—whatever he was investigating and his brother's well-being—were linked in Nate's mind.

"Is there something in Connecticut?" I say.

Nate closes his eyes and opens them again.

"Something that—" My voice dries up, and I have to swallow.

"Something that explains why you were hurt?"

Eyes close and open.

"Something that could put James in danger, too?" I don't want to tell him James was shot at, not with him in this condition.

His eyes close again and just barely open this time. I can see the strength draining out of him.

"I understand," I say, taking his hand in mine again. "We'll go to Connecticut and find out who's behind this. We'll catch them, and James will be safe."

Nate squeezes my hand, and his head sinks back into the pillow. His lips twitch, like he's trying to say something or maybe just smile, and then he closes his eyes.

"Nate?" I put a hand on his shoulder. "Nate, wake up!"

I panic, sure he's dead, but then register the continued beeping of his heart monitor. He's still alive, just unconscious. A doctor rushes into the room with James, Vivianne, and Finn at his heels. It feels like Nate and I have been alone for hours, but it couldn't have been more than a minute. Vivianne falls into the chair beside him, taking his hand, while the doctor checks the machines hooked up to Nate and lifts his eyelids to check his pupils.

"What happened?" Vivianne says. "He was awake?"

"F-for a little while," I say with difficulty. I'm still trying to process what just happened. I have no spare brain cells left for speech.

"Is he okay?" James asks. "Why isn't he still awake?"

"It's common for someone to slip in and out of consciousness after a trauma like this," the doctor says. "The fact that he woke up, even for a short time, is a good sign."

Vivianne turns to me with a fragile look of hope on her face. "Did he say anything?"

"He wouldn't have been able to speak with the ventilator in, I'm afraid," the doctor says, sparing me the need to fumble for words. I don't know what to say yet. Should I just tell them everything, despite how far-fetched it sounds?

Or would they just think I was crazy, like before?

I realize James is watching me very closely.

"Did he communicate anything to you, Marina?" he asks.

I swallow. Even if they *did* believe me, do I want all these people to know what Nate said? Is it safe for him and James if they do?

"No," I say softly. "He tried to talk, but he couldn't."

Vivianne and the doctor accept this and turn back to Nate, but I can tell from the look in his eyes that James sees right through the lie. I can't meet his gaze anymore and look away.

"Hey, you okay?" Finn says, touching my elbow.

Nate lies there, as silent and still against the sheets as he ever was, and I say, "I'm not sure."

Vivianne rests her head against Nate's shoulder and begins whispering, talking to Nate or God or maybe both, and the doctor continues his examination. James just stands there, staring at me.

"Agent Morris?" he calls suddenly.

Morris, who's been stationed outside the door, pops his head into the room.

"We need to talk to whoever's in charge of the investigation," James says, eyes locked on mine. "Now."

FIFTEEN

marina

Morris goes to get his commanding officer. With the Capitol Police, Secret Service, FBI, and God knows who else involved, I have no idea who's leading the investigation.

"What is it, sweetheart?" Vivianne asks once Morris is gone.

"I just think it's time we get some answers," James says, his eyes not leaving mine.

Morris returns a few minutes later with Agent Armison. Without giving the man a chance to speak, James says, "I want to speak to whoever's in charge."

"I'm sorry, Mr. Shaw," Agent Armison says, "but I don't think that's possible at the moment; Assistant Director Richter is currently in the field. However, I'm sure we can get someone from his office to come and update you on—"

"I don't think you understand." James might as well be chiseled out of granite. "My brother was shot. I was shot at. Director Nolan eats dinner at my house once a month, Justice MacMillan was at my sixteenth birthday party, and the White House chief of staff once borrowed swimming trunks from me when he was staying at my house on Martha's Vineyard. So when I say I want to speak to the person *in charge*, that's exactly what I mean. I suggest you quit treating me like a child and get this Richter here before I pick up the phone."

I stare, having never suspected this side of James even existed, and Finn whistles low under his breath. He doesn't chastise him the way he did me when I got a little short with a nurse, but maybe that's because James is genuinely frightening at this moment. Who *is* this person?

Vivianne sits up, and all of a sudden she's a fierce attorney again instead of a grieving fiancée. "I have some questions as well," she says, "and I imagine Alice Shaw does, too. Should I get her?"

Armison's steely expression wavers. Even he doesn't want to tangle with Alice. "I'll make some calls," he says in a clipped tone.

When he's gone, the doctor tells us what we might expect from Nate in the coming hours, but Vivianne is the only one really listening. James is watching me and I'm trying to pretend I don't notice, while Finn darts looks at both of us.

Connecticut. The only reason Nate would have to bring my attention to Connecticut would be the investigation he was conducting while he was there, which, if it was under Nate's purview, would almost *have* to be something to do with the intelligence community. Why would he remind me of that unless he thought it was related to his shooting? Why would that have been his very first message, one he struggled so hard to convey, if it weren't important?

And why would he tie James to it if he weren't in danger, too?

It may be crazy, but I feel the truth of it in my bones. Those people—whoever they were—*were* shooting at James. They came after Nate, and now they're coming after him.

"Marina?" James says softy. "Can I talk to you in the hall?"

I nod. I have to get James out of here. If someone from the government was responsible for all this, James isn't safe here.

Once we're out in the hallway, James takes my hand. "What did he say to you?"

"He signed," I say. "*C-T.* Connecticut."

The information means something to him. His eyes start to move quickly around the hallway the way they do when he's thinking very hard about something. He explained it to me once, how different eye movements signal someone accessing different parts of their brain, but it looks like he's searching for the places where his invisible puzzle pieces fit together.

"I think all of this has something to do with the investigation he was working on over the recess," I continue.

James frowns. "How did you know about that?"

"He told me. The night you came home." I neglect to mention what he said about James's increasingly odd behavior. I twist my fingers into his sleeve. "I think we need to go, now."

"Why?"

"I don't think we should meet with anyone in charge," I say. "I'm afraid that . . . that . . ."

"Hey, it'll be okay, kid." James tucks a loose strand of hair behind my ear. "I have some questions for this Richter guy, but then we'll figure everything out."

"Please, I don't think it's a good idea."

"It'll be fine," he says. "Trust me."

What choice do I have? I try to ignore the pit in my stomach and say, "Okay."

James kisses my forehead. "Don't tell anyone else about Nate yet, okay? Let's go back in."

I nod and follow him back into the hospital room. Vivianne barely notices us, she's so focused on Nate, but Finn says, "Everything okay?"

"Fine," James says.

"Yeah, fine," I echo. Finn shoots me a questioning look that I ignore.

A half hour passes before Agent Armison reappears in the doorway. He says the agent in charge has arrived and leads us to a staff room at the end of the hall where we can meet with him in private. When we enter, a surprisingly young man—no more than forty—in a sharp gray suit stands to greet us.

James gives him a once-over. "You're the person in charge of the investigation into my brother's shooting?"

"I am." The man offers his hand to James. "Chris Richter. I understand you want to talk to me. I came over as soon as I heard."

James doesn't shake his hand. "What agency are you from? You're not FBI."

I don't know how he can tell, but he says it with certainty. His uncle was once the director of the CIA, so he must recognize signs I don't.

Richter smiles. "Very astute. Given your brother's work on the Intelligence Committee, it was thought that someone with a higher clearance level should coordinate the investigation."

"What are you, CIA? NSA?"

"I'm with the DNI." I don't know what that is, but James and Vivianne both nod like it answers all their questions. Richter turns to Vivianne. "You must be Ms. Chase. I'm sorry to meet you under such awful circumstances."

Vivianne shakes his hand. "Mr. Richter."

"And these are?"

"My friends," James says.

"Perhaps they'd like to wait outside while we talk?"

"I'd prefer they stay."

Richter smiles. "Whatever you'd like, Mr. Shaw. Now, how can I help you?"

We settle down in plastic chairs at the small dining table in the staff room, Chris Richter on one side and the four of us on the other.

"So, you think Nate's shooting was related to his work on the Intelligence Committee?" James asks.

"We're exploring that possibility."

I take a good look at Richter. If there's one skill I learned from my mother, it's how to size someone up with a glance. I noticed the quality of his suit the moment he stood, but closer up I get a better picture. Not only is it *not* the standard-issue Men's Wearhouse preferred by most government employees, but it's hand-tailored and expensive, even for a man in his position. His haircut is precise, done recently, and his hands are square and strong but not rugged. He doesn't wear any jewelry, not a wedding ring or even a watch. He holds himself well, and his smile is warm and genuine.

I dislike him instantly.

"I'm glad you asked to meet with me," Richter says. "It gives me the opportunity to tell you myself that we've determined the incident here last night had nothing to do with your brother's shooting."

Vivianne sighs in relief and rubs a hand across James's shoulders, but he frowns. "Based on what?"

Richter leans forward. "I really shouldn't be telling you this, but I know how frustrating it can be to be kept out of the loop when it's your life at the center of things. We have CCTV footage of the people who shot at you last night—"

Just like Finn said they would. Now they'll know I wasn't making things up. "People?" I say. "So there *were* two of them?"

Richter turns his attention on me for the first time, and there's a hint of evaluation in the look that unnerves me. Maybe he sees my resemblance to the girl who shot at James.

"That's correct," Richter says. "Two males, both around twelve or thirteen."

"What?" I shake my head. "That's not right—"

"Our technicians are working on refining the images right now," Richter continues, as though I hadn't spoken, "but it seems pretty clear this was a case of gang activity. Nothing to do with you, Mr. Shaw; just an unfortunate coincidence."

Liar. My clammy hands curl into fists under the table.

"You're sure?" James says. He looks between me and Richter, a fine line creasing his brow, but I can't tell which one of us he believes.

"Very. However, just in case, the Capitol Police are going to continue to keep an eye on you. I hope you won't find that inconvenient."

"Not at all," Vivianne says. "We appreciate it."

"Of course. We want to do everything we can to make sure James stays safe," Richter says. "Now, I'm sure you have lots of other questions."

"Yes." James folds his hands in front of him on the table, and the tips of his fingers are red from squeezing his fingers so tight. "I want to know how the hell a shooter was able to get into the Mandarin's ballroom."

Richter barely blinks. "That's something we're looking into."

"*Looking into?*" James says. "There was a massive security breach in the vice president's protection, and you don't even know where the problem happened yet?"

"James, honey." Vivianne puts a hand on his, but he slips from under her grasp.

Meanwhile, Richter has gone tight, and the casual smile has slipped off his face. "I understand your frustration, Mr. Shaw, but I'm afraid I can't get into specifics with you. However, I can assure you that the Secret Service did everything they were supposed to."

"Obviously not," James says, "or my brother wouldn't have a machine breathing for him. What about the security cameras in the Mandarin? Have you gotten any footage of the shooter from them?"

"Unfortunately, the relevant cameras were nonfunctioning at the time of—"

To my left, Finn snorts.

"And that's not suspicious?" James says. "The shooter was obviously aided by someone on the inside. Are you looking into *that*?"

"James, please!" Vivianne says. "Mr. Richter, I'm so sorry."

"It's quite all right; I understand emotions are high. We have several solid leads, Mr. Shaw, and I assure you we're doing everything we can." Richter stands and reaches into his wallet. "Unfortunately, I have to get back now. Here's my card; please feel free to give me a call at any time. I'll be in touch. Mr. Shaw, Ms. Chase."

As soon as Richter is gone, James balls up the business card in his fist and tosses it across the room.

"What were you thinking?" Vivianne says. "I've never seen you act like that before."

"It makes no sense that a gunman was able to get to the ballroom from that service exit." James stands and begins to pace from wall to wall. Nate once told me they had to replace the carpet in his bedroom every couple of years because he wore right through it. "The place was swarming with Secret Service. No way that entrance would have been unsecured like that."

"So what are you saying?" Finn asks.

James stops. "I think someone in the Secret Service was involved."

"*What?*" Vivianne says. "James, that's—"

"How else would the gunman have gotten so close to Nate and the vice president?" James says. "How else would all those doors off the service hallway have been unlocked when they should have been secured? How else would the shooter have gotten away, and without a single camera picking him up? Nothing else can account for all of that."

"But Assistant Director Richter—" Vivianne begins.

"Richter is covering the government's ass," James says. "Why else wouldn't he even entertain the *possibility* of collusion? No. I don't trust him, which is why we can't tell him what Nate said to Marina."

"What?" Vivianne's eyes go wide, and she grabs my hands. "He talked to you? What did he say?"

I look at James, and he nods. "It's okay."

"While everyone was out of the room," I say, all attention suddenly on me, "Nate signed a few words to me. *Air*, which I don't understand, and *CT*. Connecticut."

Vivianne seems to shrink into herself. "What does that even mean?"

"Nate was holed up in his office for days while we were in Connecticut," James says. "Normally he spends the recess doing events and pressing flesh, but he was working on something he wouldn't tell even me about."

"The night you got home," I say, "he told me he'd been investigating something. Did he say anything to you about it, Vivianne?"

She covers her eyes with one hand. "No. He didn't."

So why would he tell me, the kid next door, and not his own fiancée? The only reason I can think of is because I spend the most time with James. If this really has something to do with him, I was in the best position to notice the changes Nate warned me about.

"I think maybe . . ." I take a deep breath. "I think maybe whatever Nate was working on has something to do with why he was shot."

"Like he was getting too close to something," James says.

"Stop it!" Vivianne stands. "Both of you! This isn't a spy novel. This is real life, and Nate is *dying*!"

Her voice rises hysterically at the end of the sentence, and I feel as though I've been slapped across the face. The blow knocks me back a step.

"I'm sorry," I whisper, and I really *look* at Vivianne. Her skin is dull and her eyes shot through with red. I realize she's been here all night, dealing with Alice and the others, watching the man she loves fight for his life with no sleep or support. Suddenly I see just how thin it's worn her.

"He's not dying, Viv," James says stiffly. "He's not, so don't even say it."

Vivianne sighs. "I'm afraid you can't think your way out of this one, sweetheart. You need to take advantage of the time you have with Nate while you still can, instead of wasting energy on these crazy conspiracy theories." She shrugs, slowly, like the weight of worries on her shoulders makes it hard to move. "Who cares what he may or may not have said if he never wakes up again?"

James's voice is tight and small. "Nate would care. *Especially* if he never wakes up again."

Vivianne's lower lip quivers, and she presses her hand to her mouth to hide it. Tears are filling her eyes, but she refuses to let them fall. I want to disappear. Finn and I shouldn't be here for this; it's too personal and too raw. It shouldn't have been me that Nate communicated with. It should have been James or Vivianne, and he should have told them he loved them. My guilt at being the one who happened to be in the room is suddenly suffocating.

"Why don't you get some sleep, Vivianne?" Finn says softly,

taking a step toward her. "The nurses should be able to set up a cot for you. Want me to go ask them?"

Vivianne swallows, and when she speaks, her voice is thick. "Yes. Thank you."

Finn leads her from the room, and James watches them go.

"I don't think I've ever seen Viv cry," he says.

The room is silent without them. James leans back against the counter and rocks slightly, running his fingers over and over his lips as he thinks. I pull fluffy pills of wool off my sweater and try not to let the silence crush me.

"I don't know what to do," James suddenly says. "Maybe Viv is right and I'm being irrational, but . . . Marina, what am I supposed to do?"

"I don't know," I whisper. Useless.

Finn returns. "Viv's asleep. She was exhausted. She wanted me to tell you she didn't mean what she said."

James nods, but I'm not sure he believes him. I know I don't. Vivianne meant every word, but she was wrong. Nate told me what he did because it was important to him that we know.

"I guess it's back to the waiting room and Cousin Alice," James says.

Finn and I follow him out into the hall, and I say tentatively, "What about Richter and the Secret Service? What about Connecticut?"

James looks torn. "I . . . I'll call Bob Nolan. Have him look into it."

Finn raises an eyebrow. "The director of the FBI? How are you two such pals?"

"He went to Princeton with my dad."

"James." I catch his wrist and pull him to a stop outside the waiting room. "I know this is a terrible time, but I think we should go to Connecticut and find out what Nate was working on. Today."

"*What?*" Finn says.

"I know it's seems crazy," I say, "but we can't trust anyone else to do it. Not even Bob Nolan. What if you're right and Richter is involved in some cover-up? If he searches the house first, he could destroy evidence that points to the person responsible."

James looks back toward Nate's room. "But what Viv said . . . I can't leave here now."

"How far is the drive?" I say. "New York's only four or five hours, and Greenwich can't be much farther. Vivianne would barely even be awake by the time we got back."

"Marina," Finn says, reproach in his voice. "He wants to be with his brother."

"I know, and I wouldn't normally ask you to leave, but . . ." I pause. "James, I'm afraid the people who shot Nate might want to hurt you, too. I don't believe for a second that what happened in the parking lot last night was a gang shooting. We have to find out who they are and stop them."

"If that's true, you should just tell the police," Finn says.

"They wouldn't believe me!" I say. "And I don't trust them to keep James safe anyway."

"What makes you think someone's after me?" James asks.

"You were *shot at*! And Richter's lying about who did it, I know he is."

179

Finn groans. "Not this again, M."

"Shut up, Finn! I know what I saw!" I snap. "James, please. Nate asked me to look out for you. He told me his investigation has something to do with you."

"He said that?" The worry lines on James's forehead deepen.

Basically. "Yes."

James looks back at Nate's room and then into the waiting room, where Alice and Aaron and Julia and Uncle Perry are sitting in silence.

"Okay, let's do it," he says. "It's what Nate wants, and that's enough for me. I can't go with Morris and Spitzer on my ass, though, so we'll have to lose them."

"You know this is nuts, right?" Finn says.

"Maybe, but I can't do anything for Nate here," James says. "Maybe I can help him there."

"What if someone really is trying to kill you?" Finn says. "You really think now's the time to ditch your protection?"

"What if they can't be trusted?" I say. "We're driving straight up and back, and we'll only get out at the house in Connecticut, which is safer than almost anywhere."

Finn sighs. "Fine, but I'm coming. You're both acting like lunatics, and I don't trust you out in the world alone."

I narrow my eyes at him. "Fine."

"Okay," James says, fishing his car keys out of his pocket. "Here's what we do."

SIXTEEN

em

Finn and I park across the street from the hospital and wait. My gut is churning. Finn rifles through our backpack and comes up with a Snickers. He offers me half, and I have to pretend I'm not hungry, even though I haven't eaten since yesterday. I can't tell him what's really wrong: the acute flash of memory that threw me back into my prison cell, how I had the perfect opportunity to end all of this by putting a bullet into James through that window, or how I hesitated because Marina was beside him. I should tell him, but I can't.

I hate myself.

I must look as sick as I feel, because he puts a hand on my knee. "It's going to be okay."

I look at him. *Really* look at him. For so long, he was only a voice to me, and now he has a body and a face once more. I want to memorize every expression so that no one can ever take them away from me again.

I try to smile. "When did you become so trusting?"

"Around the same time you became so cynical, I guess. Now try to inhale. It's good for you."

"Yeah, yeah." The front door to the hospital slides open, and Marina steps out. I hit Finn in the shoulder. "Look!"

Marina runs to the street and flags down a cab, the younger Finn on her heels. The photographers and news crews still camped outside the hospital don't even look up, and the two of them climb in and drive away.

"Where are they going?" Finn asks. "Just the two of them?"

"I don't know." I'm glad I didn't take that Snickers, because my stomach is turning flips. "But it means James is alone inside."

Before, Finn and I had to wait for James to come out of the hospital on his own because we can't make a move on him while the three of them are together. We can't risk coming face-to-face with our younger selves; the fabric of time might not be strong enough to survive it.

But if James is alone again, it's our best chance to do things right this time.

"He'll be protected in there," Finn says. "He'll be with Nate, surrounded by armed guards."

"I'm not saying it'll be easy. But I think we have to try, don't we?"

"You're crazy, but let's do it."

We wade through the mobs of press and supporters, who pay no more attention to us than they did our younger selves, and approach the entrance of the emergency room. I stop short near the front of the crowd. I'm close enough to see through the sliding glass doors. Beyond them, there's now a portable metal detector manned by two officers.

"Okay," Finn says. "Change of plan."

"What's the new plan?" I say.

"I don't know yet."

We both stand there, thinking. A girl from the crowd hands me a candle, and I stare into the flickering flame.

"The ambulance bay?" I whisper.

Finn shakes his head. "Too conspicuous. Plus, it'll be guarded, too."

"Maybe you could distract the guards, and I'll slip around the outside of the metal detector?"

"Too risky. It might work with one, but not two."

I sigh. "Then we have to leave the gun. Find something inside to use instead."

The crowd shifts and presses against us, and Finn wraps his arms around my waist and rests his chin on my shoulder. I'm not sure if he's doing it to comfort me or so that he can lower his voice even further from the whisper we've been speaking in. "You realize that a best-case scenario for that is a scalpel or a hypodermic needle, right? We'll have to kill him up close, if not with our bare hands."

I drop my eyes to the sidewalk. Looking at someone down the barrel of a gun and actually spilling their blood with your own hands are two very different things. "Yeah, I know."

"Okay then," he says softly.

We go back to the car and stash the gun in the glove compartment. As we weave our way back through the crowds to the hospital entrance, I pass off my candle to an empty-handed mourner. Finn and I pause to look at each other before we enter the hospital, and he gives me a tight little smile. I nod, and we step forward together. When the glass doors slide apart, we're hit with a blast of warm air that makes me realize just how cold I've been. One officer offers me a bowl for keys or change without looking at me, but the other has a faint frown line across his forehead as he looks between Finn and me.

"Yep, we're back," I say, dropping my cell phone into the bowl.

"We basically live here now," Finn says. "So if you ever want us to take over for a little while . . . ?"

The officer laughs. "That's tempting. I'll let you know."

He waves us through the metal detector one at a time and hands me back my phone.

"Take it easy," Finn says.

The officer nods at us. "You too."

"Well, that wasn't so bad," I say as we walk toward the elevator. "If only Vivianne and James paid as little attention to Marina and Finn as the officer at the door did."

"We'll move fast," Finn says, "before they realize something's wrong. Besides, what are they going to do? See our different clothes and slightly aged faces and say 'It must be Marina and Finn from the future! Stop them!'"

"Good point."

"All we have to do is get close to James for a second," he says. "We're still enough of Marina and Finn that it shouldn't be a problem."

We walk along the hallway, glancing at the doors of each

trauma room as we pass. They're all occupied. At the end of the hall there's a water fountain, and I pretend to drink from it while Finn leans against the wall next to me.

"You're awfully fake thirsty," he says.

"I'm waiting for one of the rooms to clear," I say. "Here, you drink for a while."

We switch spots, and Finn takes a drink while I keep my eye on the trauma room doors. We can't just stroll in there and ask to borrow a blade or needle, so we'll have to sneak in when one's empty.

The bay doors two rooms down from us suddenly swing open, and a doctor and nurse wheel out an ashen-faced man with a leg that's so badly broken, I feel myself pale a little. They take him to the elevator, which will no doubt take them up to the surgical floor for his leg to be set. Finn looks at me and nods, then heads for the room they just vacated. He stops short at the doors and then backs away, waving me over.

I join him and see there's a nurse still inside, tidying up the room. I step forward while Finn stands flat against the wall beside the swinging doors

"Excuse me, nurse?" I say.

She looks up. "Yes?"

"Can you help me?" I put a wobble into my voice.

She comes closer. "What is it?"

"My dad." I rub a fake tear from my eye. "My dad just had a heart attack, and I think they brought him here, but I don't know where he is. . . ."

The nurse steps toward me, into the hall, leaving the trauma room empty. Behind her back, Finn silently slips in.

"Just go ask there at the desk," she says, nodding to her right. "They'll be able to help you."

"Where?" I say.

"Right there." She points. "See that desk with the computers and the nurses?"

Behind her, Finn has found a tray of surgical tools next to the bed, and he plucks up a scalpel. It flashes with a reflection of the overheard lights as he hides it up his sleeve.

"Oh, right," I say. "I'm sorry. I'm such an idiot."

"That's okay, dear."

Finn moves toward the door, and I pull the nurse into a hug. She stiffens in surprise, but doesn't push me away.

"Thank you so much," I say tearfully as Finn sneaks out of the room and begins walking in the opposite direction down the hall. "I really appreciate your help."

The nurse pats my back and pulls away. "You're welcome, dear. Take care, now."

She goes back to the trauma room, totally oblivious, and I check to make sure that no one's watching us before catching up with Finn at the stairwell.

"Nice work," he says.

"You weren't too bad yourself."

We take the stairs instead of the elevator. That way, we can slip into the crowd on the third floor instead of having the doors open on us, exposing us for everyone to see. The less time they have to look at us, the less they'll be able to pick out the details that just aren't right.

I think about the scalpel concealed in Finn's sleeve with every step. Will he be able to do enough damage to James in whatever time we have that they won't be able to save him here in a hospital? Finn gets queasy about fast food because of something he once read about how they slaughter the chickens. How will he slice his former best friend's throat?

My chest is heaving by the time we reach the landing, and it's not entirely from how out of shape I am. I put my hand on Finn's arm when he goes to open the door between the stairwell and the corridor.

"Wait," I say. "Let me catch my breath."

"You okay?"

"Yeah," I say. "Just need a second."

I put a hand on the wall to steady myself. It's not true; I'm not okay. I'm caught in James Shaw's gravity again, my world always revolving around his, and this time the closer I get to him, the sicker I feel. There should be relief or even a vengeful kind of joy to ending his life and snuffing out Cassandra forever, but I can't stop picturing him lying beside Marina, holding her hand in his own, and it scares me. What if I blow this again? How many people will suffer because of my weakness?

Finn brushes the hair away from my face, his cool fingers lingering at my cheeks and temples, calming me.

"Put your hair up," he says. "They'll definitely notice that."

"Good call." I sweep my shoulder-length hair back into a ponytail. It's at least six inches shorter than Marina's.

"Ready?" he says.

I take one last deep breath and nod. I can do this; I have no choice. Finn pushes open the stairwell door, and I try to summon

Marina's attitude: insecure but territorial, well-meaning but oblivious. My heart is racing, and for a moment I can appreciate the irony of worrying that I'll be caught impersonating myself. But then we're walking toward the waiting room, where I recognize Cousin Alice and Uncle Perry, and there's no room left in my head for anything but the plan.

Finn sticks his head in the room. "Is James with Nate?"

"I thought you two left," Uncle Perry says.

"No, just went to get some new clothes." Finn gestures down at himself.

"James?" a voice calls. All these years later, I still recognize the sound of Vivianne's voice. A shudder goes through me as I remember what happened to her. What *will* happen to her if we're not successful.

I wait, every muscle tensed, for James to respond, to step out of whatever room he's in. But nothing happens.

"James?" Vivianne calls again. She's headed down the hallway and spots me at the waiting room. She comes straight for me, and I force myself to stand rigidly still and not bite my lip or back away.

"I didn't realize you two were back," she says, and her eyes, which keep darting around the area, barely take me in. "Do you know where James is?"

I shake my head, and she pushes past Finn into the waiting room. "Has anyone seen James?"

No one has.

"Oh God," Vivianne whispers. She turns and runs in the direction from which she'd come. "Agent Morris!"

"He probably went for some coffee, Viv!" one of the Shaws—I vaguely recognize him as Aaron—calls after her. "I'll go check the vending machines."

"I'll check the bathroom," Finn says. He grabs my wrist as he passes me, and I let him pull me to the little side hallway where the restrooms are.

"He's not here," Finn says. "He must have snuck away the same time Marina and Finn did."

"He'll be meeting them somewhere. I should have realized there was no way she would leave him here," I say. Down the hall, doors slam and people shout. An agent runs past us. "Let's get out of here."

We head for the stairwell. As we pass the waiting room, Finn says, "Not in the restroom. We're going to check the cafeteria."

"You two stay right here!" Alice Shaw barks. "Let the officers handle this. I won't have any more teens go missing from under my nose. Come, sit."

Finn and I exchange looks. We can't stay here. The Capitol Police will be shutting down the building any moment. There's really only one choice, though our younger selves won't thank us for it.

When Alice turns her attention to questioning the woman beside her, we turn and make for the staircase.

"Stop!" Alice yells after us, but we don't even pause.

We thunder down the stairs and dodge through the crowds in the emergency room. At the opposite end of the room, an officer gets a radio call. I push Finn forward. We can't afford to be locked up in this building while they search for James. Somewhere behind us, I hear someone running, but there's no time to look back. Finn and I squeeze through the crowd and make it to the front door.

"We're really leaving this time," Finn says to the officer from before. "I promise!"

He takes my hand and pulls me out with him, and we disappear into the sidewalk vigil.

Once we're back in the car, I say, "Marina's house?"

"He knows that's the first place they'd look for him."

"You're right." Time is ticking away from us, each second separating us from ourselves more and more. "Where would he go?"

I stare ahead, trying to think, and a figure in a black coat steps out of a Starbucks and into my field of vision. It could be anyone, but I recognize him even before a familiar BMW pulls up to the curb and Marina climbs out of the driver's seat to let James take over the getaway car.

marina

I take the steps up to my front door two at a time. I need to grab some clothes and food, tell Luz where I'm going, and then Finn and I will take James's car back to the hospital to pick him up. If everything's gone according to plan, he'll have lost his protective detail.

The lights upstairs are on, which is unlike Luz, but I have too many other things on my mind to think much about it.

"There are bags in the pantry," I say to Finn as we walk inside. "Grab whatever you want from the kitchen. I'm going to run down to the laundry and get some—"

"Marina? You home?"

I freeze.

She *can't* be.

"Is that . . . ?" Finn says.

My mom turns the corner into the kitchen, looking perfectly fresh, beautiful, and *here*. I can't do anything but stare. She hugs me, and the familiar smell of her perfume turns me for a moment into the little girl who hovered over her shoulder while she sat at her vanity and got ready to go out.

"Mama?" I say in a small voice. "Why are you home?"

"We came as soon as we heard." She lets me go and seems to notice Finn for the first time. "Who is this?"

"It's Finn, Mom. You know, James's friend?"

"Oh," she says, looking him up and down. "You go to Johns Hopkins, too?"

"He goes to Sidwell with me."

Her expression doesn't flicker, like the smile is painted on to her face. "Well. That's nice. Maybe Finn would like to go upstairs?"

She makes it sound like a question, but I know it's not, and Finn seems to as well.

"Yeah, of course." He backs away from us. "I'll just go . . . uh, up to Marina's room?"

"That's fine," Mom says. I'm not crazy about the idea of Finn being in my room and quickly try to remember if I've left anything embarrassing like underwear lying around, but Finn turns and sprints up the stairs before I can suggest another location.

"How well do you know that boy?" Mom asks, brushing my hair back behind my ears like she always does whenever it falls into my face.

"Not very well," I say. "We just came to . . . get some things for James. Some food and stuff."

"All right. Daniel!" she calls. "Marina's home!"

"Dad's here, too?" I say. "Why didn't you answer my calls?"

"There wasn't any time, hon." She puts her arm around my shoulders and leads me to the living room. "Daniel? We're in here."

"Be right there!" Dad's voice comes from the direction of his study.

She sits me down on the sofa and rubs her hand up and down my arm. It's weird. "Mom, what's going on?"

"There's something we need to discuss," she says as my father walks into the room. His slacks are creased from the hours on the plane; he obviously didn't shower and change immediately upon arriving home like Mom did.

"Marina." He bends and kisses my forehead. "How are you doing?"

"Not good," I say, even though that should be obvious. How am I going to get out of this house now? They'd have a joint aneurysm if I told them I wanted to go to Connecticut. Maybe I can tell them we're spending the night at Finn's again—without mentioning *where* Finn lives. "I've been with James at the hospital since the shooting—"

"Luz let you go to the hospital last night?" Mom stiffens.

"With a shooter on the loose and the media circus around that place? Sometimes I swear that woman has no sense."

I bristle. "She didn't *let* me. I just went. I couldn't leave James there alone."

Mom smoothes a wrinkle out of my jeans. "That's something else we need to discuss—"

"Amanda." Dad gives her a look. "Another time. The truth is, Mimi . . ."

I cringe at his baby nickname for me, and he perches on the edge of his chair so he can put a hand on my knee. That plus Mom's arm around my shoulders makes me nervous.

"I know this isn't the best time, but unfortunately it's something we can't put off," Dad says. "Your mother and I have thought a lot about this, and we've decided that it will be best for us to separate for a while."

I stare at them. Is this really happening?

Are they really doing this right *now*?

"Separating?" I say. "You mean you're getting divorced?"

Dad and Mom exchange a look. "That's right, sweetheart," he says.

"I . . . Why are you telling me this?" I stand up. "I just watched Nate get shot, and you came home to tell me you're getting a divorce?"

"The timing is awful, honey," Mom says, "but we couldn't put it off anymore."

"Why not?" I say. "How long have you known?"

Years, probably. I try to remember the last time they seemed happy together, and at first I draw a blank. A picture eventually rises in my mind of the three of us in Paris. I was watching a street vendor make crepes with his little squeegee, and when I turned around, I caught my father leaning down to kiss my mom, their lips smiling against each other's. I was twelve. I sink back to the couch.

"A little while," Mom says. "We went out of town to sort out the details so you wouldn't have to be a part of it, but then your father got called away for a meeting."

"I leave for Rome in the morning," Dad says.

"I'm going to go visit your grandparents in New York while he's gone," Mom says, "and I'm taking you with me."

"What?" I whisper.

Dad squeezes my knee. "We don't want you here with everything that's going on right now."

"You want me to leave?" I say. "Now?"

"It's for the best, sweetheart," Dad says. "I'm going to be in Rome for at least a week, and we can't possibly leave you alone here with that insanity next door."

I swallow my rising panic. "Then can you stay? I can't leave James—"

Dad shakes his head. "I have to go. They're expecting me."

I turn to Mom. "*You* don't have to go. Stay here with me."

"It's best if we go to New York, honey," Mom says. "I think we could all use a little time away. You know your grandmother's good friends with the headmistress at Spence, and the semester is just starting. I thought we might take a tour and see if you like it."

"*Why?*"

They both just look at me, like they can't find the words. It takes a long time for the truth to filter through my foggy brain. I turn to Mom.

"We're moving?" I whisper.

"Nothing's definite," she says, "but I'm considering it. I know it will be an adjustment for you, but you've always loved New York, and your grandparents and Aunt Celeste are there. Think of all the new opportunities you'd have in a city like that."

My throat closes up, and I have to force the words past. "But I don't want to leave."

"Nothing's for certain yet, honey," she says. "I just want you to keep an open mind while we're there."

"I'm not going."

Mom sighs. "Marina. I know it's a difficult time, but I'm only trying to do what's best for you—"

"Bullshit!" Suddenly the fog over my brain is gone, and I'm angry. So angry that I'm shaking, like all the rage inside of me is trying to explode outward, pushing at my skin.

"Honey—"

"You didn't come back here for me." My voice breaks. "You don't care about how hard the last twenty-four hours have been for me. You came to pack me up like a piece of luggage."

Mom's face hardens. "That's enough, Marina. This isn't easy for any of us."

"Sweetheart . . ." Dad steps toward me.

I try to blink the tears back, but I can't. I step out of Dad's reach, backing out of the room.

"I hate you," I say, meaning it. Finn is waiting for me at the base of the stairs, one of my tote bags slung over his shoulder. I hate him, too, for overhearing whatever he did.

"Let's go," I say.

"Mimi!" Dad says after me.

"Let her go, Daniel," I hear Mom tell him as I run from the house, Finn somewhere behind me.

SEVENTEEN

marina

We go next door and retrieve James's car, a white hand-me-down BMW from Nate. He should be sneaking away from his protection right now, and we'll pick him up. I only just got my learner's permit, but Finn asks me to drive anyway.

"Hey, Marina . . ." he says as I'm pulling out of the Shaws' driveway.

"Can we not talk about it?" I say. I'm on the verge of tears and fighting hard to keep them back. I can't talk, contain myself, and not hit things with James's car all at the same time.

"Sure."

"Don't tell James, okay?" I say.

"I won't."

Finn texts James when we're a minute from the hospital, and he emerges from the Starbucks across the street just as we pull up. He takes the driver's seat, and I climb into the passenger's.

"Everything go okay?" I ask, trying to keep my voice light and even.

"Our boy's a genius," Finn says, patting his shoulder. "Those cops never had a chance."

"In all fairness," James says, "a four-year-old could have made that escape. They weren't keeping too close an eye on me since we were still in the hospital. I said I was going to the restroom and then just took the stairs and left."

I hear the conversation, but I'm not really paying attention. I keep thinking about my parents. I used to joke with Tamsin and Sophie about the inevitable divorce all the time; it's practically a rite of passage for a teenager. But maybe I never really expected it to happen, because this feels like a punch to the gut, sudden and shocking.

What am I going to do? If they have to split up, I'd rather live here with my dad. He and I don't fight the way Mom and I do, even if that's mostly because he's never home. He's a total work-aholic, like he still thinks he's that lower-class kid from South Boston who has to scratch and claw his way to the top. And that's just why Mom would never let me live with him. She's been try-ing to mold me into a miniature her ever since I was born; she's not going to give up now. I could live with that if she just stays in D.C., but if she takes me away from my friends and Luz . . . from James . . . I can't bear it.

I hate this. I hate them. And I *really* hate that I can feel Finn's eyes on the back of my neck.

"Marina?" James says.

I shake myself out of my thoughts. "Yeah?"

He hands me his phone. "Can you text Viv for me? Just tell her I'm okay and sorry and I'll be home soon? After that we need to take the SIM cards out of our phones; otherwise they could use them to trace our location."

"You think they'd do that?" Finn asks while I start the text to Vivianne.

"No idea, but I'd rather not risk it."

"What if . . . they need to get a hold of you?" Finn says. We all know what he means. *What if Nate dies?*

James's jaw tightens. "We'll be back by morning."

James drives through the rest of the afternoon and into the evening, only stopping once for gas. I spend most of the trip staring out of the window, trying not to think about what I can't stop thinking about. None of us talks much.

"You okay?" James asks me as we cross the border into New York.

No, I'm not. I want to cry out all my troubles to him and let him comfort me, but even I'm not that selfish. "Yeah. Fine."

"It's just you've had that look on your face ever since you picked me up," he says.

"What look?"

"The Marina-is-suffering-in-silence look, where you grit your teeth and pinch your lips together like something might escape you at any second and you're trying to hold it back."

"I have no such look."

He smiles. "Sure you do. You had it on your face the entire time I tried to teach you how to sail last summer, and it's the look on your face basically any time your mother talks."

"You do totally have that look, M," Finn says from the backseat.

I shoot him a glare. He's not helping.

"I know you, Marina," James says softly. "You can't hide anything from me."

Oh, but I can. If he only knew.

"I'm fine," I say. "Really. Don't worry about me."

James must see he'll get nowhere with me now, so he lets it drop, and we spend the rest of the ride in silence. It's dark by the time we roll into Greenwich, Connecticut, one of those lush old towns that CEOs and neurosurgeons return to after a long day's work in Manhattan. Just like Georgetown, but colder. The house is on the outskirts of town, protected by a gate with a guard posted there twenty-four hours a day. James slows to a halt beside the guard station, rolling down his window as the guard steps out.

"Mr. Shaw," the man says. "I'm so incredibly sorry—"

"Thanks, Mark," James says. "We shouldn't be here long, but if anyone comes looking for us—*anyone*—please tell them you haven't seen us."

"Whatever you want, sir."

"And give the house a call if anyone comes by, will you?"

"Yes, sir."

James thanks the man and rolls up his window. The driveway from the guard station to the house is a mile long and takes a couple of minutes. Finn swears softly in the backseat as we finally clear the trees and the house comes into view. James insists on calling it a house, but it's really more of an *estate*. Even Mom would be impressed.

"My great-grandfather built it," James says, offering the words up like an excuse.

"It's beautiful," I say. It's a three-story stone building in the Gothic style, with high arched windows and ivy climbing the outer walls. It's like a house out of a movie, where its inhabitants would wear corseted silk dresses and throw lavish parties with fountains of champagne.

"It's *okay*," Finn says, and a brief smile touches James's lips as he parks the car in the circular driveway.

We climb out and approach the massive front doors, which are made of carved oak. James unlocks them and disarms the beeping security system, and then he just stands there in the foyer, in the dark.

"Where do you think we should look?" he says.

I take a step inside and immediately trip on a small landing. Finn's hand comes out of nowhere to grab my elbow. "You okay?"

"Fine," I say as I grope the wall for a light switch. "Thanks."

I find the panel and turn on every light. James squints and looks around like he's never seen the place before.

"Where did Nate do most of his work?" I ask.

"His study. Upstairs."

"Okay," I say. "Let's start there."

James leads us through the foyer to the wide marble staircase that curves up to the second floor landing. He doesn't turn on a single light as he goes, so I do it in his wake, and Finn and I exchange glances.

"Where's the staff?" I say as James leads us down a long hallway.

"They always get the week off after a recess," he says. "This is it."

He swings the door to Nate's study open and stands there in the hallway, looking inside, Finn and me peering over his shoulders. I don't know what I was expecting, but the room is a relief. There's nothing distinctively Nate about the dark walls or heavy furniture. It smells like wood polish, not Nate's cologne, and there's no half-drunk mug of coffee or uncapped pen on the desk waiting for him.

It's just a room.

I step past James and head for the filing cabinets in the corner. I pull open the first door with a rumble and start to shuffle through the hanging folders. Tax return, tax return, tax return . . .

"Hey, it's okay," I hear Finn saying softly. I look up. He and James are still standing in the doorway, and Finn has a hand on his arm. "We're here to help him."

James says something back that's too quiet for me to hear. I realize it may just look like a room to me, but James has probably seen his brother sitting in that chair, flipping through these files, working on that computer, a thousand times.

Finn smiles. "I know, but we don't have much choice, do we?"

James laughs softly and steps into the study, opening up the second filing cabinet. My eyes meet Finn's briefly. I never understood why the two of them were friends, beyond the fact that Finn didn't have anyone and James always appreciated people who weren't impressed by his last name. But maybe it's simpler than that. Maybe it's that Finn has this magical ability to make you smile even when things are grim. James can use that.

Finn settles down behind the computer, somehow bypassing its security measures when James says he doesn't know the password. He clicks around while James and I pull stack after stack of documents from the filing cabinets, laying them out across the Persian rug. All we find are dry bits of paper—old tax returns, invoices, bank statements—that couldn't have anything to do with a man firing two shots into Nate's chest.

I close a cabinet door a little more forcefully than I mean to, and the slam of metal on metal reverberates through the silent room. "There's nothing here. What about his bedroom? Or the living room?"

James sighs. "Maybe."

"Or maybe there's nothing to find?" Finn says.

"No." I stand up and stretch my stiff legs. "Nate wouldn't have wasted energy telling me to come here if it wasn't important."

"But he didn't actually tell you that, did he?" Finn asks.

I open and shut my mouth before I'm able to collect the words. "Not exactly. There wasn't time. But it's what he meant, I know it."

Finn looks skeptical, but before he can say anything, James abruptly stands and walks out of the room.

"Where are you going?" I call after him.

"Kitchen. I'm starving."

Finn and I follow James downstairs, and he assembles the ingredients for peanut butter and jelly sandwiches. James spreads the peanut butter with quick, hard strokes that rip the bread, and after two mangled pieces, he picks up the entire loaf and hurls it across the room with a guttural cry. I jump, and Finn winces.

James buries his face in his hands, and for a moment there's no movement or sound outside of his labored breathing.

Then Finn steps forward and takes the knife smeared with peanut butter out of James's hand. He sticks it back into the jar and collects the bread off of the floor. He dumps the dirty slices into the trash and calmly starts making sandwiches with the clean ones.

James sits on the floor in the corner of the room, rubbing one hand against his forehead, his lips moving silently as he talks to himself.

I stand frozen at the counter, so unsure of what to do that I can't do anything.

Finn puts a peanut butter sandwich on a paper towel and slides it over to me. He puts one beside James, who doesn't even look up at him, and then sits beside me at the counter to eat one himself.

When our eyes meet, he gives me a small shake of the head, his brows drawn close together. He's worried. I look away and take a bite from my sandwich.

The jangle of the telephone on a side table cuts through the air, and we all start. James jumps to his feet and crosses the room to look at the caller ID.

"It's Vivianne," he says.

The sandwich turns to sawdust in my mouth, and I push the rest of it away.

"I think you should answer it," Finn says.

James shakes his head. "She's just trying to figure out where we are."

Finn's voice is soft. "You don't know that, man."

"We'll be home in a few hours," James says, and he stands there beside the phone until it stops ringing.

I shred my paper towel into little squares. God, why did I bring us here? Everything seemed so clear before, but now I feel muddled and ashamed of dragging James away from his family at such a time. All because of one odd conversation with Nate in the snow and a couple of letters he signed to me that I might not have even interpreted correctly. Maybe I really am losing it.

And James, he's . . .

Finn finishes his sandwich and starts to tidy the kitchen island, replacing the jars and loaf of bread and wiping away the crumbs. "We should probably head back now, huh?" he says.

In my mind, I hear the crack of gunfire, see the blood and the scattering of people. James is *safe* here. I may not be sure of anything else, but at least I know that much.

"There are still places we haven't looked," I say. "We could still find something—"

"Damn it, Marina! This wild goose chase of yours has gone far enough," Finn snaps. He turns to James. "I'm sorry, man, but she's not doing you any favors by pretending there's some neat solution to all of this. The truth is, the world is just a fucked up place sometimes."

I'm not sure why I feel so wounded by the words. Maybe because they sound so true. But before I can figure it out, I hear myself flinging words back at Finn.

"No one made you come with us," I say. "You could have stayed in D.C. *Alone.* As usual."

Finn's jaw tightens as the tension between us builds like gas in need of a single spark.

"He should be with his brother right now, and you know it," he says. "Don't take your guilt out on me—"

"I'm only trying to—"

"Stop, stop, stop!" James cries. He's rocking back and forth on his feet, fingers clenched in his hair. "I can't think!"

Finn and I exchange alarmed glances at the outburst, suddenly on the same team again. Thick, choking silence fills the air. I reach hesitantly for James. "Are you okay?"

"The safe." James suddenly goes limp. "I'm so stupid."

He rushes from the room without waiting for either of us.

"This isn't good, M," Finn whispers. "He's really starting to worry me. This isn't normal."

"*James* isn't normal," I say, stuffing my own worry down. "He just thinks differently than we do. He's fine."

"Maybe, but—"

"No buts! He's fine!"

We catch up to James on the third floor. He opens the door to a darkened room and flips the light switch, revealing a massive bed with a dozen pillows arranged perfectly against the headboard, a vanity littered with little bottles and brushes and a strand of pearls, and fine antique furniture in need of a good dusting.

"It's my parents' room," James says, and I shiver, recognizing the room for what it is: a mausoleum. It looks like it hasn't been touched except for an occasional cleaning since the day they died. "I saw Nate coming out of here one morning last week. He never comes in here."

James walks to a bookshelf across from the bed and pulls at a book. A whole section of what looked like leather-bound volumes turns out to be a panel covering a small wall safe.

"Cool," Finn whispers.

"Do you know the combination?" I ask.

"No, but Nate was terrible with numbers. He would have picked something he could remember."

James punches in several combinations. Nate's birthday; his birthday; their addresses in Georgetown, Martha's Vineyard, the Chesapeake, and here. Each is followed by a blinking red light and a deepening of the wrinkles on James's forehead.

"You have any other houses?" Finn asks.

"Don't think so."

James tries a few more combinations, and in the heartbeat between the numbers going in and the light turning red, I hold my breath. It's here, I know it. Whatever it is Nate sent me to find, it's in this safe. I see Finn looking at me from the corner of my eye, but I won't look back at him. He may think this is a waste of time, but I'll stand here while James enters numbers all night if I have to.

Two more combinations and the light turns green. James exhales. "Mom's birthday."

The handle makes a heavy clunking noise as he turns it and pulls the door open. Inside is a jewelry box, several stacks of foreign currency, and filing folders full of documents. On top of everything, one corner bent like it was shoved inside hastily, is a manila envelope. James reaches for it and holds it lightly in his hands, like he's trying to weigh its contents.

"Open it," I say.

He bends the brads that hold the envelope shut and pulls out the stack of papers inside. His eyes sweep across the top page, widening more and more as he reads.

"You were right, Marina," he says.

I lean in so that I can see the sheet over his shoulder. It's an e-mail, and I scan it quickly. I see Nate's name, and James's, and the bottom is signed *CR*. I check the e-mail address at the top to see who wrote it.

Chris Richter.

The three of us are so stunned that it takes us a moment to recognize the dim sound of the phone ringing in another room.

EIGHTEEN

em

Finn pulls the Honda off to the side of the road a hundred yards from the Shaws' guardhouse and kills the lights.

"What do you think they're doing in there?" I say.

"Don't know. Maybe they just wanted to get out of the city?"

"Well, they'll probably want to get some sleep, so I doubt they'll leave before morning. Which means it's going to be a long night for us." I pop my seat back and ball one of the spare shirts Connor gave us under my head. "Ugh. I'm so sick of this car."

"Me too. We should steal a new one soon. They'll be looking for this one."

"Can we get one with leather seats? And a better stereo?"

"You bet." Finn unbuckles his seat belt. "Come on, let's get out of here for a while."

"What?"

He opens his door, which lets a frigid blast of air into the car. "Hurry up!"

"It's freezing!" I say, but I'm already zipping up my hoodie as far as it will go and climbing out of the car.

Finn hops up onto the hood and offers me a hand. "It's nice and toasty up here."

"You are such a weirdo." But I climb onto the hood next to him. It *is* warm, from hours of the engine running and heating the metal. He lies back, folding his hands under his head, and I do, too.

The stars are shocking. It's been so long since I've seen them, and I swear they've multiplied in my absence. Out here, away from the city, they're like tiny explosions of light. Thousands of diamonds lodged in the atmosphere.

"Wow," I whisper.

"Yeah. I'd forgotten they were so *bright*."

We sit in silence, staring up at the sky, and after a few minutes Finn takes my hand and rubs it in his own to warm it.

"What are you thinking about?" I ask.

"Connor's pancakes."

"Mmm. And hot chocolate."

"Oh God," he groans. "I could kill you for making me think of hot chocolate right now. I'd do anything for some of that."

"You started it with your pancake talk!"

"You asked! And besides—"

The world spins underneath me, and the rest of what Finn says gets lost. I know what it is now, but I'm not sure if that makes it easier to take or even more terrifying. I just have time to grip Finn's hand before the chain wraps itself around my middle and yanks me out of the present.

It's dark, only the faintest blue safety light from the hallway creeping in through the window of my cell door. Taminez, one of our usual night guards, turned the lights out a long time ago, but I haven't been able to sleep.

Finn, of course, has been out for hours. The jerk.

I hear footsteps outside and sit up on my cot. A soldier I don't recognize slides open my cell door, and the doctor walks in.

"Thanks, Greggson," he says. "You can leave us."

So it's going to be one of those nights.

The soldier salutes and shuts the door behind him. The doctor sits down on the floor of my cell, facing me. It's strange to see him there on the concrete floor in his white lab coat and expensive slacks, looking up at me. It makes him look small. I pull the blanket tighter around myself and wait.

His eyes drop to his lap. "I miss you, Marina."

I hate these nights. I think I hate them more than anything else.

"I'm right here," I say. "You're the one who's gone."

"I understand, you know, why you hate me." He examines his hands closely. "I've done terrible things."

"Do you want my forgiveness? Is that why you came here?"

"I don't know. Maybe." He takes a shaky breath. My God, is he crying? "Maybe I just needed to be with a friend tonight."

"I'm not your friend," I say. "You can hold me here forever and confide in me every night, but I'll never be your friend again."

"Marina, it's not like you think," he says, and the desperation in his voice is palpable now. "If you knew what I know . . . It requires some terrible sacrifice, but we're doing good things—"

"I'm tired. Can I go back to sleep now?"

He reaches for me. "Please, I *need* you to understand—"

"Good night, doctor."

His hand hovers in midair, trembling, and falls to his side. He moves like an old man as he gets to his feet and knocks on the door to be let out. The soldier I don't know reappears and slides the door open.

The soldier I don't know.

"Where's Taminez?" I say. "It's his shift."

The doctor stops but doesn't look at me.

My stomach clenches. I suddenly realize why the doctor is here. "Oh God. What did you send him back to do?"

"I didn't have a choice," the doctor says, and the door closes behind him with a clang.

"Em!"

I blink and inhale. The world rights itself, and I see stars, real ones.

"Em, wake up!" Finn's voice is choked. "You're breaking my fingers."

I feel Finn's hand in mine. I'm squeezing it with all of my strength. I drop it, and he cradles the appendage to his chest.

"Damn, girl," he says. "When did you get so freakishly strong?"

"I-I'm sorry." I push myself into a sitting position and rub my eyes. The memory may have been a brief one, but the effects of it are lingering the longest. I can still feel the dread in the pit of my stomach and see the shadow of my cell walls in front of my eyes.

"You okay?" he says. "What did you see?"

I shake my head. I don't want to talk about it. "How long was I gone this time?"

"Ten minutes," he says. "Maybe fifteen. It felt like forever."

I shiver. The hood of the Honda is cold beneath us, and the chill of the night has seeped into my bloodstream. "What's happening to us?"

"You . . ." Finn hesitates and shakes his head, and I realize how pale he is. "While you were out, you sort of . . . *flickered* for a second. Like a hologram or something. I was afraid you were going to disappear." He touches my cheek. "Like, really afraid."

"I'm sorry," I whisper. I try to imagine how scared I'd be if I thought Finn was disappearing and leaving me to face all of this alone, but I stop myself because it's too horrible to even think about.

He smiles. "I think I can forgive you."

"James always said time must have a mechanism for fixing paradoxes," I say. "Maybe it's trying to figure out where we actually belong. Maybe it's trying to erase us."

"Each flash seems to be lasting longer and longer," Finn says. "Do you think that means—"

I nod. I may not be a scientific genius, but I feel the truth of it. Time is coming for us, and coming fast. "We don't have much time."

That's when the police cruiser passes us, headed toward the Shaw house.

NINETEEN

marina

James runs for the phone, and Finn and I follow. He takes one look at the caller ID and swears. He grabs the receiver.

"Mark?" I hear the guard's faint voice on the other end, and James swears again. "Thanks." He hangs up and runs for the stairs, calling behind him, "The cops are on their way up to the house!"

"It's okay!" Finn shouts after him. "We just won't answer the door!"

"Yeah, but the car is out front!"

Finn and I chase after James and catch him by the front door. I snatch the car keys out of his hand.

"Let me," I say. "They don't care about me. You stay here."

"Marina—"

"Shut up and turn off the lights," I say. "They'll be out of the trees any minute."

I dash out of the door and toward the BMW. As I slide into the driver's seat, I glance at the driveway, but it's still clear. I start the car and realize I have no idea where to take it. There's a garage at the side of the house, but the door is closed. I flip open James's visor and his glove compartment, rifling through the contents a little wildly, but I don't see a remote control. I could just drive it around to the back of the house, but what if the cops see tire tracks in the grass?

I look at the driveway again. No sign of anyone yet, but it won't be long. I imagine I can see the glow of headlights through the trees.

Screw it. It's dark, and I don't have any other choice. I press my foot to the gas and pull off of the driveway, bumping over the curb and onto the lawn. I try to visualize the car floating, tires barely touching the grass as I drive around the side of the house and park the BMW at the back, out of sight from the driveway. I run up to the back door and knock, and Finn's right there to let me in.

"Nice driving," he says.

"Hilarious." I struggle to catch my breath. "Where's James?"

Finn leads me through the dark house to where James is standing behind the front door. Seconds later, headlights sweep across the front of the house, and Finn grabs my wrist, pulling me away from a window. We press ourselves close to the wall so that we can't be seen.

Outside, a car door closes. We hear the crunch of hard-soled shoes against gravel, and a motion-activated security light turns on. The knock against the door is like an explosion, echoing through the house. It makes the chime of the doorbell that follows it sound delicate and sweet.

"Mr. Shaw?" a voice calls. "This is the state police. Are you inside?"

James inches toward the peephole and looks out.

"Mr. Shaw, we just want to make sure you're safe," the cop says. He presses the doorbell again.

James continues to watch through the peephole, and we stand, frozen. I try not to breathe. After a minute, James whispers, "They're leaving."

We're silent, and beyond the door is the crunch of gravel, the closing of a car door, and the roar of an engine. We hear the cruiser pull away, and James steps away from the peephole.

"They're gone," he says.

"Well, that was terrifying," Finn says. "I don't think I'm cut out to be a fugitive."

"Let's give them a few minutes to clear out, and then we're going back to D.C.," James says. He holds up the file folder. "Someone needs to see this."

"I knew Richter was hiding something," James says as he guides the car back toward I–95 South. As soon as we got on the road, he reassembled his cell phone and called Vivianne to tell her we were on our way home and to call off the search dogs. He didn't tell her about the file folder we found.

I click on the dashboard light and read the printed-out e-mail exchange that was at the top of the folder again.

FROM: Chris Richter <christopher.richter@dni.gov>
DATE: November 16, 2013 3:48:02 EDT
TO: Joshua Schweiger <joshua.schweiger@air-online
.org>

He's gonna have a big future.
> Our source in his office says yes. He's protective,
doesn't trust us. What do you want the kid for?
> > I want him. Will the congressman be an
impediment?
> > > James Shaw. IQ 168. Briefly institutionalized after
the death of his parents in '08, still under psychiatric
care. Skipped 4th and 8th grades. Graduated first in
class from Sidwell at 15. Completed his BS in Science
at Georgetown University in eighteen months. Currently
working on his PhD in Applied Physics and Mathematics
at Johns Hopkins, under the mentorship of Dr. Ari
Feinberg. Doing his dissertation on some aspect of relativity, real secretive.
> > > > Just do it.
> > > > > You want me to look up the grades on his
report card?
> > > > > > Everything. Especially his education.
> > > > > > > What do you want?
> > > > > > > > Can you get me info on the Shaw kid?
The congressman's younger brother, James.

I look closely at the e-mail address: joshua.schweiger@air.org. *A-I-R*. Nate wasn't trying to tell me he couldn't breathe; he was trying to tell me something about an organization Chris Richter works with.

Underneath the e-mail are photocopies of pages in James's handwriting, shadowy lines of formulas and theorems that could be written in Chinese for all the sense they make to me. It reminds me that I have the pages James was writing in the hospital in my front pocket. He seems to have completely forgotten about them. He'll only lose them again if I give them to him now, so I make a mental note to hand them over once we get home.

Along with the e-mail and photocopies are a dozen more documents. There's something that looks like an official government report, almost half of which has been blacked out with a thick marker, more e-mails, something that looks suspiciously like photocopies of medical records with James's name at the top, and notes Nate was making for himself of the goings-on of the SIA, another acronym agency I've never heard of. Whatever they were up to, Nate didn't like it.

"This must be the investigation Nate told me about," I say. "He was looking into something called the SIA, or maybe the AIR? It's hard to tell which one, but it sounds like they were going to offer you a job. Who do you think they are?"

James shrugs. "A subset of the CIA, maybe? Richter could be overseeing them as part of his job at the DNI. My uncle once told me the Agency has several covert arms that do the kinds of things even the CIA can't be seen to be doing."

I shiver. "Creepy."

"But those pages from my notebook," he says. "That's what really concerns me. I don't know why Nate went looking for those."

"What are they?" Finn asks. He reaches for the stack of papers, and I reluctantly pass them back.

"It's some of the latest work I've been doing for Dr. Feinberg." James veers a little too sharply into the next lane, and I brace myself against the armrest. "I made a big breakthrough recently, but I didn't tell Nate about it. He doesn't like my research, thinks it isn't healthy for me to be so focused on the past."

"Where do you think he got them from?" Finn asks.

"Don't know. Maybe Dr. Feinberg, or maybe he went through my things."

I catch a flash of James's thin, straight handwriting as Finn flips through the pages. I have a sudden realization that makes my heart sink, even though it shouldn't matter after everything that's happened.

"Is that breakthrough what you were going to tell me about?" I say. "The night you came home?"

James nods but doesn't look away from the road. "Yeah."

"What is it?" Finn asks.

"It's something I've been working on for a long time. I'm finally starting to make some real progress, and those pages there are the crux of my formulations."

"What are they for?"

"Travel in the fourth dimension."

"Huh?"

James's gaze flicks into the rearview mirror and back again. "Time travel."

I've listened to James talk about this for years, so it doesn't faze me, but Finn clicks off his seat belt and scoots up between us. "Say *what* now?"

"I know it sounds ridiculous, but I think it's possible, and Dr. Feinberg agrees. When I finish those formulas, I'll prove it." James's fingers tighten around the steering wheel until his knuckles turn white. His passion has always been one of the things I love most about him, but it worries me, too. I've learned a lot about James these last two days, and I see more than ever now how he's like forged metal, strong but brittle, unable to bend.

"What happens when you prove it?" Finn asks.

"We fix the world."

Only four little words, ones I've heard from James a thousand times before, but for some reason they unsettle me to my core this time.

"What do you mean?" Finn asks.

"Imagine what we could change," James says, "if we could use time. The wars that could be averted, the natural disasters that could be planned for. We could erase so many terrible, senseless things."

"Wouldn't that be dangerous?" Finn says. "You don't know what you could accidentally change. You could, like, kill your grandfather and then you'd never have been born, right?"

James smiles dryly. "Time isn't quite that simple. For one thing, it isn't linear, the way we perceive it. And the current research suggests there's some unknown variable that eliminates threats to time, like the paradox you're talking about. My theory is that time has a sentient element. It fixes events in place to stop paradoxes from happening. So, in theory, if I were to go back in time to kill my grandfather, that event would become fixed by my action. Because he's dead, I would never be born, but a remnant of me from my original time, a kind of shadow, would always be there to kill my grandfather and ensure he stayed dead."

Finn blinks. "I didn't remotely understand that."

"Yeah," I say. "Could you use smaller words?"

"Those *were* my small words."

"It still sounds dangerous to me," Finn says. "So much could go wrong."

"There are risks," James concedes, "but progress is always dangerous, isn't it? Most of the time, walls don't get dismantled brick by brick. Someone has to crash through them."

Someone has to crash through them. A pall descends over the car. It sounds so foreboding.

Finn raps his knuckles against the back of James's skull. "Then I guess it's a good thing you've got such a hard head."

I roll my eyes. Trust Finn to lighten the mood.

"Ow!" James says, but he's smiling. He swats at Finn blindly. "You're lucky I'm driving."

"I'm not," I say. It's so good to see James smile that I want to prolong the moment. I go to knock Finn on the head, but he dodges deeper into the recesses of the backseat.

"Stay away, woman!"

Spurred on by James's laughter, I unbuckle my seat belt and try again. Finn catches my fist midswing, and I pull back, but he doesn't let go.

"Hey!" I kneel in my seat for better leverage and pull, but his hand is tight around my wrist now. "Let go!"

"No, you'll hit me!"

"How old are you two?" James says.

Finn yanks my hand, and I tumble into the backseat with a shriek. Despite my squirming, he manages to catch me in a headlock and muss my hair. I elbow him in the stomach, and I hear James laugh again over the sound of Finn's grunt.

"You want a piece of this?" Finn says. "You think you can take me, Marchetti?"

Distantly, I hear the sound of James's cell phone ringing, but now I'm too focused on trying to pry Finn's fingers off my wrist. I bend his pinkie back until he yelps and lets go, and then I throw myself at him. It seems only fair that I get to mess up his hair, too, but he's too strong and keeps wrestling me away. I accidentally jam my elbow into his ribs and am shocked when he lets out a girlish, shrieking giggle.

"Oh my God," I say, breathless, "you're *ticklish*?"

He points a finger at me, suddenly very serious. "You stay away from me."

I grin and launch myself at him, and the two of us are engaged in such an intense battle that I barely notice the car slowing at first. When I do, I glance at James in the rearview mirror and see that his face has gone ash gray.

"James?" I say. Finn tries to tickle me under the arms, and I slap him away. "Stop it. James?"

The car continues to slow, and James steers it to the shoulder of the highway. I scoot forward, and Finn sits up.

"What's wrong?" I say.

James puts the car into park with one hand and holds the phone to his ear with the other. "I'm here."

I can hear the person on the other end of the line, a tinny little sound stretched thin by hundreds of miles of air, but I can't distinguish any words. Instead, I watch James's face. His expression is an open book to me, because I took the time to learn the language many years ago. What I see makes my throat go dry. I clamber back into the front seat, Finn forgotten.

"Yeah . . ." James says. "Okay . . ."

My hands start to tingle, like they do whenever I get really scared. James once told me it's because my blood vessels are constricting, sending all the blood to the core of my body in case I have to run or fight. I clench my hands into fists to try to get the feeling back.

The cell phone slips out of James's grasp and clatters to the floor of the car. He doesn't move, doesn't grab for it or even seem to notice it's gone. His hand hovers, empty, by his ear.

"James," I whisper.

He turns to look at me, slowly, his face unchanging. His eyes are wide, mouth open, frozen.

Then, like a dam breaking, he crumbles into sobs.

TWENTY

em

Finn and I follow at a distance, far back enough that when James's BMW shifts onto the shoulder and stops, we have time to stop, too. Finn flicks off our headlights, and hopefully we're far enough behind them that they won't notice us.

"Do you think they have a flat?" I say when the other car doesn't move for several minutes.

One of the BMW's doors open, and the younger Finn climbs out.

"Damn, I'm good-looking," Finn says, and I smack him.

The driver's door opens next, and James steps out. His shoulders are bent inward, and he keeps one hand braced against the car for support.

The smile dies on my lips. "It's happened."

"What?" Finn squints at them. "It's not supposed to happen for four more days."

"Something's changed."

Finn bends his head. "Poor James. Poor *this* James."

I'm not sure what to say. The James in front of us is just a boy. He doesn't deserve this.

But I also can't forget that this is one of the moments that sets the future as I know it into motion.

The two boys switch places, James moving into the backseat of the BMW, where he's quickly joined by Marina, and Finn slipping behind the wheel.

"Shit," my Finn says, shifting our car out of park. "He doesn't know how to drive."

The BMW jerks forward and starts to pick up speed along the shoulder. It finds a gap in the traffic on the highway and veers sharply into it. Finn winces and follows. The BMW stays in the right lane, doing ten miles under the speed limit, which sends the cars behind it flying into the left lane to pass. Its right blinker is still on, a pulsing beacon in the dark. It pulls off at the next exit and into the parking lot of a Holiday Inn. The younger Finn parks twenty feet away from the nearest car.

"Good call, kid," Finn mumbles. The BMW is straddling two spaces.

We watch from the far end of the lot as Marina helps James out of the car and into the hotel. Finn fetches a couple of bags from the trunk and follows them inside. Then there's nothing, only darkness and silence.

"Nate was a good man," Finn finally says.

"The best." I close my eyes and picture Nate the night before the fund-raiser, waiting in the cold at his car to see that I got inside all right. Smiling and raising his hand when I waved at him from my open door.

"You okay?" Finn asks.

"Sure," I say. "I mean, nothing's really changed. He's been dead to me for four years."

"I know, but . . ." Finn takes my hand and brings it to his mouth, kissing my knuckles.

My heart goes hot and seems to melt, spreading warmth through my whole body. How long have I loved Finn? It crept up on me so gradually, I don't know if I can even pin the moment down. Was it the day in the cells when, after a particularly brutal interrogation, he managed to make me laugh by telling me about the time his father had to call the fire department when he got his head stuck in a storm drain? Or when we were still on the run and I woke up in the back of the cereal truck that was smuggling us across the state line to find his sweatshirt tucked around me while he sat shivering in his T-shirt?

Or had it started even before, back when I was still Marina and thought I couldn't stand him?

Finn jerks his head toward the entrance of the Holiday Inn, and I turn to look. Speak of the devils. Finn and Marina are walking out together.

"Where are they going?" I say.

They're headed straight for us. Finn and I duck down behind the dash. I don't know what exactly will happen if my younger self and I ever come face-to-face, but James was always insistent that the fabric of time was too delicate to survive the paradox it would create.

Their shadows pass over our heads, and we hear Finn speaking, but neither takes any notice of the battered blue Honda. They pass us, and we gradually sit up and watch them walk across the street and into a Denny's.

"They'll be gone ten minutes," Finn says. "At least."

I nod, suddenly queasy. "It's our best chance."

"I'll do it." Finn pops open the glove compartment and grabs the gun. "He's going to be devastated, and I don't want you to have to see it."

I touch his cheek. "You're a pretty sweet guy, Finn Abbott, you know that?"

"I may have heard it once or twice."

I swallow down the hot ball in my throat. "But I can't let you do this alone. We're a team."

"Em—"

"No way. Besides . . ." I breathe in and take the gun away from him. "I feel like I owe it to him, in some weird way. It should be me."

With our younger selves safe inside the Denny's, Finn and I walk into the hotel. I feel about a million years older than the pair who walked out of here, but I hope we won't look it to an overworked desk attendant in the middle of the night.

"Hi," Finn says, flashing his most charming smile at the woman behind the desk. "Sorry, I'm a moron. We checked in a few minutes ago?"

The woman nods. "Sure."

"Our friend is back in the room," he says. "He's got a bad cold, so we went out to get him some medicine. I'm hoping he's fallen asleep by now, the poor guy."

"Oh, bless his heart," she says. It's been years, but I still marvel at Finn's ability to win people over so quickly.

"Yeah. So, I was wondering if you could make us another copy of our room key?" he says. "We forgot ours, and we don't want to have to wake him up to get back inside."

"No problem," the attendant says, already punching something into a computer. She slips a key into an envelope and scrawls *126* across the front, so we won't even have to pretend to have forgotten which room we're in. "Here you go. I hope he feels better."

"Thanks so much." Finn takes the key. "You have a nice night."

"You too."

"Well, that was easy," I whisper as we follow the little signs with arrows that lead toward room 126.

"No, that was very dangerous and daring, and it was only through my extreme charm that we pulled it off."

Even at this moment, he can make me smile. "My mistake."

Soon we stand in front of the door to 126. It's on the first floor at the back of the hotel, practically in the corner, which is good. If something goes wrong, we'll have a better chance of getting away. But hopefully everything will go right, and escape won't be a concern.

Because we won't exist anymore.

"Ready?" I say, more to myself than Finn.

I raise the key to the door, but before I can put it in the lock, Finn slides his hand around my neck and pulls me against him, muffling my squawk of surprise with his lips. He kisses me like I've never been kissed before. *Kiss* is too small a word for it. It's like he's pouring every ounce of love and lust and regret, every moment of pent-up longing from months in a cell, into me. I press up into him, and when he pulls away to rest his forehead against mine, I'm dazed and out of breath.

"Now," he whispers, the words ghosting over my lips, "I'm ready."

I palm his cheek and nod, trying to memorize the color of his eyes in these last few seconds. I was wrong before. They're not just blue. In the center, right around his pupil, is a tiny ring of greenish yellow you can only see this close, like a secret. I have to remember that.

He nods, and I let my hand drop from his face so I can reach for the gun in my belt.

TWENTY-ONE

marina

Finn and I slide into a booth to wait for the cheeseburgers we ordered to go. I said we should have a pizza delivered to the room, but James needed a minute alone to call Vivianne. I didn't want a repeat of what had happened at the hospital, so we left him sitting on the bed, pillow held against his chest, staring at his phone.

"His whole life is going to be different now," I say. "What's he going to do?"

"I don't know."

"He's all alone."

"He's got Viv, and you. He'll *always* have you."

There's an edge to his voice, and it turns my thoughts dark. *Not if I'm in New York, he won't.* I haven't turned my phone back on, and once Mom and Dad realize I'm not coming home, they should leave without me, him to Rome and her to New York. But I can't put moving off forever if my mother's determined to do it, and just thinking about it makes me feel like the foundations that hold me together are cracking.

"He has you, too," I say.

"Yeah, but it's not the same."

"What do you mean?"

He shifts in his seat. "Nothing."

I grab the bowl of sugar packets and begin sorting them: blue, pink, white. Blue, pink, white. "I was always jealous of James, you know. He only had Nate, but Nate really loved him. You know he missed his first session as a congressman to go to James's science fair? He was always there for him."

Finn pulls the sugar bowl from my hands and slides it away. "Your parents are assholes. You don't deserve them, and they definitely don't deserve you."

I stare at him, shaken. "I-I'm not talking about me. I'm talking about James."

"I know." He looks down at the sticky Formica tabletop. "Just thought it needed saying."

I don't know how to respond. It's like he reached deep inside of me and pulled my darkest and most fearful thoughts out of the muck and into the sunlight for everyone to see.

In a *Denny's*.

em

I pull the gun from my belt and check the safety. When I'm ready, I slip the key card into the lock. It beeps softly, and Finn pushes open the door. I step in first, gun extended, and he follows me. Together we creep inside, and I hear Finn slide the chain across the door after us. We steal past the bathroom, the closet, and refrigerator. With one last breath, I turn the corner into the main area of the room.

It's empty.

A door opens behind us. We spin around, and I instinctively hide the gun behind my back.

"Hey, guys," James says as he comes out of the bathroom. "Where's the food?"

He doesn't know we're not them. Either grief or his natural inattention to people has blinded him to the changes time has carved into us. The scars on Finn's face, the hollowness of my cheeks.

"I . . . it was closed," I say. God, why am I lying? Why am I dragging this terrible moment out any further? I glance at Finn, expecting to see the thought mirrored back at me in his expression, but his eyes have gone soft and sad as he looks at James. I understand the spell that's fallen over him. It's hard to remember the doctor and the cruelty of his ambition when you're standing so close to the boy he was when he was our best friend. When he was our James. I still feel it, too.

"James . . ." I say, my voice choked.

"You okay?"

"How can you ask me that?" I whisper, forgetting the gun behind my back and Finn standing a few feet away. Forgetting everything but the sweet boy I loved so much for so long. "After what's just happened to you, how can you worry about me?"

"It happened to you, too." James steps toward me and envelopes me in a hug. It happens so quickly that I don't know how to stop it, and I'm not even sure I could. I bite my lip as hard as I can and try to remember what Finn said, how this James—who is so real and solid against me—is already dead and gone. I think of how many tears Marina will shed and all the different ways he'll take her to pieces. All the people who will die.

But I had forgotten what it feels like to have his arms around me, how small and protected it makes me feel. I can take this moment to say good-bye, can't I? Haven't I earned that much? I tuck the gun into my waistband and wrap both arms around James, closing my eyes and inhaling the familiar boy-and-detergent smell of him, suddenly sixteen and desperately in love with him again.

I open my eyes and find Finn staring at us, his expression heavy and unreadable.

"I'm sorry," I whisper, not totally sure which one of them I'm talking to.

"God, Marina, you're shaking," James says. He holds me tighter, cupping the back of my head. He runs his fingers gently through my hair.

The hair I hacked short, watching the long, dark locks pool at my feet like orphans, just before we were discovered and dragged off to those concrete cells.

James's hand pauses at the edge of my hair—which only hangs to my shoulder, not halfway down my back like Marina's—and I stiffen. He pulls back and looks at me with eyes that are suddenly sharp. He stares at me for a moment and then scrambles away, wheeling backward until he hits a wall.

"Who are you?" He looks back and forth between Finn and me, taking in our borrowed clothes and the changes the years have wrought on our faces. "Who the hell are you?"

Finn holds his hands in front of him like James is a frightened animal who might charge. "It's us, Jimbo."

"Bullshit."

"It's us," I repeat, taking a step closer to him. He flattens himself against the wall, trying to move every atom as far away from me as he can. "It's just not the us you know. Not yet."

"What are you talking about?"

"You did it," Finn says. "The fourth dimension. You figured it out."

"Shut up! You're a . . . This is a trick. It's a trick . . . or something." James can't seem to catch his breath. He turns to leave, but I'm too fast for him, wedging myself between him and the door.

"Look at me, James," I say. "*Look* at me."

He raises his eyes slowly to mine. I'm not sure what he sees there. The seriousness of my expression, the thinner, harsher planes of my face, or maybe a glimpse of my anguish, but it convinces him. The truth hits him like a blow, doubling him over.

"Oh God," he breathes. "It's really true?"

"Yeah," Finn says. "Sorry, man."

"Sorry?" James laughs, and his whole face changes. "This is incredible! I really did it, you're really from the future! How far?"

His happiness is like a needle, sharp and bright, right through my heart. "Four years."

He throws his arms around us. "I can't believe you're here! We're going to change science; we're going to change the *world*!

Oh my God, Nate—*Nate*." His eyes widen. "If you could come back here, then I could—"

"Stop!" I can't take it anymore. I shake James's arm off of me and press a fist to my mouth to stop a sob escaping. I have to stop this now, before he starts talking about using time travel to save Nate's life.

"Marina, what . . ." James stops, and uncertainty creeps into his expression. "Why did you two come back?"

I look at Finn, who seems suddenly old to me, as old as I feel. Then I look at James, who is lit up from the inside, so alive and beautiful and *James*.

"We came to kill you," I say.

TWENTY-TWO

em

James stares at me.

"What?" he says, the shocked remnants of a smile still on his face.

"James . . ." I whisper.

"I don't understand. Why—" I pull the gun from my belt, and he swallows the rest of the sentence with a gulp. "Jesus Christ, Marina."

"I don't go by that name anymore." I lift the gun. "I'm sorry, but I have to do this."

"Wait! Stop!" James moves away from me and toward Finn, who must seem friendlier since he doesn't have a weapon aimed at his head. "I don't understand. What's going on?"

I should pull the damn trigger and be done with it. I hate that my last memory of this world will be James looking at me like that, but I can't fail again. I tighten my finger on the trigger. Pull it, I tell myself.

Pull it!

"Wait!" Finn throws a hand in front of James's chest, and I release the trigger. My heart is pounding. I might have been able to do it, and I'm simultaneously enraged and thankful for the interruption. "He hasn't done anything yet. He at least deserves to know why." Finn turns to James. "I'm sorry, man, but the future is an awful place. The machine changes everything."

"It *ruins* everything," I say. "And you become so scary, James."

"What?" he whispers. "No."

"We've tried every other way to prevent it happening," I say. "Previous versions of us tried to convince you to stop your research, burned your notes, got rid of people who helped you, you name it. Nothing worked. But this?" I nod at the gun. "This has to work."

His face darkens. "Oh my God. It was *you*. Outside the hospital. You're the ones Marina saw."

I nod.

"And my brother?" His voice rises to a break on the last word, Nate's name hanging unspoken in the air like a ghost.

"Not us," Finn says.

James holds his head between his palms, like the press of his thoughts is painful. "No. No. No. I don't understand."

"We know you never meant to become a monster," Finn says, "but you did. You couldn't help it."

"I can't let you hurt her again," I say, raising the gun.

"Marina, wait!" There's a bright flash of panic in James's eyes when he realizes I really do mean to shoot him. "We can talk about this! Whatever I am in the future, I'm not that person right now, here in this room."

I clench my jaw. "No. This is hard enough for me already."

Finn stands next to me, laying a soft, steady hand on my shoulder.

"I don't get this." James raises his hands in surrender and looks around, but there's nowhere for him to run. "You're my best friends. I would never hurt you."

In my mind, I see the doctor sitting in a chair across from me while hot, sharp electricity sizzles through me. I endured it because the pain was the only alternative to dying, and, as much as I couldn't understand why sometimes, I didn't want to die. But the feeling of helplessness, being so powerless in my own skin, was worse than every bruise and scar. I wonder if James knows that now, with my gun pointed at his head.

He must see something in my expression, because his voice is soft and heavy when he speaks. "My God. What did I do to you?" He takes a step toward me, like he wants to take me in his arms again.

"Don't come any closer!"

His eyes fill with tears. "Marina, please."

I swallow. "I'm sorry, James. I'm so sorry."

My finger begins to tighten on the trigger. In a fraction of a second, there will be sound and blood and then nothing. I still don't want to die, but Marina will live. That fierce, loyal, innocent girl who just wants someone to love will get the life I never had, and that's more than enough.

There's a bang on the door. I flinch, and James uses the opportunity to leap at me.

"James?" Marina calls from the other side of the door. "Can you let us in? Our hands are full."

James is trying to wrestle the gun from my grasp. I twist, and the back of my knees hit a bed. I topple backward, him on top of me. I keep hold of the gun, but James has me pinned painfully to the mattress, his forearm across my neck. I hold the gun over my head to keep it out of his reach, but I can't get it pointed at him.

Finn pulls James off of me, and I gasp for air and roll away from the boys. Finn is strong, but James is bigger and fueled by pure terror; the fight won't last long.

"James?" I hear the sound of a key in the card reader.

"We have to go!" I hiss at Finn.

The door starts to swing open but is jerked to a stop by the chain.

"Jimbo, open the door!" the younger Finn calls through the crack.

I run to the window and pry it open. I could try to take a shot at James now, but I'd risk hitting Finn. And Marina, God, she's only a few feet away. I can't bear it. I kick the screen out onto the parking lot below.

James knocks Finn back with a clumsy but powerful punch to the jaw. He scrambles to his feet. "You can't be in the same place they are, can you?"

He runs to the door, and Finn runs to me. Finn jumps into

the bushes four feet below and lifts his hands up for me. I take one look back at James, who is struggling with the chain on the door but looks up at me at the same moment.

"I'm sorry," I say, "but this isn't over. We won't stop."

I jump into Finn's waiting arms, and together we run.

TWENTY-THREE

marina

"James?" I shift the soft drinks and vending-machine food Finn and I got on our way back to the room into the crook of my right arm so I can wiggle the fingers of my left through the gap in the door. Inside I hear shuffling and a muted bang, whispers. "What's going on?"

Silence.

"James!" I cry. "You open this door right now!"

"Move your hand."

I sigh in relief and pull my fingers free, and the door closes and then opens. James's face is red, which I expected, but it looks oddly sweaty and flushed, like he's been running a marathon instead of crying. He stares at me like he's seeing me for the first time. Finn pushes past him, not seeming to notice anything amiss.

"Burgers all around," he says, dumping the Denny's bag on the rumpled floral coverlet of the nearest bed. I lay my load of junk food in a pile beside it.

James stalks past us, grabbing my tote off the floor and his coat from the back of a chair. "Let's take them to go, okay? I think we should get back on the road."

"What?"

"We should keep moving," he says. "I don't want to stay here."

"You've had a shock." I try to catch him and hold him still, halt his frightful momentum around the room, but he keeps slipping through my grasp. "You need to get some rest."

"What I need is to get the *fuck* out of this hotel room!" He's visibly shivering, his entire body quaking like he's freezing from the inside out. He slams the side of his fist against the wall, and I jump, suddenly frightened of the stranger in front of me. James sees it and bows his head. "I'm sorry, Marina. God, I'm so sorry. But please, I need to leave."

Finn steps between us and puts a hand on James's chest. "Okay. We'll go. It's okay."

James's voice is thick when he says, "Thank you."

We go back to the car—the burgers cooling, forgotten, in the backseat beside Finn—and James drives like the devil is on his heels. I'd feel safer if *Finn* were behind the wheel again. The speedometer approaches the triple digits, and he weaves around other cars, eyes flicking into the rearview mirror every few seconds. I'm too scared to ask him what's wrong or even speak to him. This quiet, smoldering James reminds me uncomfortably of the day of his parents' funeral, when the rage in his eyes as he hit that lamp seemed like it could burn a hole right through me.

Finn doesn't share my concern. He's flopped across the backseat, dead asleep, his mouth hanging open ever so slightly. When

I notice, I roll my eyes, but I end up watching him longer than I mean to. He looks so young when he's asleep; I can almost see the little boy he must have been once.

"Marina?" James whispers.

It's the first word he's spoken since we left the hotel. "Yeah?"

"Do you think I'm a bad person?"

"*What?*"

"Is there evil in me?" He searches the road in front of him like it could give him answers. "Could I become a terrible person someday?"

"James." I'm too shocked to even find words. I put a hand over his where it rests on the console. "You're the best person I know."

"I want to be good." His lip starts to wobble, and he raises a hand to his mouth to cover it. "I want to *do* good. I want to help people."

"I know—"

"That's what everything in there is about." He nods his head at the manila folder at my feet. "It's what I've worked for all these years."

"James, I *know.*" He's not hearing me. Whoever he's talking to, it isn't me.

"I wish Nate were here." His voice cracks. "I need him."

"Everything's going to be okay."

"No," he says, looking at me for the first time. His pupils are so big that they're like black holes, just the way he explained them to me, so deep they swallow all the light around them. "It's not going to be okay, Marina. *Nothing* is going to be okay, ever."

I pull my hand back. "You're scaring me."

"I know. I'm scared, too." He clenches his hand around the steering wheel. "I've been scared of so much stupid crap in my life. Making a bad grade or not fitting in. God, I was scared of *you*. And it was all such a waste. None of it matters a damn now that the *real* scary shit is here."

"Why were you scared of me?" I whisper.

He doesn't look at me. The streetlamps fly past outside the window, outlining his silhouette in orange and then plunging it into blackness again. The pulse mimics the beat of my heart.

"Don't make me tell you now," he says. "Not like this."

Hope balloons up inside of me until I could be floating, but I pop it and come back down to earth. I know how that conversation will go. He'll look at me and say, *I love you, Marina. Like the sister I never had. I was scared to tell you, because the people I love tend to go away.* And I will try to smile and tell him I love him, too, like a brother, and then I'll cry myself to pieces and never, ever tell him the truth. I can already feel the pain of it, the hot burn of misery somewhere behind my eyes.

But, oh God, what if I'm wrong? What if my crazy, racing heart is right?

James reaches for my hand. "Just don't leave me, okay, kid? Please don't ever leave me."

I squeeze his fingers. "Never. You're stuck with me, Shaw."

I think he tries to smile. "I'll hold you to that, Marchetti."

TWENTY-FOUR

em

I stare at the dashboard for at least an hour as Finn drives, following the speeding lights of the BMW. I've been turning the dilemma over and over in my mind, examining it from all angles and probing it for a weakness, but it's impenetrable.

"It's over," I finally say. "Now that he knows, he won't let Marina or Finn leave his side, and the doctor will send someone back tomorrow to hunt us down, if time doesn't erase us first. We're done."

"Probably."

I look down at the gun in my lap. I don't know why I haven't put it away yet. I touch it with one fingertip. "Even if we manage to get him alone again, I don't know if I could do it. I've had three chances now, and I've failed every time."

"Three?"

I look up, realizing what I've said. *Stupid.* I glance at Finn and the angry red bruise rising on his jaw. "There was . . . while you were asleep in the car at your house. I watched Marina and James through a window."

"Together?"

"They were just sleeping," I say softly.

Without a word, Finn jerks the wheel violently. We veer off the highway and down a small exit ramp.

"What are you doing?" I yelp. "We're going to lose them!"

"I don't care. You said yourself we've as good as failed already."

He drives us into the parking lot of a gas station and gets out of the car, slamming the door behind him. The sound reverberates through my body, like he screamed without ever opening his mouth. He disappears inside the garishly lit station, and I sit frozen in the car, shame pressing me into my seat, making me feel small.

He's gone a long time. At first I try to keep track, counting the seconds in my head and watching the windows for his fair head. But eventually I give up. I rub my hands across my arms to keep off the chill creeping in through the broken window we taped up with a trash bag.

When he finally comes back to the car, at least a half hour later, he's clutching two cups of coffee and has a plastic bag dangling from one wrist. He opens the door and slides back behind the wheel.

"I'm sorry I lost my temper," he says. "But please don't talk to me yet."

I swallow and nod.

He hands me a cup, which is deliciously warm in my hands, and dumps the contents of the bag. Two turkey sandwiches, potato chips, and a package of Oreos. God, how many times did I dream about Oreos in that cell? How many times did I tell Finn that the biggest regret of my life was not eating more of them when I could, because I'd been stupid enough to worry about the sugar and fat? My eyes suddenly burn. I lift the coffee cup to my mouth and use the movement to cover my brushing away tears.

"You're still in love with him," Finn finally says, calmly. I wish he would yell at me or shake me. It would be easier to take than him sounding so weary. So *sad*.

"Finn—"

"I knew it," he says. "I should have always known it, and maybe I did, but when I saw you with him in that hotel room, the way you held on to him . . ." He traces his fingers across the thin scar on the back of his right hand, a nervous habit. He got it while changing a flat somewhere in South Carolina. It would've healed properly if he'd gone to a doctor to get it stitched up, but he didn't want to slow us down. "I know loving someone doesn't ever completely go away, but it's hard for me. I see the way Marina is with him, and it *still* tears me up inside. I can't take it from you, too. I can't always be the consolation prize for you, Em. I just—I love you too much."

I'm a fish on dry land, gawping and gasping.

"I know you care about me or whatever," he continues, "but if you're still in love with James, I need to know. I deserve that much."

"Finn—" I say, reaching for him.

I don't get to finish the sentence. The pulling starts behind my navel, and I'm overwhelmed by terror. Not this again. I don't want to relive another moment. But I have no choice; I'm swept up by the tide and thrown back with such force that the world blurs around me.

I open my eyes, not realizing I'd closed them. I'm sitting on the back porch of the house in West Virginia, looking out over the mountains in the distance, which are black silhouettes against the slate-gray sky. Everyone else is inside, arguing around the dining room table. Again.

The door behind me slides open, but I don't bother turning around. I know, maybe from the way the air around me changes, who it is. Finn sits down on the steps next to me.

"You okay?"

I nod. "Just needed a break from all the screaming."

"No kidding."

"Have they decided when to go public yet?"

"Maybe in another few hours."

I glance back at the group around the table, Jonas at the head. We met Jonas a few months ago when the three of us were being smuggled across state lines by the same trucker, and we've been with him ever since. He was a demolitions expert the FBI brought in to consult on the evidence from the Philadelphia bombings, but he decided he needed to get out of Pennsylvania when he discovered military-grade explosives deep in the crater at the Sunoco refinery. With what we knew plus what he knew, we began to piece together what's really been happening in the country these past three years. The bombings, the mysterious deaths, the sudden about-faces by politicians and military leaders: they all lead back to Cassandra.

Then we met Rina, and Sahid, and a handful of others. Rina

owns this house deep in the Blue Ridge Mountains, miles from the nearest neighbor, and we've been here for weeks, digging into the SIA and pooling our information. There's a faction of the government responsible for what's happening, and we think we can prove it.

If we could only agree on how.

"Do you think it'll make any difference?" I say. "Going public with what we know?"

"Probably not," Finn says, "but we've got to try."

"I don't understand why he'd want this." I lean my head against a post. "He wanted to make things *better*. Does he really think bombs and checkpoints and mass arrests are better?"

"I'm not sure we'll ever understand." I see him studying me. "You look tired."

"I am." I rub my dry eyes. "I haven't slept in two days. For such a little woman, Jocelyn snores like you wouldn't *believe*."

He grins and wiggles his eyebrows at me. "You can always come share my bed."

I roll my eyes and push his shoulder, but it's not like we've never done it. There was the first truck that took us out of D.C., hidden behind a pallet of cereal boxes. It was the dead of winter, and we huddled together for warmth during the ten-hour drive south. Then there were a half a dozen gross little motels with only one bed where I took pity on him and didn't make him sleep on the floor, even when he offered. And the last time, when we were crashing with a friend of Rina's and ended up sharing the pullout, I woke up in the middle of the night with Finn's arm slung around my waist and his lips grazing the back of my neck, and I didn't move. Just stared into the darkness, pulse racing, hoping he wouldn't wake up.

"You'll probably snore worse," I say.

"Probably. You want to switch beds? Jocelyn won't bother me."

I shake my head, and the ends of my new, shorter hair brush my cheek. I do it again.

"Feel weird?" he asks.

"Yeah. I can't believe I did it." I was looking in the mirror yesterday morning and suddenly couldn't stand the sight of myself, so unchanged on the outside when I felt so different on the inside. I found the shears behind the bathroom mirror and began to hack, feeling oddly satisfied as the hair pooled in the sink and at my feet, discarded remnants of my old life. "I must look kind of crazy."

Finn touches the edge of my hair, rubbing the strands between his thumb and forefinger. "I like it. It suits you."

I feel the warmth of his breath on my face as he says the words. When did he get so close? His knee is touching mine, and his knuckles are brushing my neck as he touches my hair.

"Em?" he says.

I can't quite meet his gaze. "Yeah?"

"I'm really glad you don't hate me anymore," he says, "'cause I can't imagine doing this without you."

"I never *hated* you."

His face brightens. "Yeah?"

"Yeah."

He leans toward me, closing the inches between us, and my mind sort of—stops. All I can think is Finn Abbott is about to kiss me. And I'm about to *let* him.

A sharp crack rips through the air. Finn and I whip our heads toward the house and see bodies dressed in black pouring in through the front door, which hangs awkwardly on its hinges, the jam splintered. They raise guns and shout.

"FBI!"

"Oh God," I say, feeling every ounce of strength seep out of me. "He's found us."

Finn pulls me, limp and unresisting, to my feet and pushes me down the porch steps. "Run! Get out of here!"

"Come with me!" I say. Inside, the SWAT team is forcing our friends to their knees and sweeping the rest of the house. They'll be on us in seconds.

"Go!" Finn hisses. He walks back into the house, his hands held up in surrender, to give me precious seconds to get away.

I turn and run blindly for the woods. I make it less than twenty feet before a hand reaches out of the darkness and grabs me. The house is surrounded; I never had a chance. My captor yanks my hands behind my back and cuffs them, and he drags me, slipping and stumbling, toward the front yard. Finn, Jonas, and the others are kneeling in the mud, and Finn winces when he sees me. One of the officers hauls him to his feet.

"What are you doing?" I say. "Where are you taking him?"

"Em, it's okay!" he says.

"Finn!"

They drag him into the darkness, away from the rest of us.

"Finn!" I scream. There are heavy hands on my shoulders, and I struggle against them.

"Em, wake up!" Finn yells as they drag him away. I see his lips moving, but the words make no sense. The hands shake me.

"No," I sob. "Stop!"

Finn is shoved into the back of a van, and he's gone, but I still hear his voice. "Em, it's okay! Open your eyes."

I blink. The hands on me are gentle and warm. I blink again, and this time the mud and the mountains dissolve. I realize I'm inside the Honda, safe, four years in the past. Finn is hovering over me, one hand on my face, his eyes wide.

"Hey," he says softly. "You back?"

"Yeah." I sit up shakily. My tongue is dry and tacky, so I reach for my coffee cup, but it's gone stone cold.

"It's getting worse, isn't it?" Finn says. He sits back and pushes a shaking hand through his hair. "You were gone a long time. I thought—"

"It's okay, I'm here," I say, putting a hand on his knee. I glance at the clock on the dash. I was out for over half an hour. "Jesus."

"What did you see?"

The memory rolls over me, so fresh I can still smell the wet grass and automotive fumes. I wrap my arms around Finn's neck and try to shake the image of him being dragged away from me, dig my fingers into his skin to reassure myself he's really here.

"I'm so sorry," I say. "I love you, Finn, and I hate myself for not saying it until now."

He seems to have caught my trembling, and he places a sweet, shaky kiss to my lips. "I think I can forgive you."

I hug him again, holding on to him until our breathing aligns, but the peace it brings me is short lived. My worries creep back in, the way the cold creeps into the car when the heater isn't blasting.

I keep seeing him being dragged away. Me powerless to stop it.

"But . . ." I say.

Finn sighs. "But."

"I do still have feelings for James," I say. "It's too easy to remember the girl I was when I loved him. I don't know if I can do it. I know I *should*, but so far . . ."

"I've been selfish, letting you take responsibility for pulling the trigger." He tucks a loose strand of hair behind my ear. "The truth is, I kind of love that you can't do it. That's who you are, Em. If it were easy for you, you'd be no better than him."

"But Marina," I say. "And Finn. They'll suffer if we fail."

"We'll think of something." He presses a kiss to my forehead, then my eyebrow and my cheek, each one warmer and more lingering than the last. "And we won't give up."

"Finn . . ." I whisper, my body growing heavy as his lips continue to move across my face.

"We've already lost them." The languid kiss he leaves at the corner of my mouth sends a shiver up my spine. "Pointless to try to catch up. We should get some rest."

"Rest," I murmur.

He kisses me, finally, on the lips, pulling the breath out of me until I'm gasping and dizzy. He pulls away and slides the car into drive. With one hand, he takes my own, lacing our fingers together, and with the other, he steers us toward a motel across the street.

TWENTY-FIVE

marina

We arrive at James's house as daylight is beginning to turn the edge of the sky pink and orange. It's hard to believe it's only been two days. The world's been so flipped on its head that day is night to me, my eyelids growing heavier as the sun comes up.

I catch a glimpse of my house as James pulls into the garage. The lights are off, and there's no car outside. Maybe my parents are already gone. I'm not sure if the hollowness I feel is relief or disappointment.

I shove Finn awake in the backseat, and we stagger out of the car while James is already unlocking the door to his house. He doesn't seem sleepy at all, like he's fueled by something purer and more primal.

"He okay, you think?" Finn asks as he climbs out of the car.

I sigh. "I don't know. He was saying some weird stuff while you were out."

"Oh, uh." Finn looks at the ground. "Really?"

I narrow my eyes at him. He *was* asleep, wasn't he? He glances back at me, unmistakably guilty, and I smack him. "You're terrible!"

He rubs his arm. "Your talking woke me up! Believe me, that was the *last* conversation I wanted to eavesdrop on."

He walks past me into the house, and I frown at his back before following him. Inside, James is moving from room to room, shutting all of the curtains so that not a crack of daylight comes through. He passes me on his way from the living room to the dining room and throws the lock and dead bolt on the front door on his way.

"Everything all right?" I say.

"It's going to be fine. I've just got to . . . make some calls. So just make yourselves at home."

"Now that you mention it"—Finn scratches his fingers through his unwashed hair—"I could use a shower."

I try to smile. "I'll say."

"Ha-ha."

"You can use the first guest bathroom," James says. "There's shampoo under the sink, and you can borrow clothes out of my closet."

Finn nods and heads upstairs.

"Do you mind if I lie down in the blue room?" I ask. "I don't want to go home right now."

"Sure."

I turn to trudge up the stairs, and James comes with me. Halfway up he loops an arm around my waist, and I lean into him.

"Tired?" he says.

I nod and look at him out of the corner of my eye. He's acting surprisingly normal, the frantic curtain-closing aside. Nate is *gone*, but James isn't crying or pacing or pulling out his hair. He looks focused. Energized.

"You should get some rest, too," I say. It can't last. This is some weird James-style denial that will only make the breakdown that much worse.

"I will."

We walk together toward the blue room, which I've always thought of as mine. I'm sure I've spent more nights in the mahogany bed with the blue damask comforter than anyone else. I pause only to toe off my shoes before collapsing face-first onto the mattress.

"Are there fresh sheets?" James asks, as if that matters.

"I don't care." I crack one eye open and see James closing the curtains with the same care he did downstairs. I roll over and shimmy myself under the comforter. "They're clean."

"Good." He sits down beside me and pulls the covers up to my chin, tucking them around me like I'm a little girl.

"Thanks, Mom," I say. "So, who are you going to call?"

"Dr. Feinberg. I want to find out if he gave my notes to Nate. Plus, there are some . . . other things I need to talk to him about."

"Okay," I say, not knowing how else to respond.

"And I'm going to call Bob Nolan at the FBI. I don't want Richter working on Nate's case. If Nolan sees the stuff we found, maybe he'll do something about it."

I run a hand down his arm. "I hope you're right."

"I hope so, too. In any event, nothing should happen for a few hours, so get some sleep."

He leans down and kisses my forehead, and the moment lingers. He pulls away slightly, like he's realized what he's doing, and our breath mingles for the space of three shallow breaths before his lips sink onto mine.

His lips move against mine once, slowly, but other than that we're both still, our lips just pressed against each other. It probably seems peaceful from the outside, but my insides are rioting. Something strange happens in my chest, like my heart breaking open and spilling heat into my body, tingling through my limbs. I want to move, open my lips or touch his face, but I'm frozen.

Then James puts his hand on my chin and tilts it toward him, deepening the kiss, and I crash through my paralysis. I've figured it out, why I couldn't take all of Sophie and Tamsin's seduction advice. It's because I didn't want to. I didn't want to *seduce* James, to trick him and his hormones into wanting me. I wanted him to want me all on his own. Like this.

I run my hands up his broad back and into his hair, on the opposite side from his stitches, and make a mess of it the way I've imagined doing so many times. Nate's dead and I'm leaving, and all I want is to drown myself in this moment until I've crowded out everything else. James picks up on my urgency, and his gentleness slips away, becomes fumbling hands and messier kisses. He pulls at my sweater, fingers curling in the hem.

"Is this okay?" he whispers.

"Shut up." I press the words against his lips and drag his shirt over his head. Mine quickly follows, and then there's skin on skin and the world narrows to the places where we touch. I strain toward him and pull him closer, back into a kiss, wanting to disappear under the weight and heat of his body on top of mine.

James turns his head away from me. "Sorry. Sorry. I shouldn't have."

"What?" I whisper.

He stands and gathers his discarded shirt and shoes. I sit up, crossing my arms over my chest. "James—"

"Sorry," he says, not looking at me.

And then he's gone.

em

I wake, squinting into the light. I'm not sure where I am, but the thought doesn't bring panic like it should. I try to shift away from the sun and realize there's someone beside me. My cheek is resting on Finn's bare chest, which rises and falls with his breath, the quiet thump of his heart in my ear.

Oh yeah. *Rest.*

The motel room is tiny, with peeling paint and a carpet that would cause my mother to drop dead on the spot, but the mattress is soft and the sheets are clean and cool. The person beside me isn't half bad, either. I have no desire to ever get out of this bed. The world can go to hell outside our locked door; I'm not leaving.

Finn lifts a hand and runs it through my hair, his touch featherlight and gentle. I close my eyes and enjoy the tingle his fingers send through my scalp. When he kisses the top of my head, I look up at him and smile.

He narrows his eyes at me. "I thought you were asleep."

"So *that's* why you were being so sweet."

"I don't know about that. . . ." He kisses me, and maybe I should be self-conscious about my unwashed hair and unbrushed teeth, but I'm not. Not now.

"This was a good idea," he whispers, "if I do say so myself."

"Yeah." I sigh as the cold air comes creeping in again. "But—"

"No! Not yet. No buts yet." He kisses me silent. "Let's at least eat our complimentary continental breakfast first."

"I'm pretty sure it's afternoon."

He glances at the clock on the bedside table. "Damn, cheated! Oh well, we'll have to find something else to do instead."

I'm laughing when he kisses me this time, and I feel the imprint of his smile against my lips. His words are warm in the air between us as he kisses his way down my neck. "God, you don't know how I dreamed about this. All those nights with that wall between us when all I wanted was to touch you."

My face flushes, which is stupid. It's stupid to get so embarrassed and trembly over a few little words. I hide my face against his shoulder.

He flops back against the pillows. "But it's probably time to get serious again, huh?"

I burrow a little closer to him. "Probably."

"So, what are we going to do?"

"We'll stake out James's and Marina's houses," I say. "If they're not there now, they will be soon."

"But finding them is the easy part, isn't it?"

"Maybe I was wrong before." I push myself up on my elbows. "Maybe we didn't try hard enough to convince James to give up on Cassandra. He's seen us now. If we could make him understand how bad things get—"

"We've already tried that," he says gently. It was number one on the list, the very first thing that some previous version of Finn and I tried and failed at. "Besides, when have you ever seen James let something go?"

"Never." I lie back down. "I know. You're right."

Finn sighs. "Maybe we give up. We weren't up for it this time. Maybe the next version of us will be."

"Do you think we've done that already? Do you think other versions of us have gotten the same note, come back here to kill him, and given up?"

"Maybe." He runs his fingertips up my back and smiles. "We could drive down to Florida. Lie on a beach somewhere and get drinks with umbrellas in them while we wait for time to erase us."

"Doesn't sound like a bad way to go," I say, picturing the scene, the sway of the surf and the sun beating down on us. I haven't been warm since we came to this time. The cold has settled into my bones now, my marrow. But the vision fades. It's replaced with a picture of Marina, who I've finally—*finally*—learned to love. My stomach turns. "Four years later and I'm still so selfish. I can't kill

James because of how badly it will make *me* feel, when so many other lives, even Marina's, depend on it."

"Hey." Finn puts a hand on my face and makes me look at him. "You're not selfish. You're a loving person who wants to believe in the good in people, even after all you've been through. If you were selfish, it would have been easy to kill James."

"Maybe."

Finn sits up and looks at me seriously. "You talk about Marina like she's a different person from you, Em. You *are* Marina. You are that same loyal, determined, infuriating girl. It's time you started seeing how great you are, just like you wish Marina could see it. I mean, look at me. I think I'm *fantastic*."

I smile. "You *are* fantastic."

"I know!" He kisses me. "And so are you."

"I'll take your word for it." I sigh and, with great effort, climb out of the soft, safe bed. "We'd better get moving."

TWENTY-SIX

marina

I must be really tired, because even with a noxious cocktail of anger, shame, and lingering arousal churning in my stomach, I'm out in minutes. A knock on the door wakes me, and I drag myself up through sleep to waking. Did I dream it? James kissing me, his hands on my bare skin, him running out with no explanation?

Finn's standing in the doorway. "James just got a message from Richter. He's going to meet him at a restaurant downtown in an hour, and he wants us to go with him."

"*What?*" I push myself into a sitting position. My head is heavy and spinning. When did this all happen? How long was I asleep?

"He's acting really weird, right? Even for James? It's like he thinks—"

"There's still something he can do that will make a difference?" I say.

"Yeah." Finn sighs. "I can't keep running along after him,

262

waiting for the breakdown. I've barely been home in two days. Can you talk to him?"

I climb out of bed and straighten my clothes. "I'm sure as hell going to try."

"Oh, and by the way," he adds, "the family has descended, and Alice is pissed at us."

"Great."

I find James downstairs at the kitchen island, drinking a cup of coffee in big gulps. He's showered and changed, but from his bloodshot eyes, it's clear he hasn't slept. Nancy Shaw-Brookline has arrived, and her three children are squabbling over crayons at the dining room table. Alice, who has probably never done a dish in her entire life, has unpacked the entire contents of the refrigerator and is scrubbing the inside with barely controlled mania, while Vivianne, who has her eyes closed and is rubbing her temple, is on the phone with what sounds like a catering company. I listen in confusion until I remember.

Of course. The wake.

"Who are you?" Alice says, turning from the refrigerator as I enter the kitchen.

James puts down his empty coffee cup and answers without looking at me. "That's Marina, Alice. You've met her about a dozen times. She was at the hospital, remember?"

"Oh yes, the one who ran away from me like it was some kind of game we were playing."

"What?" I say.

"Was she also with you when you disappeared last night?"

Alice says as though I never spoke. "Poor Vivianne could have really used your support—"

James squeezes his head. "I said I'm sorry! There were things I needed to do!"

"I don't know what could possibly be more important than being with your family at such a time. . . ." Alice's words become muffled by the refrigerator as she sticks her head inside and continues scrubbing. James pours himself another cup of coffee and screws up his nose as he downs the first gulp of bitter liquid.

Vivianne hangs up with the caterers. She looks . . . blank. Like whatever used to animate her features is gone. She could be a glass-eyed doll.

"I wanted to go to city hall to get married, you know," she says to no one in particular. "Nate's the one who talked me into the big wedding."

None of us can look at her.

"I'll never be his family now," she says, and then she picks up the phone to continue her calls. Nancy goes to put an arm around her, and even Alice pauses in her cleaning to pat her shoulder. James just stares at the floor and drinks his coffee.

I grab his wrist and pull him out onto the back patio, where two-day-old snow turns to slush beneath our feet.

"What has gotten into you?" I say. "You called Richter? You know getting yourself killed won't bring Nate back, right?"

James puts his cup down on the railing. "So you're done with the soft-touch approach, then?"

"Well, it hasn't been working very well!" I say. "I don't know what's going on in that brilliant brain of yours, James, but you're really starting to worry me. Finn too. Why on earth would you want to meet with Richter after what we found? What happened to going to Director Nolan?"

James crosses his arms and looks out over the frozen yard. "Things changed."

"What things?" I have to stop myself from shaking him until he talks sense. When he doesn't answer, I ask, "What did Dr. Feinberg say? Did he give Nate your notes?"

James hurls his coffee cup down at the icy flagstone, where it shatters. I yelp and jump back. "Dr. Feinberg didn't answer his phone! He's *gone*, Marina. No one's seen him for two days."

"M-maybe he went out of town—"

"No. It's Richter." James goes quiet, his rage disappearing as quickly as it bubbled up. "There's no one else. He has to be the one who helps me."

I blink back tears of frustration. "Helps you *what*?"

"Marina, please." James approaches me, and I have to curl my toes into the ground to keep from backing away from him. He puts his hands on my face, and for one dizzy moment I think he's going to kiss me again, but all he does is look me in the eye. "Please. I have to talk to Richter, but I can't do it alone. I need you with me."

"But what if he's dangerous?" I say. "What if he wants to hurt you?"

"He doesn't."

"How do you know that? Everything we've found points right at him—"

"I *know* Chris Richter didn't have anything to do with the

people who shot at me." He runs the side of his thumb over my cheekbone. "Do you trust me?"

"Yes," I whisper. What else can I say? James is the only person in the world who's never let me down.

"Then please come." He kisses me lightly on the lips. "You promised you wouldn't leave me."

My resolve, like a house without a solid foundation, begins to crumble. "Okay."

"Let's go," he says. "If we're quiet, no one will even notice us leaving."

"We're leaving now?" I say. "But what about Vivianne and your family? They need you here."

James shrugs me off. "I can help them better this way."

He takes me by the hand and leads me back through the kitchen, where no one so much as looks up at us, and into the foyer to collect our coats. Finn is sitting on the stairs, waiting for us.

"Going somewhere?" he says.

"To see Richter."

Finn looks at me with hardness in his eyes. Like I failed him.

"Well, do what you want, I guess," he says, "but I'm leaving."

"What?" James says.

"Marina thinks she's helping you by letting you run around in denial, but I can't do it anymore." He stands. "You need to be still for a minute and mourn your brother, man. And I need to go home."

"You can't," James says. "I need you to come with me."

"I'm sorry, Jimbo, but that's not—"

"You don't understand." James grabs his shoulders. "I *need* you with me, Finn. You can't leave me, not until this is over. You can't!"

"Whoa!" Finn shakes James off. "What's up with you?"

"I know it seems like I'm acting crazy right now, but please believe me when I say there are good reasons for everything I'm doing." James says. "You can't leave me now, Finn. Neither of you can. It's important."

"I have to get home," Finn says, but the resolution in his voice has wavered.

"And you will soon, I promise," James says. "I just need you to come with me this last time."

Finn huffs out a sigh. "Fine. But this is it, and it's only because I'm worried about you."

"Thank you."

"James!" Alice calls. "What are you doing in there?"

James pushes us toward the door. "Just go."

I pull on my coat. "Shouldn't you tell them—"

"It's better this way," he says, and he closes the door on Alice calling his name and sprints for the car.

Finn catches my sleeve and whispers, "What the hell is going on?"

"I don't know, but . . ." I watch James's back. "The last time James cracked, after his parents died, I didn't see him for three weeks. I can't let that happen again."

"You're not helping him by going along with his crazy."

I pull my sleeve out of Finn's grip and turn to follow James. "He'd be there for me."

em

The front door to the Shaw house opens, and the three teenagers climb back into the BMW.

"See?" Finn says, popping his seat into an upright position. "Told you we'd find them again."

"You're so smart."

"You're lucky to have me around."

Finn cranks to life the gray Chevy we swapped for the Honda in the parking lot of the motel, and we follow them into the crowded streets of D.C. They drive downtown, to a leather-and-wood-paneled restaurant of the kind frequented by lobbyists and power players, and we find a parking spot at a meter across the street to wait. Each second seems to drag more than the last.

"I don't like this," I say after fifteen minutes have passed. "What are they doing in there? They get a craving for filet mignon?"

"Yeah, this is weird."

I bite a thumbnail that's already worn to the quick. "What if we really pushed James over the edge? What if all he took away from seeing us was that he succeeds in making that damned machine someday? With Nate gone now—"

"It's all he'll be able to think about." Finn stares across the

268

street at the restaurant. "How he'd be able to save him."

"He won't care about anything else we said. God, what if we only made things *worse*?" I curl in on myself, resting my forehead on my knees.

Finn strokes my hair. "This saving-the-world thing is pretty hard."

"Yeah, and we suck at it."

The weight of the future settles on me, threatening to cave in my chest with each breath. It's too much for one tiny person. Marina will have to mop up my mess someday. She'll find a note in the drainpipe of her prison cell and come back to this moment to try again to save a younger, more innocent version of us. Every single second of this time is a fresh new failure.

Finn's hand on my hair stills. "Oh my God."

I sit up so quickly that the blood rushes from my head and makes me dizzy. "What?"

Finn's eyes roll back in his head, his bruised and unshaven jaw clenching and unclenching like he's biting back scream after scream. I touch his face, but he doesn't turn toward me, can't see me anymore. He's gone.

I look at the restaurant. A valet in a bright red vest is climbing into a silver car, and its owner is walking through the front doors. I only catch a glimpse of his profile before he disappears inside, but it's enough.

It's him. It's the director.

TWENTY-SEVEN

marina

James drives us to The Hamilton on the corner of F and Fourteenth Street and hands the key over to a valet. The hostess shows us to a leather booth in the back corner, which has a RESERVED sign on it. Fifteen minutes later, she returns with Richter at her heels.

"Thanks, Sherry," Richter says as he slides into the booth. "I'll take a sparkling water when you get a chance. What would you kids like?"

"We're fine," James says. The three of us, me sandwiched between the boys, sit squashed on the side of the booth opposite him.

"My deepest condolences about your brother, Mr. Shaw," Richter says once the hostess has left. "He was a great man."

"Thank you," James says, tossing away the words to move on to what really matters to him. "How's the investigation coming?"

"We're making progress. I'm sorry I can't be more specific right now." I glare at Richter with such heat, I think he must be able to feel it, but he keeps his level gaze on James. "Was there something in particular you wanted to speak with me about?"

"Actually, there was." James pulls out the manila folder and drops it onto the table with a *thwack*. "This."

"I'm sorry, I don't—"

"I found it in my brother's things," James explains. "It contains an e-mail exchange between you and a colleague where you ask for information about me and then wonder if my brother will be a 'problem.' Nate was monitoring your e-mail as a part of his investigation into the SIA, the covert organization *you* work for, and somehow you were the one put in charge of his shooting?"

My breath catches painfully in my chest. What is James thinking, laying everything out like this? If Richter did kill Nate, a congressman, in a ballroom full of people and Secret Service agents, he won't hesitate to kill us. This whole time I've been trying to keep James from cracking, but maybe he already has and I didn't notice.

Richter flips open the folder and glances over the first page. "So, you think I had something to do with the congressman's shooting?"

He asks it so matter-of-factly, in the same tone of voice he used to ask if we wanted something to drink, that I shiver. I swear the temperature in the restaurant has dropped.

Richter may be cool, but James is made of ice. "*Someone* had to help that shooter access the Mandarin ballroom. What had Nate done? Was he getting too close to something you wanted to keep hidden?"

Finn's hand finds mine under the cover of the table, and he

squeezes my fingers hard. I don't have to look at him to know his face contains as much barely concealed terror as my own.

Richter's eyes widen, and for the first time his face doesn't look like a carefully cultivated mask. "Shit, James. Look, you know your brother was a bulldog when it came to intelligence, and you know how small the community is. It was inevitable that someone the congressman had investigated at some point would end up heading the investigation."

"So you're telling me it's a coincidence?"

I have to stop this conversation before he gets us all killed. "James—"

But he doesn't even look at me, and Richter cuts me off as though I hadn't spoken. "That's exactly what I'm saying. It's true, your brother and I disagreed on things. To be honest, I thought he was a sanctimonious prick who was more interested in scoring political points than keeping the country safe." James quivers with rage beside me. "But, Jesus, I wouldn't shoot him over it! That's how things work in our world; people disagree, and it isn't personal. God knows I think *worse* of most politicians."

He's a liar. I feel the certainty of it pulsing through my veins, but he's a smart liar. Give in a little rather than denying it all outright; I learned that with my parents years ago. Admit to skipping tennis practice so I'd seem more believable when I swore I hadn't gone shopping on the credit card instead. Something is beyond wrong here.

"And me?" James leans forward. "What was your interest in me?"

A smile touches Richter's lips, like he thinks he's won something.

"I was interested in the work you're doing at Johns Hopkins. I still am. I thought you might like to come do it with us."

"Why would I do that?" James's voice is thrumming with more intensity than it had even when he asked about Nate's death. I glance at Finn and see he's frowning. What is James after? Who *cares* why Richter wanted to work with him?

"Because we have resources you won't find at your university or in the private sector," Richter says. "We think your research could have very real consequences for the world. Could help make things better."

Without knowing it, Richter has said the magic words. I look at James. His jaw has relaxed, the thin line of his lips softened. The uneasiness in my stomach turns into dread.

"You're not listening to this," I say, turning far enough toward James that I can't even see Richter out of the corner of my eye. I drop my voice. "Nate had a file on this guy, and I'm sure he had his reasons for not telling you he was asking questions about you."

"Marina's right. If Nate thought you should work with him," Finn adds, "he would have told you."

Richter leans back against the booth, clasping his hands on the table in front of him. "Thanks, kids, but I think James understands the situation better than you do. I'd still like to work with you, James. I think you and I could make a great team."

"Let's go," I say, ignoring him. "Please."

"No, we still have a lot to discuss. Now that—" Richter reaches into his jacket pocket for his humming phone. "Excuse me, this may be important. I think you'll want to stick around for this, James. Hello?"

Richter stands and walks a few paces away from the table, talking quietly into his phone, and I use the opportunity to take James's hand. "Come on. We'll go to Director Nolan like you wanted to before. Something's wrong here."

"Marina's right, man," Finn says. "This guy's a creep. I don't trust him."

James presses the heels of his hands to his eyes. "You guys don't understand. There's more at stake here than—"

"Then let *us* help you!" I say. "Or Director Nolan or the vice president or *anyone* else. Not him."

James wavers. I thread my fingers through his, ready to drag him out of the booth if I have to, when Richter hangs up his phone and turns to look at us.

"James, we have your brother's shooter in custody."

TWENTY-EIGHT

em

Chris Richter is inside that restaurant with Marina. Some previous version of me got to kill him, and I wish it had been me. If I were aiming a gun at him, I never would have hesitated.

Nausea overwhelms me, and at first I think it's from fear, but then I'm jerked away from the present, flying and falling and unable to scream.

I'm in my cell. The director stands above me, his jacket off and his hands in his pockets.

"Where are the documents?" he asks.

I touch a tongue to my swollen lip, which tastes of iron and salt. "Go to hell."

He nods at the young man in uniform beside him, and the soldier strikes me again. White-hot agony explodes through my head, turning my vision black at the edges.

The director crouches in front of me, studying my face. I stare back at him through one eye, the other already swollen shut. He can't really think this is going to work, can he? They've already put me through much worse than a beating, and I haven't talked.

No. He must just like it.

"I suppose you think the documents are your trump card," he says, his voice soft and a little pitying. "That I can't let anything happen to you until I find out what you did with them."

I raise my chin. "Wouldn't want them to fall into the wrong hands. Hell, the Chinese could be building a rival to Cassandra as we speak."

The soldier hits me again, in the stomach this time, and I can't stop the coughing moan that heaves out of me. Next door, Finn hollers my name, the sound of his fists against the metal door echoing down the hall.

"It was a decent plan for a silly little girl," the director says, "but I'm starting to think you have no idea where those documents are, and I won't let you play this game with me much longer. The biggest mistake you made, Miss Marchetti, was *vastly* overestimating how much I give a damn about you or the Chinese or even our good friend Dr. Shaw. I could kill you at any moment and not think twice about it. The only reason I've let you live this long is you were a useful tool for making sure James didn't stray from our mission, but I don't need to worry about that anymore."

I struggle to keep my hard, expressionless mask in place. The director's most powerful weapon has always been his particular brand of brutal honesty. Bruises fade, but words like that fester.

"Give me the documents," he whispers, "and I'll consider making it quick. Otherwise . . ."

"Em!" Finn yells next door. "Em!"

The director smiles slowly while Finn's voice fills my cell. His meaning is clear. He would make it slow and painful, and he would make Finn watch. I'd die with his screaming in my ears, knowing he was next.

If I was lucky. If it wasn't the other way around.

The cell spins and melts, and the world goes white around me. I try to move or scream, but I'm frozen. Maybe I'm even dead. I wake up thrashing in the front seat of the car. Finn is still rigid beside me, his eyelids fluttering wildly, trapped in a memory of his own.

Oh God. We drove James right to him.

TWENTY-NINE

marina

James's hand drops from my suddenly limp grasp. Nate's killer, caught. The rush of emotion the words send through me is so intense, I feel like I've grabbed a live wire and can't let go.

I turn to look at James. He looks pale and cold, like someone pulled from a frozen lake after falling through the ice.

"Who?" I say, because he can't.

Richter slides back into the booth and tucks his phone into his pocket. "His name is George Mischler. He's Secret Service."

"Oh my God," I say, turning to James. "You were right."

Richter nods. "I've had my eye on him from the beginning. Outwardly, of course, I couldn't seem to be suspecting one of our own people until we had proof. That's why I had to dismiss your concerns about the shooter having help from the inside, and I apologize for that. My team just arrested Mischler in his home, where they found the credentials he used to gain access to the building and a handgun matching the caliber used in your brother's shooting. We're running ballistics now that will more than likely prove it's the same gun, and I'm confident he'll make a full confession soon." Richter leans forward, nearly laying his hand over James's but deciding not to at the last moment. "I know it doesn't bring your brother back, but I hope knowing his killer is going to jail for the rest of his life will be of some comfort to you."

"Can I really trust you?" James says softly, his voice like a plea.

"Nate still had a file on him," Finn, braver than me, says. "If he has something to hide, he could've framed this Mischler guy."

Richter throws up his hands. "James, listen. I'm sure your friends are trying to help, but this is fantasy. Mischler had access; he has the gun. Once we finish searching his home and computer, I'm damn sure we're going to find the motive, too. You've got to trust me on this. We got the guy, and I'm not your enemy. I don't blame your brother for being overprotective, but I want to work with you, that's all."

James rubs his temples. "How can I be sure?"

"Let's go," I say, wrapping my hand around James's arm. I don't know why we're still here, still talking to this man. James can't really be considering working with him, can he?

"We've got a picture," Richter says, "from a surveillance camera across the street from the Mandarin. It shows Mischler leaving the hotel ninety-seven seconds after your brother was shot."

James looks up. The worry lines etched into his forehead go smooth, his tortured expression becoming one of resolve. "I want to see it. Once I've seen it, then we can talk about . . . other things. Working together."

I gape. *"What?"*

"I'll go get the car," Richter says. "You won't regret this, James."

Richter slips out of the booth, and before he's out of earshot, Finn says, "Are you insane?"

"I can't explain it to you guys right now," James says, "but I've got to know, for sure, if I can trust him."

"Then have him send you a scan of the picture," Finn says, "but you don't need to go running off with him. Nate knew this guy was bad news, Jimbo. You can't seriously be thinking about *working* for him."

"I only said I'd discuss it."

"Let's just go!" I say. "Why even talk about it?"

"Because it might be important!" James slams his fist into the table, sending the silverware jumping. "Look, I don't expect you two to understand."

"Oh, right, because we're too stupid to grasp it?" Finn says. "Marina and I have gone along with a lot of crazy shit the past twenty-four hours, James, but teaming up with this guy? You really want to go make sweet, sweet scientific research with him?"

"You can't trust him," I say. "He's a liar; we *know* that. You're vulnerable right now, and you shouldn't make any decisions that—"

"I'm not a child, okay?" James says. "I know what I'm doing. So either you trust me, or you don't."

"I'm sorry, man," Finn says, "but I don't. Not right now."

James looks at me, and Finn too. I feel the weight of their gazes like heavy hands on my shoulders, each trying to lead me in a different direction. Finn is right; James has lost perspective

280

and is acting more and more like someone I don't recognize. But James . . .

I love him. I *need* him. Can I really abandon him now? No one has ever cared about me the way he does.

Have they?

All of a sudden, the words that have been building up inside of me for years are ready to come out.

"Why did you kiss me?" I say.

For a moment, stillness and silence descend. I take a deep breath, filling myself up with it, letting it fill the emptiness the words left behind.

Finn looks down at the table, running his fingernail over a groove in the wood, pretending neither of us exists. James's mouth works soundlessly for a moment as he stares at me, and then his eyes drop to his lap.

"Marina, can we talk about this later?"

"No, I need to talk about it now. I need to know why."

He shrugs tightly, still unable to meet my gaze. "I don't know. We were both upset. It just . . . happened."

"Do you love me?" I ask. I can't believe how easily the words come out of my mouth now.

Finn gets up and walks away. I only hear him leave the table, because my eyes are fixed on James.

"Do you?" I say. "Because I love you, James, and I think you know it."

He flushes. "Of course I love you."

"Like a sister? Or like something else?"

"I don't know!" He reaches for my hand and takes it by the

fingertips. He runs his thumb down my index finger. "Sometimes I think maybe . . . but I'm just not sure. . . ."

Sometimes I think maybe. God, the wildfire of hope those words would have lit in me a few days ago, but now I'm just angry. I pull my fingers from his grasp. "Then why did you kiss me? If you knew how I feel and you weren't sure, why would you do that to me?"

"I don't know!"

"Unless . . ." My skin goes cold. "Unless you did it to keep me with you. Give me just a little hope, and then I'd never leave, right? I'd go along with anything. Kissing me was just the *X* factor in your equation."

I scoot back, away from him, and he reaches for me. "Marina . . ."

But he doesn't deny it. I don't think he *can*.

"I love you, James," I say, "but I can't keep doing this. It's not good for either of us. Go with Richter if you like, but you'll have to do it without me. I don't trust him, and I won't be a part of it."

I stand, and James grabs my wrist. "Marina, wait."

I stop, because a little piece of me can't help hoping. I turn to look at him, and know, to my shame, that he could break my resolve with a single word.

"Please," he says. "Please don't leave me alone."

Stupid girl. I bite the inside of my lip to keep it from wobbling.

"I'm sorry," I say, and walk away.

THIRTY

em

Richter emerges from the restaurant alone and goes to the valet stand. My stomach cramps at the sight of him, like my body has come to associate his face with pain. I look at Finn, but he's still somewhere else. I hold his rigid hand in my own.

Richter gets in his car when the valet brings it around, but he doesn't drive away. He lets it idle, sending fogging plumes into the cold air. Each moment he lingers, my body grows tighter and tighter.

"Leave," I whisper. "Leave!"

But he doesn't. And a few minutes later, Marina and the younger Finn step out of the restaurant. Without James.

Marina's nose and ears are red; she's been crying. Finn's movements are abrupt and angry as he steps off the sidewalk and flags down a cab. He and Marina climb inside, and off they go.

"Oh God." I shake Finn's shoulder. "Wake up! They've left him! Please, Finn!"

But I know it won't do any good. There's only me now. I fumble for the gun in the glove compartment.

James steps out of the restaurant. His eyes are fixed on the idling car, and he nods at Richter behind the driver's seat. I have maybe a ten-second window before he gets inside and they drive away.

My fingers are heavy and clumsy as I reach into the glove compartment. I'm not going to make it. I get the gun in my hands and throw open my car door. James has already stepped off the pavement and is making his way to Richter's passenger's seat.

I stand up and raise the gun over the roof of the car, aiming it at James, who has a hand on the door handle. He looks up at me. Our eyes meet.

I pull the trigger.

Nothing happens.

James flinches and scrambles into the car.

I look down at the gun. It's jammed. Stupid semiautomatic piece of crap.

"Damn it!" I slam my fist into the roof as Richter's car speeds away. I toss the gun onto the floorboard of the car and run down the sidewalk after them. I need to at least see what direction they're going. I reach the corner and see they're headed down Fourteenth Street, away from downtown. It's late afternoon; traffic will be building up soon. It might slow them down enough for me to catch up. Can I get Finn out of the driver's seat of the car? He's probably got fifty pounds on me, but if I can push him—

A hand claps over my mouth.

A tight arm around my torso makes it impossible to struggle.

For a split second I think Finn's woken up and this is his perverse idea of a joke. Maybe four years ago it would have been, but not now. Then I recognize the feel of the body against my back, the smell of fabric softener and expensive shampoo in my nose. I begin to writhe and scream against the hand over my mouth.

"Easy, kid," the doctor says into my ear. "I'm not going to hurt you."

I try to kick, but he's too tall and strong. He holds me practically off the ground, his arm like a steel band around me, keeping my arms pinned to my sides.

"I could kill you right here," he says, his voice soft and warm against my chilled skin, "and that wouldn't stop you, would it? You'll just keep trying. So what choice do I have but to get rid of *her*?"

Marina. I whimper against his hand.

"It hurts, doesn't it?" His voice is thick. "I would have understood if you'd tried to kill me. I've done everything I could to convince you of the good I'm doing, but I know you're having trouble seeing it. But that boy? Who is such an innocent? How could you, Marina? How could you do that?"

I close my eyes against my burning tears.

"Now you'll know how it feels." He releases me, and as I draw breath to scream for help, I feel the sting of a hypodermic needle and the world goes dark.

I wake up on the sidewalk with an ache in my neck and Finn frantic beside me.

"Thank God," he breathes, pushing the hair out of my face. "What the hell happened?"

For a moment, I can't speak for the wild, choking sob rising in my throat. "The doctor is back."

"What?"

"The doctor! He's gone after Marina and Finn."

Finn goes gray. "Why them? Why not just kill us?"

"Because he knows we'd only come back and try again," I say. "If he kills them now, before Cassandra is built—"

"He'll never have to worry about us," Finn finishes. He slams his fist into the concrete. "I programmed Cassandra to say we traveled back to the seventh. He shouldn't have come back until tomorrow."

I struggle to my feet, and Finn helps me. "He must have come early, thinking he could kill us the moment we reappeared in the warehouse."

"Then something tipped him off that we'd already come and gone." Finn's hand tightens around my elbow. "You don't think . . ."

"Connor." How else could he have known we were already here, unless he got the information from our man on the inside? "If he did something to him—"

"He'll never be there to help us escape again," Finn says. "This is our last chance."

"Come on!" I start running for the car, Finn at my heels. I don't slow down, even though I'm so sore from being knocked out that it feels like I'm breaking apart at every joint. "You have to go after Marina and Finn, keep them safe. Call me the moment you find them. I'll get James."

I throw open the driver's door to the car, but before I can slide in, Finn catches my hand. The look in his eyes stops me cold, but it takes me a moment to realize why.

I'm either going to kill James or the doctor's going to kill Marina, which means this is it for us.

He kisses me softly on the lips. "I love you."

I take one last second to memorize his beautiful face. "I love you, too."

He hands me the keys to the car. "See you on the other side."

THIRTY-ONE

marina

In the cab with Finn, I turn on my phone. We're almost to my house, but my mother could be leaving any moment, if she hasn't already. I have to get out of this city. Everything else pales next to my need to get as far away from James Shaw as possible right now. I dial Mom's number without listening to the three voice mails I already have from my parents.

"Marina!" She picks up after the second ring. "Are you okay?"

"I guess," I say. There are no words for what I really am.

"You're in big trouble, young lady."

"I know," I say, "but I'm on my way home. And I want to go to New York."

Something in my voice softens her. "It's going to be good for you, honey. I really believe that."

It doesn't matter. At this moment, nothing does. "I'll see you soon."

"You okay?" Finn asks softly when I hang up.

I shake my head. The fury that burned inside of me has gone, leaving me cold and empty. It feels like the time I cut my foot on a broken bottle. The ER doc gave me an anesthetic so he could stitch it up, but I *knew* the pain was still there, lurking behind the numbness, waiting for me.

"You did the right thing," Finn says.

I turn to him. "Did I? I abandoned him when he needed me."

"Maybe that's what he really needed. Something to shock him into some sense."

Or maybe it will make everything worse. Maybe he'll start acting even more recklessly, and I won't be there to stop him. "I hate myself."

"Hey, don't say that."

"It's true." I cover my face with my hands. I don't want him to see me cry. "I've never been any good for anyone. James is the only person besides Luz who really cares about me, and I left him. I'm mean and selfish and shallow and ugly, and I never do anything right, and—"

"Stop!" Finn pulls my hands away from my face, his fingers firm around my wrists. "M, don't say that."

"Nobody loves me, and why should they?" I'm half wild now, the tears thick in my throat. I try to pull my arms out of Finn's grasp, but he holds tight. "How could they?"

"Marina." He puts his hands on my face, thumbs brushing the tears from my cheeks, and guides my gaze up to his. "That's not true."

For once there isn't the smallest trace of humor in his ocean-colored eyes.

The cab comes to a sudden, screeching halt in the middle of the street. It pitches me forward, and I slam my head against the back of the driver's seat. Black dots pepper my vision, and the world swims before me. I'm distantly aware of Finn yelling at the driver, but all I can think of is a song I learned in kindergarten.

Buckle up your safety belt,
Every time you ride.
Don't forget, not even once,
Safety belts save lives!

My head is throbbing, but it's such an absurd memory that I laugh. Finn's hands are on my face again.

"Marina? You okay?"

I touch my forehead, and my fingers come back clean. "Yeah, I think so."

The driver's door is open, and he's standing outside the cab, hollering at something, waving his arms in the air. I crane my neck to see through the windshield. My vision is still dark around the edges, but I can clearly see the black car parked across the middle of the street, blocking the entire road.

Finn is checking me for injuries, so he doesn't see the door of the black car open or the man who steps out of it. Tall and slim, with neat dark hair and pale skin. I close my eyes and rest my pounding head on my knees.

"Oh God," I moan. "I think I really *am* hurt."

Finn puts a hand on my head, stroking my hair, and normally that would be bizarre, but it doesn't even rank in the strangeness of this moment.

His hand freezes. "What the hell?"

Then there's a bang, deafeningly loud. I know exactly what it is. I bolt upright and see the cab driver staggering to the ground, and the window beside me splattered with fine red droplets. I try to scream, but the sound lodges painfully in my throat. Through the haze of blood, I see the man I thought was a hallucination walking toward us, gun at his side. I don't understand how he can be here, how he can have killed a man in cold blood.

Because it's James.

He's James, and he's not James. He's definitely not the James I ran away from barely twenty minutes ago. My vision tilts and whirls. This person has James's face, but it's twisted into an alien expression, the corner of his mouth curling upward as though in distaste and amusement at the same time. His eyes are too sharp, his hair too short, his body too tall and broad.

A shiver goes up my spine. I'm hallucinating, I must be.

I sit frozen in my seat, staring at not-James through the bloody window, but Finn flies into movement. He grabs me around the back of the neck and shoves my head below the window of the cab, covering me with his arm. As we cower there, he kicks open his door and crawls through it, pulling me after him.

"We've got to get out of here," he whispers. We crouch on the pavement, keeping the cab between us and the gunman. Finn looks around us for an escape route.

"Did you see him?" I say. "Did you see—?"

Somewhere there's the squeal of tires and the slam of a car door.

"Marina, run!" a familiar voice cries.

Finn yanks me up by the wrist and sprints for the gap between two houses across the street, dragging me after him. I throw a look over my shoulder, expecting the impact of a bullet at any moment, and what I see stops me dead in my tracks.

The James who isn't James is running toward us. But before he reaches us, he's tackled by another man.

By Finn.

The same Finn who's holding my hand is wrestling not-James to the pavement.

My deadweight jerks Finn back as he tries to run. He turns and freezes at the sight.

The two men in the street continue to fight. The dark-haired man with James's face is taller and stronger, but the fair man who looks like Finn is quick. He twists the gun out of the dark-haired man's grip and sends it skittering across the pavement. The dark-haired man hits him across the face with a loosely curled first, the thick *thwack* of it ringing through the quiet street. Then he removes something from his belt, a black rectangle that fits neatly into his hand and shows a tiny glint of metal in the light.

"Marina!" not-Finn cries, his eyes never leaving the weapon. *"Run!"*

The dark-haired man jabs what I think is a Taser into the fair man's side, and he convulses once, his body arcing up off the pavement like a puppet jerked on its strings, before collapsing back to the ground, his eyes closed, mouth agape.

The real Finn comes out of his shock before I do and yanks on my wrist. The two of us run, the slapping of feet like thunder behind us as the dark-haired man comes after us.

"Faster, Marina!" Finn yells.

"I can't!"

Finn darts into the gap between the houses, pulling me so fast behind him that my feet barely skim the ground and each step jolts the joint of my shoulder. I'm not going to make it. I know I'm not.

"Just go!" I pant.

"No!"

A hand closes around my other arm. I scream.

"Marina!" Finn cries.

The scream dries up on my lips as I look up into the face of the man who caught me. This close, looking into those light brown eyes, there's no denying it.

"I'm sorry," James says, and I feel the jab of metal against my stomach before the world upends and goes black.

THIRTY-TWO

em

Finn goes to steal a second car so he can catch up with Marina and his younger self, leaving me with the Chevy. It jerks underneath me as I pound the gas and then the brake. James and Richter have an enormous head start on me, and the odds of my finding them are staggeringly slim. My only hope is that they turned onto Fourteenth Street, the major route from downtown to Virginia, because they were headed out of D.C.

I drive perilously fast, gunning the car up to fifty through the crowded center of downtown when there's a break in traffic, dodging around slower-moving cars, and running red lights. My hands shake against the steering wheel, and I'm convinced that any second I'm going to collide with something or someone.

I watch the other cars as I drive, looking for Richter's silver sedan amongst the traffic. I spot a silver Lexus at a stoplight in front of me. Richter was driving a Lexus, wasn't he? I weave my way through four lanes of traffic toward it, but then I catch a glimpse of blond hair and oversize sunglasses in a side mirror.

There's no way I'll find them.

I stay on Fourteenth Street as it takes me out of D.C., toward the Pentagon. There are silver cars all around me. There must be more silver cars in the world than any other color. I speed past them, glancing at the occupants with no real hope of finding who I'm looking for.

Then the cars around me grind to a halt. For the first time ever, I thank God for D.C. traffic. I pull off onto the shoulder and start to drive, slowly, scanning the cars that are deadlocked in the actual lanes. If they were headed this direction, I may be able to find them.

The traffic is thick and slow for miles. I've driven two, maybe three, on the shoulder when I see a silver Lexus ahead in the far left lane. I slow to a crawl as I approach it, even though there are three lanes of traffic between us, in case one of its occupants should see me. I squint out my window as I get close, and my breath hitches.

I'd know that profile anywhere. It's James in the passenger seat.

Now what? I didn't actually expect to find them, so I didn't think this far ahead. But I guess there's really only one plan. Kill him before the doctor gets to Marina. Whatever it takes.

I turn my blinker on and ease back into the right lane of traffic. I wish I'd heard from Finn; he should have caught up to Marina by now and called to let me know she was safe. I maneuver the Chevy so that it's two lanes over from them and several car-lengths behind, and I slowly follow them down Fourteenth Street and onto the exit for Pentagon City.

Pentagon City is like a mini downtown, full of high-rises and huge buildings that house government-consulting firms and private defense contractors. I follow Richter through the streets and watch from a stoplight as he turns his car into the underground parking garage of a nondescript office building sandwiched between two luxury apartment complexes. The only thing that catches my attention about the place is that a man in a suit is standing by the attendants' station at the entrance of the garage.

I've seen a lot of parking attendants in my time, and even the valets at my mom's favorite restaurant in LA—the ones who take over the keys of movie stars' Bentleys and Aston Martins—never wear *suits*.

I park the Chevy in a no-standing zone one street over and get out. I check my cell phone for a call from Finn—nothing—and tuck the gun inside my belt, leaving the bag with the rest of our possessions in the backseat. I don't expect to ever see the car again. Whatever it takes, I'm finding James inside that office building and ending this.

Of course, I can't just stroll in. Somehow, in my jeans and hoodie, I have to look like I belong in that sleek building for long enough to find him without attracting attention. Finn would know how to do it. I try to think like Finn, and immediately my eyes go to the pizzeria across the street.

I come out of Little Romeo's a few minutes later with a small cheese pizza—which, even in my state, I can't help but notice smells like heaven—and a bottle of Coke. I walk toward the office building, practicing my casual face along the way, which is hard to make when my heart is racing so fast. But I have to stay calm, logical. It's the only way I can help Marina.

Outside the building there's a brass placard listing the offices inside: Sheen and Goldberg Dentistry, Republic Gas and Petroleum, a few law firms, and something called the Associated Institutes of Research. AIR. The name rings a distant bell in my memory. Rina, one of the people who was taken with us at the house in West Virginia, had worked in intelligence before the world went insane. She used to tell us about all the organizations that served as front groups for different intelligence agencies, and I'm sure she mentioned the AIR. I'd bet my life that the Associated Institutes of Research is really the SIA and that James and Richter are inside.

Which is good, since that's basically what I'm doing.

I take a deep breath and push open the glass door to the lobby. I've walked into places where I had no business being dozens of times, and I know the key is to project confidence. If you look like you belong, people assume you do. I nod at the guard behind the front desk, lifting up the pizza as if to indicate I'm here on a delivery.

"Where you headed?" the guard asks, rising from his chair.

I look down at my receipt. "Sheen and Goldberg Dentistry? I'm looking for Marcy."

"Fourth floor," he says, pushing a clipboard toward me. "You'll need to sign in."

"No problem." I scrawl *Elizabeth Bennet* across the sign-in sheet. Is this the extent of the security here? Obviously the SIA has decided to hide in plain sight. "Take it easy."

"You too."

As I wait for the elevator, I look at the directory posted on the wall. The Associated Institutes of Research takes up the entire top floor in this twenty-four-story building. Once inside the elevator, I press the button for twenty-four. Nothing happens. The doors remain open, and the button stays dark. I press it again, harder. To my relief, the doors close, but the elevator remains still. Now I'm just standing here like an idiot. That's when I notice the card reader tucked in beside the emergency phone panel. Well, of course. Even if they're hiding in plain sight, they can't have just anyone posing with a pizza gaining access to the floor.

Time for a new plan.

I stand in the motionless elevator for several minutes, racking my brains for a solution. Even if I do get onto the twenty-fourth floor, there will no doubt be guards and all kinds of extra security measures. The odds of my reaching James might as well be non-existent. I need a plan that gets me near him.

All the while, a little clock ticks at the back of my mind, reminding me that each moment I delay is one in which the doctor might be doing unspeakable things to Marina as his perverse way to get revenge on me. I glance at my phone and try to calculate how many minutes have passed since Finn and I parted. He should have caught up to her by now. I should have heard from him.

Finally, with the best plan I can come up with, I jab the button for the twenty-third floor and cross my fingers as the elevator starts to move.

The doors open onto a receptionist's desk with a glass sign above it that proclaims this to be the law offices of Holden, Hewes, and Stein. I quickly remember what Finn taught me about how to get what you want from people: pay attention to them, figure out what they want and what they're afraid of. The receptionist is young, so she's probably inexperienced and a little uncertain. She's wearing a floral blouse with big hot-pink flowers on it, so she's not a stickler for rules. I need to be someone she won't find intimidating, someone she'll sympathize with and then forget.

As I step out of the elevator, I summon what I hope is a sweet, dopey smile.

"Hold, please," she says as I approach, pushing a button on the phone console and giving me a bright smile. "Can I help you?"

"I'm here to bring my dad some dinner." I gesture to the pizza. "He's going to be working late tonight."

"Who's your father?"

"Mr. Hewes." Dear God, please let Hewes be a man.

"Let me call him and tell him you're here."

"Oh, please don't!" I lean toward her, like we're sharing secrets. "He doesn't know I'm home from college. I want to surprise him."

She looks uncertain. She's probably supposed to call employees when they have visitors, but hopefully she's still intimidated by the partners and doesn't want to speak to Mr. Hewes any more than she has to. Finally she smiles. "Okay then. I'm sure he'll be thrilled to see you. You know where his office is?"

I point to my left. "This way, right?"

"That's right. Have a good evening!"

I walk down the corridor, and as soon as I'm out of the

receptionist's sight, I dump the pizza and Coke in an empty cubicle. They'll only slow me down and make me easier to spot now. I walk quickly through the office, trying to project an air of belonging and being too busy and important to be bothered, and somehow it works. Despite my ratty jeans and hair that hasn't been washed for days, no one at this high-class D.C. law firm says a word about my odd presence. I prowl the perimeter of the floor, keeping to the edges, and after several minutes I find what I'm looking for.

The staircase.

I duck into the stairwell, which is made of concrete with metal handrails and floor numbers painted in black on each landing. I climb up to the twenty-fourth floor on quiet feet and stand in front of the door. As I suspected, there's a key card panel beside it and who knows what waiting inside. I take the stairs up to the landing above, the entrance to the roof. It's locked, but I don't care about that. I peer over the handrail at the door to the twenty-fourth floor, gauging the angle and distance. It's doable. Assuming that a hundred other things I'm depending on don't go wrong.

I check my phone again as I run back to the law firm. Still nothing. Something's gone wrong, I know it. I'm still here, so Marina is alive, but I don't know how much longer that will last. I have to get to James before he gets to her.

I find the ladies' room in a secluded little hallway near the stairs. There's a fat sugar cookie–scented candle beside the sink, and I cross my fingers with one hand and grab it with the other. A cheap plastic lighter lays behind it, which may be the first piece of good luck I've had. I clutch it in my hand.

"Come on, Finn," I whisper. "Hurry."

I was in my father's office once when the fire alarm went off. Someone silenced it almost immediately, and everyone around us continued working without even looking up. Dad explained that they always sent security guards to check out the area where the fire was supposed to be, because there were so many false alarms. Something as little as a bit of dust getting into one of the detectors could set it off. Only if the guards found a fire would they turn the alarm back on and evacuate everyone.

So, for this to work, there has to be a real fire.

I find a supply closet across from the ladies' room. It's stocked with toilet paper, hand towels, and reams of copy paper. I rip into the plastic packaging over a dozen rolls of toilet paper without even bothering to check if anyone's coming. There's no time for that now.

The toilet roll catches instantly when I hold the lighter to it. I light a few more and place them on top of the copy paper. I leave the door to the closet ajar to give the fire oxygen and ensure that the smoke will find its way to a detector soon. I run back to the stairwell and climb up to the roof landing, pulling the gun from my belt and checking that the safety is off.

Then I wait, the sick pounding in my head like my pulse counting down the moments until the end. Hopefully mine and not Marina's.

The first wails of the fire alarm last less than twenty seconds before they go quiet. Just like my father's office. I count the seconds. For almost a minute there's silence, and then the alarm comes back on, louder and more piercing than before. I immediately hear the effect it has. There are footsteps all around me, and the doors to the stairwells open on all the levels below, voices spilling out, hundreds of pairs of shoes against the concrete echoing and magnifying. I peer over the edge of the handrail onto the twenty-fourth floor landing. A man in a black suit, like the one I saw at the entrance to the parking garage, is holding the door open and ushering people out.

"Take your time," he says as workers pass him. "Probably nothing. Our meeting spot is in front of the bank on the corner."

I watch every face that passes beneath me. No doubt there are multiple exit stairways, but if Richter and James happen to come through this one, I can end this right now.

After a minute or two, the steady flow of men and women slows to a trickle. They must have gone through another exit. I'll have to go to the bank on the corner. It will be harder to shoot James in a large group of people, intelligence officers no less, but I can do it.

Then a man steps into the stairwell, and even before seeing his face, I recognize Chris Richter.

"Did you see a kid come through here?" he asks the guard. "Seventeen, tall, dark hair?"

I grip the handle of the gun, which is suddenly slick in my grasp. They aren't together?

The guard shakes his head. "Must have gone down one of the other staircases."

"I need to go check—" Richter turns back toward his office, but the guard's hand on his shoulder stops him.

"I'm sorry, sir, but you need to evacuate now. It's procedure."

"But there may be a kid alone in there," Richter says, as if he gives a damn for James.

"Hoskins and Grant are sweeping the floor. If anyone's in there, they'll get them out."

Richter swears, and I see the battle in his face. If James is still in the building, he needs to find him. But if he exited via another stairwell, he needs to get to him quickly.

"You notify me the second you lay eyes on him, understand me?" he barks.

"Yes, sir."

Richter goes barreling down the stairs, while the guard lifts a sleeve to his mouth, talking into his radio. "We clear, Hoskins? . . . Roger that. I'm closing the southeast door. Mancini, you're cleared to close the northwest. See you at the bank, fellas."

The guard drops his sleeve and starts the descent down the twenty-four flights of stairs, letting the door to his floor start to swing shut behind him. I act on instinct, ripping off my hoodie, leaning over the railing, and tossing it. My good luck holds. The hoodie lands on the threshold of the door and stops its progress, leaving a two-inch gap. If James got separated from Richter, it must be because he *wanted* to be. Something tells me he's still inside the Associated Institutes of Research.

As soon as the guard's footsteps have faded in my ears, I scramble down from the roof landing and slip onto the twenty-fourth floor, closing the door softly behind me. Everything but the red emergency lights are off, which makes the office look hostile and eerie. I walk through the metal detector inside the door, setting off another alarm that joins the cacophony, and I have a moment of doubt as I creep deeper into the office. Am I letting James slip away again? Maybe I should be rushing down the stairs to the office rendezvous point to find him. But I have a tugging intuition that he's still here. For Richter to have lost him in the first place and to be so frantic to find him makes me think something must have happened between them. Did they fight? Did Richter tell James something he wasn't ready to hear?

I may be grasping at straws, but I don't think so. If James is upset, I know better than anyone how he likes to hide.

I race through the office, gun held low in front of me. I peer into cubicles and locked conference rooms with glass paneling, but I don't have time to make a thorough search. There are a hundred places he could be hidden, but the anxiety inside of me has been building with each second that Finn hasn't called to say Marina's safe. I have to find James *now*, and luckily I think I know where he'd go. The same place he used to hide at Sidwell when things got too intense for him.

The alarm goes silent as I make my way toward the men's room, which probably means the fire department is somewhere below me. I open the door to the restroom with my foot, keeping my hands tight around the gun. It looks empty. I duck down to look under the stalls, which also look empty. I kick the first open. The metal door hits the dividing wall of the stalls with a crash; there's no one inside. I move on to the next one, but before I can kick it in—

"Over here," James says.

The door to the last stall opens, revealing James sitting cross-legged on top of the toilet.

"I knew you'd find me," he says. "I need to talk to you."

THIRTY-THREE

em

"Please don't shoot me," he says, looking small and young. "I've got a lot of questions, and I need answers."

Just do it, I think, but instead I lower the gun an inch. "You've been waiting for me? Even though you know I mean to kill you?"

He nods. "I know it's crazy, but . . . Richter brought me here to show me a photograph of Nate's killer leaving the Mandarin. Marina and Finn don't trust him, so they left me, but he *did* show me the picture."

"Yeah? Who was it?" I don't know how Richter could have had the time to start his frame-up of Mischler, but it can't have been Nate's real killer either

Distantly, though, I know I'm just stalling.

James frowns at me. "Don't you know? A Secret Service agent named George Mischler."

"Oh. Right."

"Something about his face . . . maybe it's just because he's

305

the man who killed my brother, but something about him seemed wrong." I'm guessing it was the rushed Photoshop job. In my memory, Mischler isn't arrested for several more months; something must have happened to push Richter's schedule forward. "I started to feel like the walls were closing in on me. I asked if I could see the CCTV footage of the people who shot at me at the hospital, and Richter said no. Came up with some excuse about it being out of his jurisdiction now, and it was like this alarm went off in my head. Why wouldn't he let me see it? He must have seen it himself and knows that it shows you and Finn, not a couple of gang members like he said. He knows you're my friends, so why wouldn't he have had Marina and Finn arrested or at least told me about it by now?"

I don't say anything. There's only one explanation for it.

"Unless," James says, "he knows it was really *you* and not her. And if he knows that, what else does he know?"

James stands, and I raise my gun again, but he doesn't come any closer.

"I got so upset I ran in here, thinking I was going to throw up, and then I couldn't make myself go back," he says. "All I could think about was you and the things you'd told me. I've got to know *everything*, Marina."

I wince. "Don't call me that. It's just Em now."

Realization creeps into his face. "Like what Finn calls you?"

I pause. "Yeah."

"Why don't you go by Marina anymore? I've always loved your name."

"It's a silly name. It's the name of a fairy-tale princess who gets back everything she ever lost."

"God." James tilts his head at me. "Who *are* you?"

I clench my hand around the hilt of the gun. I should do it now. Put us both out of our misery and spare Marina from the monster who's coming for her. But he looks so sad and broken. Maybe it's stupid, but I think Finn was right before. He deserves an explanation for why I'm going to put a bullet in his brain. Maybe then I'll actually be able to pull the trigger.

"I will still kill you, you know," I say.

"I know. And I'll still fight."

I sit down on the cold tile floor, the gun aimed at him, and James sits opposite me.

"What do you want to know?" I say. "Make it quick."

"How does this work? If you kill me, you'll create a paradox."

"Time is sentient," I say, "like you always suspected. Actions like this become fixed in time. A shadow of me will always be here to kill you, even after I'm gone."

"And you know," he says, "that if you kill me, you'll die, too?"

I nod. "This version of me will blink right out of existence."

"So you're on a suicide mission."

"I guess, but I don't think of it that way. If I can give Marina a chance for an escape from what I've been through, what you've put me through"—he flinches at my words—"I don't mind giving up this second-rate existence of mine." What will she become if not me? Will she go to college, have children? Will she spend a year living in Europe and go skydiving on a dare and all the other things I used to dream about in my cold concrete cell?

He takes a deep breath as he absorbs my answer. "But why . . ."

The words fall off, and he pauses before trying again, his voice softer this time.

"If I really invented a time machine," he says, "then where are my parents? Why didn't I save them?"

It's a good question, one I've always wondered about myself. James never would have become obsessed with the idea of time travel in the first place if his parents hadn't died when he was a kid.

"I'm not sure," I say. "Knowing the version of you from my time as well as I do, I suspect you were afraid that if you saved them and grew up with a whole, happy family, you would never care enough about time to discover how to control it. And you're so in love with the power it gives you that you couldn't risk that. Maybe a time line exists somewhere where you made a different decision, but it isn't this one, so I still have to stop you."

James buries his fingers into his hair and looks down at the floor. "Why do you want to kill me?"

"I don't." The words come out harsher than I intend. "God, James, I never *wanted* this. But . . . things are so bad. . . ."

"How?" he says. "I need to know what that means."

I sigh and lower the gun to my lap, though I can still raise and fire it before he could move six inches from where he sits. "It starts about a year from now. You're working with Richter and the SIA. This place isn't the Associated Institutes of Research; it's the Security and Intelligence Administration, a covert subset of the CIA that works in conjunction with the Pentagon. In my memory, things happen mostly like they have so far. You meet Richter because he's in charge of Nate's case. He's interested in your work with the fourth dimension, and he has resources you can't get anywhere else. Our relationship grows strained. I don't like Richter, and I'm scared of the changes I see in you."

"What changes?"

"You become even more obsessed with your work." I imagine James at eighteen, explaining his theories to me, the passion in his voice so bright, it's almost mania. "Your idealism is one of the things I always loved most about you, but faced with the prospect of actually being able to change the world, you become rigid. You're so convinced you're right that you won't entertain any doubts. It's started happening already—do you see that?"

His eyes see past me. "The way I left with Richter even when they said I was vulnerable and he couldn't be trusted."

"It's going to get worse," I say. "A lot worse. Sometime—I'm not sure when—you'll develop the machine at a classified government lab in rural Pennsylvania. You'll call it Cassandra. That's when things will start to change."

"What kinds of things?"

"All kinds. For instance, before Cassandra, all the countries of Europe formed a single large nation called the European Union," I say. "They had one government, one currency, everything. It would exist right now, except you and Richter used Cassandra to go back in time and stop it ever happening."

"Why?" James asks, bewildered.

I shrug. "Richter convinced you it would be a threat to the United States."

"How do you know this?"

"You told me about it," I say, "during one of our midnight chats. You used to come into my cell at night and talk to me for hours sometimes. Mostly you'd want to talk about when we were kids, but sometimes you'd tell me what you and Richter were up to. Government leaders you had assassinated, terrorist attacks you either staged or stopped, natural disasters you were able to warn people about. Remember when the levees broke in New Orleans and flooded the whole place?"

"Sure," he says. "The city was evacuated ahead of time, though."

"Not originally. You made sure everyone was out of New Orleans before the hurricane hit, because you remembered the tragedy it had been the first time around."

"See?" he says, eyes widening like a child. "I do good things. That's all I want, to make things better."

"I know." For a moment, I'm tempted to reach out to him, but I wait out the urge. "I think that's why part of me has such a hard time pulling this trigger, because I know that even the future version of you, who has done so many terrible things, honestly believes he's acting for the greater good. Three years from now, a dirty bomb will go off in Manhattan, killing thousands and contaminating the Northeast."

James's voice is barely a whisper. "And I stop it?"

"Not exactly," I say. "You, and more likely Richter, think that stopping that one bomb isn't enough, because there will just be others. Instead of stopping the bombs, you need to stop the country's vulnerability to them. So you'll send people back in time—to one year from now, two years, six months—and have them set off a series of smaller bombs in half a dozen cities. Hundreds die instead of thousands, and the government pushes through dozens of new security measures that make what we have now look like mall security. A national biometric ID, no travel without authorization, electronic surveillance, body scanners in every building, CCTV on every street. It becomes impossible to do or say or buy anything without the government knowing about it. The dirty bomb never goes off, and in some ways we're safer than ever, but—"

"I've created a police state," James says, the horror palpable in his voice. "A totalitarian government."

"Richter is worse," I say. "He sees time as a weapon, something even more powerful than bombs to use against the Chinese or North Koreans or whoever he sees as a threat. I'm sure he pushed you into many of the worst things you used Cassandra for, but you were so blinded by then that you couldn't see it."

"Then why not kill him instead of me?" James demands.

"We tried that." It was number four on the list. That version of me must have been tough as nails. "It didn't work. I suspect there are plenty of equally ambitious, ruthless people who were able to take his place in your life. You *believe*, James, and no one can take that away from you. In the end, it always comes down to numbers with you. You're willing to hurt a few people to save many more."

"Are you one of the people I hurt?" he asks.

I nod. "Two years from now, Marina and Finn leave D.C. It's right after the first bomb, in San Francisco, and they're scared

Richter will want to get rid of them because of what they know. Marina has documentation of some of your calculations for Cassandra—"

James frowns. "No, she doesn't. There are only my originals and the copies that Nate made, which I destroyed."

"Well, I won't tell you where she gets them," I say. "I've been guarding that secret for years, and I won't stop now. By the time Richter comes for her and Finn, they're gone, and they've taken the documents with them."

Suddenly, the room tilts. Time grabs me around my middle. No, not now! But it's already dragging me away, sucking me into darkness.

My vision clears. I'm in my bedroom, pacing the length of the room. Finn is cross-legged on my bed.

"You're making me queasy," he says.

"So sorry my terror is upsetting your stomach," I snap. "Close your eyes."

He catches my wrist as I pass for another lap. "Hey, it's going to be okay."

"How?"

"I don't know. That's just what you have to say."

I laugh, and the brittle sound hurts the back of my throat. At least I can count on Finn to be honest.

"Sit down," he says. "Please."

I reluctantly sink onto the bed and begin to pick at a loose thread on the bedspread. When I pull it, the fabric around the string ripples through the whole length of the bedspread, highlighting the weakness in the otherwise uniform surface of the fabric. It makes me think of cosmic trampolines and tiny portals through space-time. I shudder and smooth away the wrinkles.

"I'm scared of him," I say softly. "I never thought I'd be scared of him."

"Me neither. God, we're really not imagining this, are we?" Finn says. "I mean, we all know I'm self-centered and unreliable, but if you feel it, too . . ."

I swallow. I hate him for saying it out loud. I've always secretly prided myself on my loyalty, my dogged support of the people I love. I thought James and I would be forever, that nothing could make me betray him.

"That's it, then," Finn says. "We have to leave. Get out of the city before it's too late and never look back."

Things go dark and flicker in and out, like a film reel that's come off its spool, as I'm thrown forward in time again. I'm still in my bedroom, but it's days later. I'm packing the tiny bag that's all the smugglers will allow me to take. We don't have the right papers for travel, and no one gets out of D.C. without the right papers. The armed Marines at the checkpoints see to that. Finn's parents can't help and mine refuse to, but there's already an underground network of people who can get us out for the right price.

Finn has it easy. He's living on campus at American University, so he can leave his roommate a note bequeathing him his television and stash of Cherry Coke and disappear.

I have to wait for my mother and her new boyfriend, clad in

a tux and evening dress, to leave for a charity function before I can tear through my room, separating the true necessities from things I just can't bear to leave behind. I pack my bag with a few spare clothes, a toothbrush, the wad of cash I've been pilfering from Mom's wallet one bill at a time for weeks, her best jewelry to pawn for more cash, and the four faded sheets of paper from a yellow legal pad that are my only insurance policy.

At the door, I turn and look back at my bed, the posters on my wall, the messy assortment of jewelry and makeup and gum wrappers on top of my dresser. Already it looks like another world, someplace I only lived in a dream. On my bedside table a picture frame lies facedown against the wood. I pick it up, studying the three faces that beam back at me. I suddenly want desperately to take it with me.

But there's no room. I set it back on the bedside table and close the door behind me.

I walk through the hall and down the stairs on socked feet, my sturdiest sneakers held in my hand. I've nearly reached the front door when Luz steps out of the shadows, her face lined with age and sadness.

The sight of her instantly turns me into a child again, and my lower lip wobbles. "I have to go."

"*Mija*—"

"I'm not safe here," I say. "*You're* not safe with me here."

Luz gathers me up in her arms and rocks me, and I cry the hot tears I've been holding back.

"I love you, Luz," I say, mopping at tears with my sleeve.

"*Te amo, mija.*"

My vision blurs again, and I see the outline of James's face and the tiled wall of the bathroom through the ghost of Luz. The two pictures flash one after the other, taking each other's place and melding into each other before separating.

"Marina!" James reaches for me but stops short of touching me. "*Em!*"

The world spins, and James recedes into shadow. I'm back in my cell, and the director is standing in front of me, telling me with a vicious curl to his lips that Luz is in DHS custody for suspected terrorist activities.

"Tell me where the documents are," he says.

I start to cry. This is before I learned to never, ever cry in front of Richter. Before I exhausted my lifetime's worth of tears and became dry and dead inside. I know what will happen. Enough of me still remembers myself sitting in an office bathroom to know that Richter, with James's blessing, will have Luz locked up in the FEMA detention camp on Long Island, all for the crime of loving me.

A hand on my face snaps me back to the present, and I come back to myself. I'm lying on the cold bathroom floor, looking up into James's dilated eyes.

"Em?" he says.

I roll away from him and struggle to catch my breath.

"What the hell just happened?" he says. "Your eyes roll back in your head, and you slumped over and started to sha and . . . and *flicker.*"

"It's time." I try to swallow away the dryness in my throat. "I'm a paradox, and time doesn't like that. It's trying to erase me. It will, sooner or later. I'm surprised you didn't try to take the gun."

"I did. Your whole body seized up, and I couldn't get it out of your hand."

I look down at my palm, which has a red impression of the pistol grip etched into it. "Oh."

James is obviously shaken, but he presses me. "You said Finn and Marina leave D.C."

"Right. They'll run for over a year, but eventually you'll catch them. You'll lock them up in the same facility where you hide Cassandra. You'll keep them there for . . . four months? Maybe more. And almost every day Richter will come interrogate them and ask them where the documents are."

"Interrogate?"

I just stare at him, remembering the beatings, the days on end where I wasn't allowed to sleep, the sound of Finn screaming next door. I don't think I need to spell it out for him.

"Oh God," he whispers.

"Sometimes you'll watch, but I don't think you like it," I say. "You'll have this look in your eyes, like there's a wall between what you see and your brain. I think you're trying to prove your-self to Richter, show him you're not the delicate little genius he thinks you are."

James stares down at the floor, so all I can see is the crown of his head. The dark hair that is usually so neat has grown unruly from days on the road and pushing his fingers through it again

and again. In a few minutes, when I've made him understand why I have no choice, I'll put a bullet through it.

"But sometimes at night," I continue, "when the facility is quiet, you'll come to my cell. You'll sit on the floor across from my cot, like you're doing now, and tell me how much you hate what's happening to me. If I'd just give Richter what he wants, you could change everything. You'll spend hours trying to convince me of all the good you're doing with Cassandra, the lives being saved, the disasters averted, the wonderful changes the government has been able to make. I think you *need* me to believe it alongside you. Richter wants us dead, I'm sure of it, but you make him keep us alive because you need us to believe what you're doing is right. You can't stand the kernel of doubt that we put inside of you by refusing to go along. And I think, in your own way, you miss us. You won't have let anyone get close to you in a very long time, too focused on your mission, and I think you miss the part of you that could."

"But I *know* all of this now," James says. "I won't let things happen that way again."

I shake my head. "I've tried. It doesn't work. Can you promise me you won't build Cassandra, now that you know you can?"

James hesitates.

"See?" I say. "You *have* to do it. And once you do, the rest of the story falls like dominoes. This is my fifteenth trip back in time. I left myself a list of everything I did to try to stop the future from happening. I spoke to you and to Nate and to Dr. Feinberg. I tried to get you to go to Princeton instead of Johns Hopkins, and I tried getting you expelled. I destroyed your computer and all your notes. I got rid of an engineer who helped you build Cassandra. I tried everything I could to avoid this, but nothing worked. I'm sorry, James, but you're the one who tried so hard to convince me that sometimes people have to die for the greater good."

I raise the gun, and James lunges for me.

THIRTY-FOUR

marina

My head feels heavy, like it's encased in concrete. I can't see or hear, only feel the pull of gravity against me. I try to lift my head, the muscles in my neck straining, but my chin falls back to my chest. I hear a low groan from somewhere.

Wait, was that me?

With an effort that feels like swimming to the surface in a lake of molasses, I open my eyes. When my blurry vision clears, I see that I'm inside a strange house. I look around with a mild sort of curiosity. The walls are covered in whitewashed beadboard, and the furnishings have been mismatched with the greatest of care. The paintings are of nautical scenes, and all of the fixtures are brass. We must be at the beach somewhere.

I like the beach, I think numbly.

I try to stand and find that I can't. It's puzzling. I pull myself forward only to be jerked back again. The haze over my mind slips a little with each attempt. I struggle in the chair and eventually realize my wrists are bound to the wooden slats that form the back.

"Help," I croak. I meant to scream it.

I turn and discover Finn beside me, similarly bound in a plain wooden chair, unconscious. I crane my foot to kick his leg.

"Finn!" My voice is half whisper, half sob. "Wake up!"

Finn makes a soft sound deep in the back of his throat and the muscles in his forehead contract, but he doesn't wake. He must still be swimming in the molasses.

"Finn, please," I moan, yanking at my restraints. I can't handle this—whatever this is—alone.

"He'll wake up soon," a voice says.

My head snaps to the far doorway. Leaning inside it, arms crossed casually over his chest, is not-James.

"No, no, no . . ." I screw my eyes shut. I'm not seeing this.

"He's bigger than you," the man in the doorway says, "so I had to give him a bigger shock. Shouldn't be too long now."

"Who are you?" I ask, eyes still shut. "What do you want with us?"

"You know who I am."

"No, I don't!" I jerk at my restraints until I'm sure the bones in my wrists will snap.

"Marina." I hear him move closer to me, sense him leaning down, bringing his face to mine. "Look at me."

I shake my head, lips pressed together to stop my whimpering.

He puts his hands on my cheeks, and I shudder. "Open your eyes."

I don't want to open them, but I can't stop myself. I focus on the man in front of me. He looks the same. A little older, and the angles of his jaw and cheekbones look sharper, as if he's lost weight. His hair is shorter, the cut severe. I start to tremble. Is this what going crazy feels like?

"James?" I whisper.

"That's right."

"W-what are you going to do with us?"

"Nothing yet. It's not actually you I'm mad at. *She's* the one who started all of this, but unfortunately there's no stopping her," he says. "I'm sorry, Marina, but I'm going to have to kill you."

em

James moves with astonishing speed, throwing himself at me as I raise the gun. Was this his plan the whole time? Get some answers and lower my guard at the same time? He knew exactly which of my buttons to push—the ones about friendship and loyalty—to make me go along with it.

When it comes to James Shaw, it seems, I'll never learn.

I get off one shot before he tackles me, but it misses wildly. He hits me with such force that I go flying back onto the tile floor, my head hitting with an audible *thunk*. Black stars burst in front of my eyes. James is on top of me, pinning me to the ground. I hold the gun as far away from him as I can, stretching my arm above my head to keep it out of his reach as I try to jostle him off of me. He lunges for the gun, which means taking the bulk of his weight off of my torso. I knee him in the groin and scramble away when he doubles over. The gun is upside down in my hands now. I struggle to right it, but he's too fast. He lunges at me, wrapping his arms around me and pinning my arms to my sides.

"I'm sorry," he says, the words hot against my ear, "but I can't just let you kill me. I'm going to do good things."

I try to elbow him in the stomach, but his grip around me is too tight. My only advantage is that he can't grab for the gun without letting me go enough for me to twist free.

We're in a stalemate.

One of us will weaken first. I'm afraid it will be me, and I can't just wait for it to happen. I take a deep breath and drop the gun. I give it a good kick, sending it clattering across the tiles to the other side of the bathroom. I feel James hesitate, and then he lets me go to throw himself after it. I grab his leg, clawing into his jeans as he tries to kick me free. He's sprawled out across the floor now, and I have the leverage. I can beat him to the gun. . . .

But then one of his feet connects, kicking me right in the nose. My vision explodes, and I think I hear the bone crack. My hands fly to my face, and I use the sleeve of Connor's hoodie to staunch the warm flow of blood.

When I force my eyes open, James has the gun. He points it at me, his chest heaving.

"Do it," I say. "I'll only come back."

His eyes are bright. "I could never do it. That's not what this is about."

I bow my head, thinking of Marina and how I've failed her.

All the fight seeps out of me. Does the doctor have her by now? "You'll feel different someday."

The shrill ring of my cell phone fractures the silence, and I jump. Finn. I keep my eyes on James as I pull the phone slowly from my pocket. He can shoot me if he wants, but I'm damn well going to answer it.

I flip open the disposable phone and push the speaker button. "Finn?"

James's jaw tightens, but otherwise he remains still.

"He's got them." Finn's voice is harsh and distorted over the line. "The doctor's got them."

His words sucking all the air out of the room. There's suddenly no bathroom, no gun, no James, only Finn's voice. "What happened?"

"He ambushed them down the street from Marina's house. He knocked me out, and when I woke up they were gone."

"Where did he take them?"

"I don't know," Finn says. "There's something else. He left a note beside me that says *Bring James unharmed*. Have you found him?"

"Bring him *where?*" My voice rises hysterically. "Where are they? He's going to kill them!"

Visions of blood and bone and pain float before my eyes. My grip on this world is so tenuous with Marina's life in the doctor's hands that I expect to dissolve at any moment.

"No, Em, think." Finn's voice is like a rope mooring me back to the earth. "If he wanted to kill them, he would have done it right there in the street. *We're* the ones who betrayed him, so we're the ones he wants to punish. He won't do anything to them until we're there. They're just—"

"Tools," I say. The doctor knows the best way to hurt me is through Marina. He'll do to her the things he's done to me. It took four years for all of my illusions about James to be stripped away, but he could do it to her in mere minutes.

"You've got to know where he is, Em," Finn says. "He would have told us if he didn't think you could figure it out."

I rack my brain. James had favorite places—like a café on M Street that had big squishy chairs, a preferred table by the window in the library—but nowhere he could take a couple of hostages. I have no idea where he's taken them. He'll get impatient and kill them, all because I can't read his mind.

Oh.

Panic, or maybe the multiple blows to the head, must have clogged my synapses, because it takes me a good ten seconds to realize I have another James sitting right in front of me. He still has the gun pointed at me, but it lacks conviction. The gun betrays the tremor in his hands. He's flushed and disheveled from our tussle, but his gulping breaths are too fast to be from the physical exertion alone.

"Wait there, Finn. I'll come get you." I snap the phone shut. "You must know where he would go."

"What's going on?" James says slowly, like he's taking great care to keep his voice even.

"It's you, from the future," I say. "You followed us back, and you've taken Finn and Marina."

"Why?"

"To punish me. And to keep me from doing what I came here to do."

"You don't mean I'd *hurt* them?"

"I'm sorry, but that's exactly what I mean." I almost regret having to tell him this. No one should be confronted with the depths of darkness they're capable of all at once. "He'll kill them both, because it's the only way to stop Finn and me for good."

James's face is a frozen mask of horror. What is he thinking? Is he thinking about Marina, how much he cares for her, and how devastated he'd be if something happened to her? The doctor wouldn't be, but this boy still might.

"We have to help them," he says. "I know where he took them."

"*We?*"

"You can't do it by yourself, and neither can I."

"Why should I trust you?"

"You don't have much choice, do you?" James snaps. "You can't find them without me. Look, I know you think I'm a monster, but Marina and Finn are the only people left in the world who I care about. I won't let anyone hurt them. So how about a truce until they're safe?"

I stare at him. He's not the doctor yet, but he will be one day. There's no way I can trust him.

But then I think of Marina. I imagine her crying, hurting, maybe dying, and I have no choice. I have to do whatever it takes to help her.

"Okay," I say. "Truce."

"Good. But I'm keeping the gun."

———

The stolen Chevy is still where I left it. I drive while James points the gun at me.

First we go to Georgetown to pick up Finn. As we turn onto my old street, I spot him sitting on the curb, head between his knees, like the weight of his guilt is folding him in on himself. He looks up at the sound of the approaching car, and I see an ugly red bruise rising on his cheekbone, joining the purple one on his jaw. I'm out of the car before it even stops rolling.

Finn stands to meet me, and I crash into him, throwing my arms around his neck. He staggers back but holds me close.

"I thought I'd never see you again," I say.

"I was right there," he says, "but I couldn't stop him—"

"Shh, it's not your fault."

Finn goes rigid against me. I turn and follow his gaze to where James stands, inside the open passenger's door. He's staring at us like he's understanding something for the first time. Suddenly self-conscious, I loosen my grip on Finn.

"You know I had to bring him," I say softly. "And this is *James*. Not the doctor. He's still your friend."

"I know, it's just . . ." Finn's jaw tightens. "We should kill him now, and then the doctor won't be a problem."

James shows the gun in his hand but doesn't say anything.

"Shit," Finn mutters.

"He could have killed me when he got the gun," I say, "but he didn't. He insisted on coming to rescue Marina and Finn. And since he's the only one who knows where they are and the doctor demanded to see him safe, I don't see what choice we have."

"I don't like this."

"I know. Me neither, but I'm not wasting time arguing about it."

He drops his head. "Fine. Let's go."

James hands the keys to Finn and climbs into the backseat, where he can keep the gun trained on us both. We drive eastward in silence except for the directions James occasionally gives.

"Is there a pen in the glove compartment?" James asks after we've gone twenty minutes down the road.

I frown, but James has a gun aimed at my head, so I check. "Yeah."

"Give it to me," he says. "The owner's manual, too."

I hand the items back to him. "What are you doing?"

"Don't worry about it." He adjusts so that he can write with one hand and keep the gun pointed at us with the other.

"How much farther is this place?" I ask.

"Not far," James says. "My parents had a cottage on the Chesapeake. Nate never liked to go there—the memories, I guess—but sometimes I go when I need to think. It's . . . quiet."

The word makes me shudder.

"Finn," James says.

At length, Finn meets his eyes in a rearview mirror.

"I'm sorry," he says in a small voice. "For everything. I really am."

Finn sighs. "I know you are, Jimbo. But it's not enough."

We pull up to the cottage—which is a gross misnomer, since it's a two-story Victorian with a wraparound porch and probably six bedrooms inside—as the setting sun tosses its last red rays above the waterline. The headlights of the car sweep the draped windows as we crunch up the seashell drive, and I imagine the doctor inside with Marina, watching the light beams across the curtains.

Finn kills the engine, but none of us moves.

"How are we going to do this?" James asks. "They can't see you, can they?"

"Past versions of a person can't see their future selves," I say. "At least, that was your theory. It could severely disrupt the fabric of time or even drive the younger versions of us insane."

"I'll keep my eyes closed," James says. "Then you can show him that I'm here and safe."

"What's our plan?" Finn says. "We're not just going to walk in there, are we? What's to stop him killing Marina and Finn?"

"He'll want to make us suffer first," I say. "That'll give us some time to . . ."

"To what?"

"I don't know." I press my shaking fingers against my eyes. "What are we going to do?"

A scream rips through the air, jolting us all.

It's Marina.

THIRTY-FIVE

marina

I stare up at the man who is and isn't James through hazy eyes. The jolt of electricity he gave me didn't knock me out this time, just sizzled painfully through me, like knives in my veins.

"Why are you doing this?" I say.

He's watching the windows with a frown. "I think you should scream again. I'm not sure she heard you, and I'm getting tired of waiting for them."

"Who?" I sob.

"You. You're out there, running around trying to kill me. The person who shot at James outside the hospital? That was you. The you that you'll be someday, at least."

A tear rolls down my cheek. I didn't know it was possible to be *more* scared than I was just moments ago. "You're insane."

"I know it's a lot to take in at once." He puts a hand on my shoulder as his voice attempts kindness, which makes my skin crawl. "But you know I'm telling the truth."

I close my eyes, willing this nightmare to pass. I'll wake up in my warm bed to the sound of Luz calling me down to breakfast—waffles with strawberries—and then the real James and I will go see a movie. By the time the trailers come on, I'll have completely forgotten this crazy, terrible dream.

"No," I say through gritted teeth. "You're not him."

"Yes." He brushes a stray piece of hair out of my eyes. "It's me, just a little older and wiser than the me you know."

"No, no, *no!*" My voice is beyond my control now. This isn't James. This isn't James from the future, a man who's finally solved the riddle of time and come back to knock me out and tie me up. It's impossible.

"I don't want to hurt you, Marina," he says, "but Em . . . She's the one person I always thought I could count on, and she *betrayed* me." He closes his mouth with a snap. "I need to make her understand what she's done. She's determined that only one of us can survive this, and it has to be me. In the future, I'm changing the world."

I long for James, the real James, with a sudden, wild intensity. I remember the hurt in his eyes when I walked away from him in that restaurant, and more than anything I want to go back to that moment and change things, put my arms around him and tell him that I love him and will never leave him again.

"It's going to be okay, kid," he says, the sympathy in his voice a mocking parody of my friend's. I whip my head toward him, rage momentarily eclipsing my fear.

"Don't you ever call me that!"

He looks down at me with genuine sadness in his eyes. "It's a shame you'll never understand."

Beside me, Finn coughs and raises his head.

"Oh God, Finn," I say. I think I might cry with relief at not being quite so alone anymore.

"What the . . ." he says. He looks at the man in front of us and blinks, like he expects him to disappear. He jerks against his restraints. "What the fuck is going on here?" he yells.

"We're saving the world," James says.

em

The birds in the trees above our heads leap into the air in a flurry of feathers when the scream fractures the silence. I start to run before I even consciously know what the sound is, like my body understands before my brain. It's Marina in pain, and such a thing is intolerable.

Finn catches me around the shoulders, pulling me back when I would have bulldozed into the cottage, charging through any wall or person standing between me and my younger self. I push at him and struggle in his arms.

"Let me go! It's Marina!"

"I know!" He shakes me. His grip around my arms is bruising, but comforting, too, grounding. "We'll help her, Em, but you can't go running in there."

331

James is white as a bone. "I made her do that."

"I'm going in," Finn says. "If it came down to a fight, I could overpower him."

"Me too," James says.

"No—"

"That was the one thing he asked you to do, right? Bring me along to show that I'm not hurt?" He levels a look at Finn. "If you don't, he'll hurt her again."

I press a hand to my mouth.

"Fine," Finn says. "Is there another entrance to the house?"

"Sure, there's a door around the back."

"Em, can you try to sneak up on him from behind?" Finn asks. "If we can keep him distracted long enough, maybe you can get a shot off."

"Jesus," James whispers.

"Can you handle that?" Finn asks. "Because it's that monster with your face in there or Marina. No way both of them are walking out of this one."

It suddenly strikes me how small James looks. He was always like a god to me, a giant at seventeen, someone I had to crane my neck to see, both physically and metaphorically. But although he's still a good eight inches taller than me, he's nothing more than a kid. I may only have two years on him, but I've also got ten extra lifetimes of experience. James looks soft, fragile.

"All I care about is Marina," he says.

The answer placates Finn, who gives a grudging nod. James explains to me how to edge around the side of the house to the back porch, where there's a door that leads into the kitchen. He slips a plain silver key off his key ring and presses it into my hand.

"That's not all she's going to need," Finn says.

My eyes go to the bulge barely visible under the bottom of James's shirt hem. He looks up at me, suspicion in his eyes. I know we're imagining the same thing: he'll hand over the gun, and I will point it at his head and pull the trigger. Sure, he risked everything by choosing to trust me and help me save Marina, but if there's anything I've learned from James, it's that he believes the ends justify the means. If this boy crumples dead at my feet, all my problems will be solved. Marina will be safe from the madman holding her hostage, and Cassandra will never be built.

It's what I should do. The only problem is I know now, for sure, that I can't.

Maybe it really is a sign of strength, like Finn said, or maybe I'm too much of a coward, but I can't kill the part of me that still loves James. Still believes there's goodness in the world. Thousands or more may suffer because of my weakness, but I know myself now. I just have to hope that the girl inside will be stronger when her time comes.

"It's okay," I say. "I can't do it. I wish I could, but I can't."

Inside the cottage, Finn cries out.

"Come on," my Finn says, "we've got to go!"

James pulls the gun from his belt, eyes locked on mine. Then he turns and hurls it into the woods lining the driveway.

THIRTY-SIX

marina

"James!" a voice calls from outside. "I'm coming in."

My head snaps up. I know that voice. Its ashen, wide-eyed owner is tied to the chair next to me.

It must be the man who tried to save us before, in the street. The man who looks like Finn, but older. Just like this terrible James who keeps talking about the future like it's someplace he's been.

It's Finn from another time.

We hear the front door open. "Finn, close your eyes!" the voice says.

The voice is so intense that the Finn beside me instantly shuts his eyes, and the other Finn turns the corner from the foyer into the living room. I stare at him like I wasn't able to before. His hair is longer, curling at the ends where it's tucked behind his ears, and he's grown taller and more muscled. There's a thin white scar cutting through his eyebrow, and bruises on his face from the struggle in the street. He looks *fierce*.

"You're not really the one I want to see," the older James says.

"I'm not exactly thrilled by the reunion, either."

"Marina, what's going on?" the Finn in the chair beside me whispers, his eyes still screwed shut. "Who's here?"

"Shh, it's okay!"

"Let them go," the other Finn says. "They haven't done anything."

"Neither has he, but that didn't stop you trying to kill him. I want to see him."

"You know that's dangerous."

James's lip curls. "I think I know what's dangerous better than you do."

Finn inches farther into the room. "No offense, Jimbo, but you lost perspective on that a long time ago."

"Em!" James yells, turning a circle. "I know you're out there!"

"She's not coming in, man," Finn says. "She doesn't want to see you like this, with her. It'll break what's left of her heart. Don't you get that? Don't you understand what you've done to her?"

Who are they talking about? I feel like I should know, but my mind becomes heavy and plodding when I try to think about it. Like I can't . . . can't . . .

James's eyes flare. "I saved her life. I protected her, like I protected you, and all the thanks I got—"

"Protected?" Finn demands. "You sat there and *watched* while they tortured her and she screamed for mercy—"

"Are you trying to stall me, old friend?" James says. "James! Come out, or I make her scream again! I better see him in five seconds, Abbott, or . . ."

335

He moves behind me and presses the metal prongs of the device into my side. I whimper. I don't know what the two men with the faces of my friends are arguing about—only the most vivid and terrible words stick in my mind, forming a terrifying impressionist's painting of the future—but the metal jammed into my ribs with bruising force is concrete. I shake in anticipation of the scorch of lightning through my body, and my eyes meet the future Finn's. It's the first time he's looked at me since he entered the house, and it's like nothing I've ever experienced before. No one, not even my James, has ever looked at me with such tenderness and depth, as though he's seeing straight into me. In that moment, I feel like he builds a bridge between us and sends a steady stream of warmth and strength across to me. For a second I forget about the contraption digging into my side.

Then I hear the click of James pressing a button, and I'm on fire.

em

I stare at James for one wide-eyed second and then sprint into the woods in the direction he threw the gun. The last light of the day is rapidly falling, and the underbrush is thick and choked with dead foliage and fallen branches. I look over my shoulder once and see Finn entering the house with James right behind him.

I crash through the woods, first turning over the underbrush with a long stick and then searching on my hands and knees, increasingly desperate. I pray that Finn can keep the doctor occupied long enough for me to find the gun and slip in the back door. In my frenzy, I rip up weeds and savage bushes, looking for a glint of metal. My hands are scratched and bleeding, and I don't care.

Marina screams again. I jam my hands over my ears, but the screaming goes on and on. Each second of the sound is like a white-hot poker through my chest. I have to make it stop.

As I rifle through dead leaves on the ground, the tips of my fingers brush something hard and cold. I lunge for it, my hands closing around metal. I close my eyes and say a silent thank-you.

I work my way around the house to the back door quickly. Marina is still screaming. I jam the key into the lock and slip inside.

Marina's voice grows hoarse and becomes ragged sobs. One more second of this and I will throw myself into that room. I don't care that it will ruin our only plan; I'll fire at anything that moves to stop the terrible sound.

"Stop!" James's voice rings out above the screaming. "I'm here! I'm coming in!"

marina

I slump in my chair and would probably slip off if it weren't for the bindings around my wrists. My body hums with the aftereffects of the shock, like a tuning fork slammed against the edge of a table.

"M, you okay?" Finn says from his chair, his eyes still tightly shut.

"Sh-shh . . ." I don't want him to draw their attention; he's better off silent.

My eyes water and refuse to focus, so I can barely see the boy who steps into the living room. He's just a blur, but the sight sends relief coursing through my veins.

James. My James. I'd know him with my eyes closed.

"Stop!" the older Finn says. He throws his hands out, blocking the younger James's face. "Don't look at him!"

But the two Jameses stare at each other, my James bright and beautiful, and the other James like his reflection in a dusty, cracked mirror.

The older James smiles. "It's okay. The universe won't explode."

Finn's face goes slack. "What?"

"Coming face-to-face with yourself is no bigger paradox than anything else you've done," my James says. "He lied to you."

"I thought it might buy me some time if you two ever came after me in the past." The older James smiles. "After all, the three of us were inseparable."

My James takes a step farther into the room, toward himself. "Please don't hurt them. Let them go."

"I can't do that. They're trying to kill us."

"Only the ones from your time! Do what you want with them, if that's what it takes, but Marina—"

"Marina's tried to stop us every step of the way, over and over, using every conceivable method. This girl here"—he puts his hand on the crown of my head—"won't stop until we're gone."

"Please!" my James says. My mind spins as I watch him arguing with himself. "I don't want her hurt, which means you must not, either, somewhere deep down."

"You'll learn that things change. Now, if we could stop these pathetic attempts to distract me," he raises his voice, *"while Em sneaks in the back door,* I'd appreciate it! You think I don't know exactly what you would tell her to do in this situation?"

The older Finn's expression is grim. "I guess that's why you're the genius, not me."

"Em, I swear to God, if you don't come out here right now," James calls, "I'm going to do something you'll regret!"

Silence. I quiver. I don't want to know who Em is. An impossible idea is taking shape in my mind, but I can't face it.

The older James bows his head. He seems genuinely disappointed. "Fine."

"Nooo . . ." I sob, waiting for the electric jab of the device to boil my blood again. But it doesn't come. I open my eyes and see him kneeling at my side. His fingers touch mine, and for a second it feels like an embrace, the comforting warmth of his skin. Then with a swift movement, he yanks my pinkie and ring finger back, and I hear a sick *crack*. The pain hits a moment later, and I howl.

My Finn shouts curses while the older one lunges for me. Through my haze, I feel metal prongs pressed against my neck, and the older Finn freezes.

"Stop it!" someone cries. "Stop! I'm coming out!"

The room is silent, waiting, and only my muffled sobs disturb the air. I can't think about who's coming, can't think about how familiar that voice sounded. My mind, overloaded with pain and fear, has begun to shut down, like a door closing between me and the world. I think it's trying to protect me.

"Marina," someone says. "Close your eyes."

"She doesn't have to; you can—"

"I don't want her to see this. Or me."

I close my eyes, and slow footsteps sound behind me.

"Drop the gun! Kick it over here, or I'll—" The metal prongs dig farther into the skin on the side of my neck.

"Stop! You touch her again and I'll kill you, you bastard." Something heavy hits the floor and slides across the wood.

"More empty threats, kid?"

At the sound of my nickname, my eyes fly open. It *can't* be. The older James has a gun in his hand, and he's using it to shepherd a girl to the far side of the room to stand with the others. I blink. Her back is to me, but there's something familiar about the tight gait of her walk. I feel slow and stupid as I put the pieces together. The girl turns around, and I understand why the other Finn made my Finn close his eyes. The sight of this girl, who's thin and severe and wears a hunted look on her face, makes me so dizzy and sick that I want to shut out the world until she's gone.

Because she's me.

THIRTY-SEVEN

em

Marina stares at me, and I wonder if that's horror in her eyes. I want to hide my face from her, reassure her that she will never be me. She walked away from James in that restaurant, which I could never have done. She's stronger than me already.

"Close your eyes, Marina," I say. She hesitates. "Please! I don't want you to see this."

Her eyes flutter shut. The doctor presses my gun to her head, and every muscle in my body tenses.

"Tell me where the documents are," he says.

For a moment, I can only gape. "You orchestrated all of this to ask me such a stupid question?"

"I wanted you to feel the betrayal I've felt, but I might as well take care of some business at the same time. Maybe now you'll finally answer. You never had anything to lose, but"—he kicks the leg of Marina's chair—"she's got plenty."

"What good would it even do you? Time will erase us all

before . . ." Oh, *stupid* Em. "Richter. You're in communication with him even now. You tell him where the documents are here before time eats you up, and he'll know in our future before we even left."

The doctor's unchanging expression confirms it.

"That's how he knew about your work at Johns Hopkins in the first place, isn't it? You found *him*, not the other way around," I say. "We never understood how you were able to get Cassandra up and running so fast, but it's because he's already building it, isn't he? And he must know about Nate, too. God, I'm such a fool!"

James turns to me. "What about Nate?"

I exchange glances with Finn over his head. It all makes sense now. We always wondered how the shooter was able to get to Nate, slipping past the vice president's Secret Service detail so effortlessly. All those questions go away if there was someone on the inside pulling strings, standing agents down and arranging for certain doors to be unlocked and certain security cameras to be mysteriously broken. The government's airtight case against Mischler, who we came to learn had nothing to do with the shooting, must have been all Richter's work, too.

The doctor has a hint of panic in his eyes now. His secret is so close to being exposed.

"You make me sick," I say.

He presses the gun a little closer to Marina's temple in response. "Where are the documents?"

It's so preposterous, I can't help but smile. "I don't have them."

"Then you hid them somewhere, or gave them to someone."

"Damn it, James!" I say. "I burned them years ago!"

"No." He shakes his head with quick little jerks. "No, you knew they were your only insurance policy. You wouldn't risk—"

"I got rid of them, and you *know* it." I sigh. "I think you always have."

"I'll hurt her," the doctor says, clutching the Taser in his free hand. "I swear—"

"I'm telling the truth! This was never about the documents. It was about you and me." The rest of the room recedes, until it's only the doctor and me. James and me. "As long as those papers were out there, you had an excuse to keep me nearby. If you could just *convince* me that what you were doing was right, maybe you could finally, truly believe it yourself, couldn't you? That's why you kept me in that cell for all of those months even though you *knew* the documents were gone. That's why you're here now!"

"No. *No!*"

"It's always been you and me, James." My voice cracks, and I realize I've started to cry. "That's why I can't kill you, and you can't kill me. Because even if it means the end of the world, I love you too much."

"You know she's telling the truth," Finn says softly. "I watched her torch them at a truck stop in West Virginia."

At the sound of Finn's voice, my heart breaks a little. I was so focused on James, I had almost forgotten he was there. Does he understand that my love for him, which burns white and pure and has led me through so much darkness, is so different from my lingering childhood love for James? I turn to look at him and see my heartbreak reflected in his face, but he smiles.

"What about my brother?" the younger James demands, looking from me to the older version of himself. "Someone tell me what this has to do with Nate."

My throat tightens. Even now, I'd spare him this if I could.

"It's time to tell him," Finn says.

"You shut the hell up, Abbott!" the doctor says. He jabs the Taser into her throat with vicious force, eliciting a shriek of pain and surprise from her. She keeps her eyes shut, though. I wonder if her glimpse of me horrified her so much she won't risk another.

"Don't!" I cry.

"What about Nate?" James demands.

"Em," Finn says, "we have to—"

"Stop!" the doctor says.

Marina screams as electricity shoots through her. I want to run to her, throw my body between her and the doctor, but I'm afraid of what he might do if I move. "Stop, don't hurt her!"

"Marina!" the Finn strapped to the chair shouts, pulling at his ropes. His eyes are open now, and his gaze darts among all of us in increasing panic.

"You son of a bitch!" James glares daggers at his older self. "How can you be so cruel?"

The doctor removes the Taser from Marina's side, and she sags into the chair, taking shallow breaths. His eyes as he looks on James are sad. "You'll find out."

"No, I won't." James hurls the words like weapons. "I'll never be like you. You hurt innocent people; you're everything I hate."

"Em." Finn's gaze is heavy. "He has to know. We have to tell him."

"Tell me what?" James says.

I shake my head. I can't do it to him. "No."

"The world isn't as black-and-white as you think," the doctor tells his younger self. "You'll be surprised at what you can do when you have to."

"Em, he has to know!" Finn says. "He needs to understand what he's capable of."

"Shut up, Abbott!" the doctor says.

"What do I have to know?" James says.

I shake my head. There are too many voices, too many ties and allegiances, too many paths I could take. "I can't!"

"Tell me!"

Across the room, Marina keens in pain as the doctor hits her with the Taser again.

"Stop!" I scream, my voice raw.

"What do I have to know?"

"Everyone shut up, or I'll kill her!" The doctor replaces the Taser pressing into Marina's skin with the gun.

It's the last straw for Finn. He lunges across the room and tackles young James to the floor, wrapping both of his hands around the boy's neck.

"I'm sorry," he says between gritted teeth. "I'm so sorry."

James scrabbles at the backs of Finn's hands, digging deep scratches into them, his face turning red. I sob but can't move, not to help Finn or to stop him. I know this is his gift to me. He will kill his best friend so that I don't have to, to save Marina's life.

"Get off of him!" the doctor cries hysterically. "Get off!"

I see an opportunity in his distraction. I throw myself at him, hoping he'll have let down his guard enough that I can get back the gun.

"Stop it!" Marina wails.

"James!" the younger Finn hollers, jerking so hard at his restraints that he almost overturns his chair.

I try to wrestle the gun from the doctor's grasp, but I'm no match for him. I get a decent punch in, but he shoves me away with such force that my legs go out from underneath me. I slam my head against an armoire and land in a heap on the floor, dazed. I look across the floor to where Finn has James pinned down. James is kicking and struggling, but Finn is stronger. All those months of push-ups in his cell; I can't believe it's really coming down to this. The room is all noise and movement, screaming and struggling and fire inside my head.

And then it goes silent.

It's a silence I know. The kind that's actually a sound so loud, your brain doesn't know how to interpret it at first.

The younger Finn, still strapped to his chair, slumps forward, his chest blooming red.

THIRTY-EIGHT

𝓮𝓶

"No!" I cry, my own agony like the gaping hole in Finn's chest. I struggle to my feet, like if I could just get to him, I could stop this happening somehow. The young Finn stares unseeing. His breath comes in a pulling wheeze, a bubble of blood popping on his lips when he exhales. I'm going to be sick. I turn away from the sight to look at my Finn.

He stares in horror and unimaginable pain at his younger self and the blossom of blood that is quickly soaking his shirt. He draws his eyes slowly away to meet mine. Those dark blue eyes I'll never see again. His lips start to move, but before he can speak, the Finn in the chair lets out one long, last exhalation, and my Finn fades away like early morning mist in the heat of the sun.

"Finn . . ." The word leaches from me the way blood oozes from the departed boy's wound. I always knew this was a suicide mission for both of us, but I shouldn't have had to watch him go first. The pain is unbearable. Did he know how much I loved him? Will any version of me ever see him again?

"Finn?" Marina says. "Finn!"

Hearing her cry his name shatters me. I'm not aware of my knees melting underneath me, but in the next moment I'm back on the floor with the young James's arms around me. I realize he must have caught me and lowered me down. His arms are shaking.

"How could you do that?" His voice is barely a whisper, but it gains force with each word. "You *murdered* him! You're a monster!"

"Oh God," Marina sobs.

The doctor is pale, the muscles of his jaw standing out against his skin, but he tries to put on a calm face. "It doesn't matter. He's just one person."

"I'm sorry," James says to me. "I'm so sorry!"

This has to stop. The sobs that rack my body die away, and the world goes very still and quiet around me. Finn is dead, and I have to stop this once and for all.

I look up at James, my dear James. Everything else in the room—the madman with the gun, the crying girl, the dead and bleeding boy—fades at the edges of my vision. It's only me and James.

God forgive me, I think as I raise a hand to his beautiful cheek. I love him so much, but it's not enough.

"James," I say, calm at last. "You killed your brother."

His expression doesn't change, held in place by incomprehension. "What?"

"Shut up, you bitch!" the doctor howls.

"George Mischler wasn't the killer," I say. "Richter framed

348

him. The real shooter was a man named Evan Taminez. He was a soldier assigned to Cassandra, and you sent him back in time to kill Nate."

"*Why?*" James says, wild. "Why would I do that?"

"Nate was becoming a problem," I say. "You told me one night, when the guilt was too much for you. Nate was trying to shut Cassandra down because he was worried it would be misused, and you couldn't have that."

"But . . ." James shakes his head like it will stop my words from sinking in. "But all I want is to save him. . . ."

"You do save him," I say. "It's one of the first things you use Cassandra for, but when he becomes a problem, you kill him again. You save him and kill him over and over."

The disbelief in James's expression gives way to horror. He knew something was amiss with the photograph that Richter showed him. He just saw his future self kill his best friend in cold blood. And he knows how brightly the fire burns inside of him to use time to better the world. Deep down, he knows I'm telling him the truth.

The doctor sees this, too, and he takes out his rage on Marina. He wrenches two more of Marina's fingers back, neatly snapping the bones, her screams the best possible revenge on me.

"Stop!" James cries. He looks up at his older self. For the first time I see him recognize how far he will go, how much of a monster he will become.

"I'm sorry," the doctor says, "but you'll understand someday."

Then I see the look in James's eyes change. I see the moment he decides to change the future, right here, right now.

"You're wrong," he says.

James flies at the doctor, and the two of them fall to the floor, identical twisting bodies. I scramble across the floor to Marina and start untying her with shaking hands.

"It's going to be okay," I say to the girl, even though I know it's a lie. "Everything's going to be okay. Just close your eyes, okay? Please."

She squeezes her eyes shut, tears rolling freely down her face. "What's going on?"

"Everything's going to be fine." I glance at the dead boy in the chair beside her, his body nothing but an empty husk now. "Keep your eyes closed."

One of the Jameses—I can't tell which one—bellows with rage. Another screams in pain, the thump of flesh on flesh booming in my ears as I struggle with Marina's bonds. One way or another, it will be over soon.

There's a loud crack, and one of them stands. The younger James rises, the doctor lying dazed at his feet, bleeding from where his head was rammed against the hardwood floor. James leaves him there and looks at me, his eyes red and resolved.

He raises the gun he wrestled away from his older self.

"No!" the doctor and I yell together.

"I'm sorry, Em," James says, a tremulous little smile on his lips. "I only ever wanted to make things better."

"James?" Marina cries.

"I love you, Marina," he says. "You're the best friend I ever had."

He turns the gun and points it at his own face, lifting it toward his mouth. The doctor and I both realize what he's planning to do at the same moment. I scream, and the doctor lunges up at him, one last-ditch effort to save his life. It's too late. The doctor hits James just as he pulls the trigger.

James collapses in a heap, and I drag myself to his side. He's still alive; the presence of the doctor, who's fallen to the floor in silent horror, is proof of that. The doctor didn't stop James, but he did manage to move the gun enough that the shot missed the vital part of his brain. The bullet shattered his cheekbone, but his eyes are still open. All the doctor did was ensure that James's death would be lingering and painful, and the fact that he'll die for it, too, gives me no comfort.

I grab James's hand and press it to my cheek, my tears falling onto his face. "I love you, too. You're a *good* person."

His eyes stay fixed on mine, and maybe I'm only seeing what I want to see, but I think I see peace in them. Slowly, his eyes close. Terror seizes me as I wait to drift away the same way Finn did. I never wanted to die, and I fear there will be nothing but blackness and aloneness wherever I go. I cling to the idea that Finn might be there, waiting for me.

But nothing happens. He's unconscious but still breathing shallowly. Either James's tenuous hold on life has weakened the doctor or he's just given up, because he's sitting very still and staring blankly ahead. It won't be long now, but I have a few last moments. I lay James's head on the floor gently and kiss his forehead.

Then I crawl back to Marina, who is still tied in her chair, sobbing and shaking, her eyes shut. A feeling of profound tranquility comes over me as I look at her.

"James?" she says. "E-Em? *Anybody?*"

I smooth the hair back from her face and work calmly on the knots that hold her.

"Shh," I say. "Everything's all right now. Listen carefully."

I tell her she's beautiful and perfect and she's going to be okay. I tell her she doesn't need to change herself to fit in with shallow girls or to matter to someone. I tell her everything I wish I had ever known. I tell her I love her, and I realize as I say it that I love me, too.

On the floor, James exhales his last breath.

And then so do I.

THIRTY-NINE

marina

I jerk awake. I don't remember falling asleep, but my dreams were full of running and screaming and fear. I sink back against my pillows in relief, stretching against the smooth sheets.

The doorbell rings downstairs, and I glance at the clock. It's not even nine in the morning yet. James wanted to go for breakfast and he's always early, but this is *ridiculous*.

"I'll get it!" I yell to Luz.

I stand and sway on my feet from the sudden rush of blood to my head. I feel heavy and foggy, and the tattered edges of my dreams keep brushing against my mind. I grab for them but come up with empty hands. In fact, now that I think about it, the last couple of days are a blur. I remember James in a tux, Nate's beautiful speech at that fund-raiser, and stupid Finn Abbott tagging along with us everywhere. I remember James asking me to breakfast, and vowing that I would tell him how I felt before the pancakes were finished, but everything else is a muddle.

"I love you, James," I whisper, practicing the words. God, it sounds stupid.

I trot down the stairs to the front door and throw it wide open. I have a joke about James's chronic earliness already on my lips, but I stop short.

"Congressman," I say. "Hi."

Nate looks so much like James, the same fine, strong features and humble tilt of the head. He looks up at me slowly, heaviness pulling down the corners of his mouth and his eyes puffy and red.

Somehow, I don't even have to ask.

FORTY

marina

I don't understand it. I can't. The James I knew had plans. He'd been happy. He'd smiled at me and asked me to breakfast just hours before driving to his parents' old cottage on the Chesapeake and taking his life. It doesn't make any sense.

I guess you can never really know what's going on inside another person.

But as I cried long into that first night after Nate told me what happened, the little bits and pieces of James that never seemed quite right—the sudden flares of temper, the intensity in his eyes when he would say the world needed to be changed, the way it sometimes seemed like the slightest pressure would crack him in two—began to fit together like the pieces of a puzzle, painting a different picture of the boy I thought I'd known so well. One more frail and damaged than I'd realized. Nate thinks he never got over their parents' deaths. He'd been in therapy for it for years, starting after the breakdown he'd had the day of their funeral. I never knew about that; he never told me.

At the funeral, I stand between Nate and Finn Abbott. I've spent the last two days in bed sobbing and screaming, and I have no tears left for today. I'm empty, like I died right along with James. I lean against Finn because I'm not sure I can stand on my own and glare at the sun for daring to shine today. It should be like the movies, all dark, drizzly rain and black umbrellas stretching into the distance. But the crowd at the graveside is a small one, only the people who had really known and loved James. The circus was left back at the church.

As the minister speaks, my mind slips away from where we are, the casket and the flowers and the hole in the ground. I think of the stacks of notebooks from James's room that Nate gave me because he couldn't bear to see the work James had loved so much go into a storage container somewhere. Burning tears—I guess I have some left after all—cut through the numbness shrouding me as I remember the first time James ever told me about his work. The memory rises up in front of me, as fresh and untouched as if I were reliving it.

"Marina!" My eyes are glazing over as I try to listen politely to the chatter of my mother's friends when I hear someone hiss my name. "Marina! Hey!"

A hand closes around my wrist, and I turn to find James—gangly and awkward, not yet grown into his height—behind me. He pulls me away, and we slip through the crowd of guests, each clutching a wineglass and a little plate of hors d'oeuvres. "I've been looking everywhere for you."

"Sorry, Mom was making me talk to those women on the board at the symphony with her. I think she just wanted to show me off." I look down at the party dress Mom dragged me to Neiman's to buy and forced me to wear to the Shaws' annual Christmas party. It's silver and beaded at the top, and objectively it's probably a beautiful thing, but it makes me feel like Mom's Debutante Barbie.

"Look what I swiped from the kitchen when the caterers weren't looking," James says, brandishing a half-empty bottle of champagne. "Let's get out of here."

He pulls me up the stairs onto the darkened second floor, and I find I can't resist him. He takes me into the library and closes the door behind us, wedging a doorstop underneath the crack to stop anyone else from coming in. He flops down onto the leather sofa, and I sit more carefully beside him, resting my head back against the cushion and studying him as he rubs his eyes with both hands.

"I don't know why Nate insists on throwing this damn party every year," he says. "I know for a fact he hates it as much as I do."

"It's kind of a nice tradition, though, isn't it?" I say, even though I'm sure I hate the Shaws' Christmas party more than anyone. "Your dad would be happy he was keeping it up."

"Yeah, I guess he would." James takes a swig from the bottle and tries to hide his grimace at the taste. "It wouldn't really be Christmas without the party to dread, would it?"

I smile. "Or stupid dresses to wear."

"I know you don't like it, but you look pretty."

My tongue feels suddenly too big for my mouth. The light in the room seems to change, and James looks different to me. More perfect. My breathing goes shallow, and I look down at my hands to hide the strange feeling washing over me.

"Yeah, right," I say, forcing a laugh. "I look like some senator's wife trying to show up her friends. I look like my *mother*."

"Hey, your mother is a fine-looking lady."

"Ugh, gross!"

I shove his shoulder and he laughs, and for a while we pass the champagne bottle back and forth. I've never seen James drink before; I don't think he ever has. But there's a shadow in his eyes, and he throws back the bottle like it could chase whatever those dark thoughts are away. I play along, even though I only take tiny sips of champagne and sometimes just press the bottle to my closed lips. Soon it's nearly empty, and James is loose and open, sprawled across the couch with one hand brushing my leg, and his smile gone messy and wide.

"I'm going to fix everything, you know," he says.

I have no idea what he's talking about, so I just say, "Yeah?"

"Mm-hmm." He closes his eyes. "I've been talking to this professor at Johns Hopkins about my work, and he's going to mentor me."

His words are starting to run together, and his breathing has slowed. I lean toward him and pat his cheek.

"Don't go to sleep, James!" I whisper. "Then I'll have to go back to the party!"

He cracks one eye open. "M'not sleeping."

"Yes, you are."

"No, I'm not." He sits up straighter. "I'm going to figure out time, and then I'm going to fix things."

"What things?"

"Everything. I'm going to change the world." The shadow in his eyes returns. "I'll make sure Mom and Dad never get in that car."

I feel like I've been socked in the stomach. My eyes stray to the wall, where in this same room two years ago, James threw a lamp in a blind rage that left a deep scratch in the plaster. It's gone now, long since patched up and painted over, the evidence erased so easily.

"James . . ." I whisper.

"Everything will be different then," he says, eyes closing as he rests his head on my shoulder. "I'll make everything right. I'll make everything better."

The first handful of dirt hits the coffin and brings me back to the present. James was going to make everything better, but now he'll never get the chance.

I start to cry, and Finn the Idiot takes my hand. It should feel strange and uncomfortable, but for some reason it doesn't. It actually feels . . . nice. I lean against the solid warmth of him, and he gives my fingers a squeeze.

I'm suddenly very scared. Not of the explosion, which defies my comprehension, but of what I'll have to do when it's all over. Of what this is all for.

You have to kill him.

Either Finn senses my fear or he feels it himself, because he puts his hands on my cheeks, lifting my eyes up to his.

"It's going to be okay," he says, the words barely audible above the roar.

But then things get very quiet, for me at least. Somehow I find silence in Finn's dark blue eyes. God, how did I survive so long in that cell without being able to see those eyes?

I'm hit with a crashing realization. Something so obvious, I can't believe I haven't thought of it until now. My heart breaks and spills white-hot misery into my body.

"Finn," I say, "if we can do it, if we change things, I'll never fall in love with you. And you'll never fall in love with me."

"Don't be so sure," he says, pressing his forehead to mine. "I think I was in love with you long before any of this started."

I don't know whether I want to laugh or cry. "Really?"

"Really." He presses a sweet kiss to my lips. "There's always hope for us."

I squeeze Finn's hand back, and my eyes fall closed. I feel something like the whisper of a touch to my face. Deep from the back of my mind, a voice that sounds a lot like my own speaks to me like a memory, telling me I'm strong and loved and that everything is going to be okay.

And, for some strange reason, I believe it.

ACKNOWLEDGMENTS

I must have been very good in a past life to end up surrounded by so many smart, supportive, and wonderful people, without whom I wouldn't be here.

First I want to thank my incredible agent Diana Fox. I don't know what possessed her to take me on as a client, but she made me the writer I am today, told me to write this book when I didn't think I should, and was instrumental in making it what it is. Thank you, Diana, for being such a great teacher, advocate, and friend.

Then there's my fantastic editor Emily Meehan, who saw and understood exactly what I was trying to do with this book and helped me make it happen. She and the entire team at Disney-Hyperion have been huge champions of *All Our Yesterdays*, and I don't have the words to thank these incredible people enough: Laura Schreiber, Lizzy Mason, Dina Sherman, Holly Nagel, Elke Villa, Stephanie Lurie, Marci Senders, Kate Ritchey, and everyone else at Disney-Hyperion.

I also owe a huge debt of gratitude to my amazing foreign rights agent Betty Anne Crawford, whose support and advice has gone above and beyond the call; film rights manager extraordinaire Pouya Shahbazian, who works magic; Fox Literary's Brynn Arenz and Rachael Stein for their invaluable perspectives on the manuscript; and my indefatigable publicists Julie Schoerke,

Marissa DeCuir Curnutte, and the JSK Communications team, who believed so much in this book and did so much to keep me from losing my mind.

A huge reason this book exists at all is because of the hand-holding, cheerleading, and shoulder-lending of my incredible friends and critique partners. Sara McClung is a trooper who has read this book as many times as I have, maybe more, and her insight and support was invaluable to me in writing it. Tanya Byrne was the first person who ever made me think I could actually be a writer, and her conviction never wavered, even when mine was nonexistent. Cambria Dillon and Copil Yanez were much-needed fresh eyes and endless sources of enthusiasm. And I feel confident that the D.C. MafYA is not only the best group of writers in the world but also the best people to blow off writing to go sing karaoke with. Their friendship and support has meant the world to me.

The biggest thanks goes to my family, who had more confidence in me than I ever did and who have always made me feel loved and safe in this world: my sister Annie, who is one of my first and most trusted readers; my sister Ava, who carried a copy of my truly terrible first novel in her backpack to school for weeks; my wonderful dad Ezra and stepmother Amrita; and especially my mom Lynn. I never would have written this book without her and her inability to just let me have a hobby when she thought I could be doing more. I love you guys.

And, last but not least, thank *you*.